This book is a work of fiction but includes historical
facts. The portrayal of actual characters from the period
is a product of the author's imagination based on third-
party accounts. There is no way to determine what
those persons would have actually done in this fictional
situation. Any and all characters in this book should
therefore be considered fictional. Reference to actual
historical figures has been made only to improve the
authenticity of the story.

Cover Design: Mary Holste. Side X Side Creative
Cover photo of woman: David Piechowski
Manufactured in the United States of America
First Edition

A Novel
By Mary Lloyd

CHAPTER 1

Colorado, 1893

"**STOP RIGHT THERE**, or we aim for the livestock." The gunshot was still ringing in Edwina Sinclair's ears as the faceless command came from somewhere in the house-sized rocks next to the road.

Her body clenched into a knot of fear as her husband Jerrod reined the team of mules, pulling the clumsy freight wagon to a stop.

"Just stay calm," he whispered as he leaned forward to apply the brake. "We don't have anything they'd want."

Two riders came toward them from behind the rocks. Two others came up on the opposite side of the wagon. All four had bandanas over their faces and revolvers drawn and aimed.

"Your money," the tallest one said. "Now."

The shortest one approached the wagon, and Jerrod obediently handed over his wallet. Not a huge loss, Edwina decided. After they'd finished buying supplies and equipment in Florissant that morning, there wasn't enough left in it to buy more than a few meals and a night's lodging.

"Now the jewelry."

Jerrod pulled out his pocket watch.

"But that was your father's—"

He handed it to the bandit. "He would have much preferred I stay alive," he said to her under his breath.

"Now you, little lady." The ringleader motioned with his gun.

"I have nothing." It was close enough to the truth. She wasn't going to go digging for the coins in the bottom of her valise.

"That's a mighty fine ring you have there." The bandit waved his gun toward her left hand.

She stared at him dumbly.

Jerrod turned to her. His eyes were pleading. "Give it to them, Edwina," he urged in a whisper.

"But..."

"*Now!*" The ringleader waved his gun menacingly.

She stared at him blankly as she worked at getting the ring off her finger. The stones had been her mother's and her grandmother's before that. Her father had given them to Jerrod when Jerrod had asked for Edwina's hand. She'd melted into tears when he'd given them to her, beautifully set in her own engagement ring. It was all she had left of so much now.

The bandit's frozen gray eyes, bloodshot and rimmed with red, glared at her from above the bandana. The skin near his eyes was a leathery, sick yellow-gray. Greasy blonde hair drooped to his shoulders from under a worn, sweat-stained felt hat. "Hurry up," he snarled.

Eternity passed as she struggled with the ring. Finally she got it off and handed it to the short fat one.

But still they didn't leave. The ringleader studied her and Jerrod. "Clyde, cover the back road," he said calmly. "Al, you keep watch for anyone coming from Cripple Creek." As those two rode away in opposite directions, he turned to the short fat one. "Search the load, Scoot. I'm bettin' they got more than they're lettin' on."

"How dare y—" Edwina felt Jerrod's hand over her mouth before she'd finished.

The leader cackled. "That's right, mister. You keep the missus under control."

Scoot—the short fat one—climbed into the freight wagon and worked his way from the back to the front, stepping on things as he went and half-heartedly rummaging through the boxes and bundles.

That it was happening again was excruciating. When her father had died, she'd been shocked to learn his partner had left him penniless. She'd managed to deal with that. And when Jerrod's mother had disowned him for wanting to leave St. Louis and the family business, Edwina had seen it as just one more thing she and Jerrod would conquer together. Now, they were being robbed of the little they had left. What more could the thugs want than what they'd already taken?

Finally Scoot called to the leader. "Ain't nothin' here, Rafe. Just mining tools and books, from the looks of it."

"What kind of books?"

Scoot yanked a book from the crate Jerrod had so carefully packed.

He began to spell the title. "A...s...s...a...y...i...n..g." Still holding the book in his hand, he looked up at Rafe. "What's that mean?"

"Aw, it's just mining books. Get the hell out of there."

After Scoot remounted, Rafe leveled the gun on Jerrod. "Nothing else, huh?"

"No, sir," Jerrod said quietly.

"You know what you're doing, fella." The outlaw gave a hoarse laugh. "'Sir!' I like that."

Edwina bit her tongue hard enough that she drew blood. She prayed to a God she didn't know that they would leave, but instead Rafe glared angrily at her.

"You got a right pretty woman there," he said to Jerrod, nodding toward Edwina. "Maybe we'll take her, too."

Her eyes widened in panic.

"Bet she'd be somethin'."

Edwina turned to Jerrod. His face was a sick white. She looked back to see Rafe walking his horse nearer to her side of the wagon. She let herself take a slow breath when he holstered his gun. But when she looked up at him right next to her on his horse, the look in his eyes was mean enough to freeze her soul.

He pulled down his bandanna.

She gasped.

A ragged scar ran from his cheekbone to his jaw. His thin mouth curled into a sinister sneer revealing yellowed, broken teeth. His breath was intensely foul.

"Don't like the looks of a real man?" He ran his tongue back and forth along his cracked lower lip. "How 'bout you come with me?" The words were not a request.

He pulled her head to him and pressed a hard, hateful kiss onto her lips.

She pushed away from him in panic.

"So you think you can decide?" Rafe grabbed her by her hair, which was pinned on top of her head, and yanked hard, making it come undone. He kept his hold on it and gave it another yank. "Nobody decides but me, ya hear?"

Her temples throbbed.

"Leave her alone," Jerrod pleaded. "Don't hurt her."

Rafe pulled her hair again, even harder.

She yelped in pain.

"Let her go," Jerrod's voice had changed to a firm demand. He stood up. "Let her go." He held a revolver.

Rafe let go of Edwina's hair but grabbed her around the waist. He pulled her out of the wagon and held her to his chest, her feet dangling. "You shoot me, you shoot her."

Rafe nodded to Scoot, who rode up to Jerrod with his gun drawn. "But my friend here..." Rafe continued. As Jerrod looked at Scoot, Rafe switched Edwina to his left arm, holding her like a rag doll, and drew his gun.

Edwina started to struggle, then stopped immediately. That would only make it worse.

Rafe nodded at Scoot again. "He can get clear aim."

Edwina was looking at Scoot when Rafe fired. She screamed as Jerrod fell backwards into the bed of the wagon, still clutching the gun. Blood spurted from his chest. She struggled to get free, but Rafe held her tighter, grunting with an animal satisfaction at what he'd just done.

Scoot climbed up in the wagon and lifted Jerrod's limp hand, then leaned close to him, looking at him earnestly. He looked up, first at Rafe, then at Edwina, then back to Rafe. "He's dead," he said, his tone betraying disbelief. "You shot him *dead*, Rafe."

"No!" Edwina screamed.

Her face felt the rough boards of the seat as Rafe dumped her back on the wagon.

"Get this off the road," Rafe commanded. "We gotta get outta here."

The freight wagon jerked wildly over the rough ground as they moved off the roadway and started up the nearest hillside. Edwina tried to get to Jerrod in the back of the wagon as it began to move. A burly hand pushed her back down on the seat. A wave of hysteria hit her as she tried to comprehend what had just happened. No. It wasn't real. It was a dream. Jerrod wasn't dead.

Think, she told herself. She was in the freight wagon, and Scoot was driving. There had to be something she could do. Jerrod dead? No. No. She pushed the panic away again. Scoot seemed like a real person. Would he help her? Help her what? Jerrod was dead. There was nothing left to help her with.

She made herself stay still, worried that Rafe would do even more harm to Jerrod if she moved. But her agony was too compelling to remain where she was for long. She had to touch him, to stay connected to this man who'd been so easy to love. Grasping the back of the seat, she sat up and turned to look at the back of the wagon.

Jerrod's shirt front was a wet, deep red. Blood was spattered on the boxes and bundles he'd so confidently loaded the night before. A rivulet of what had been in his veins moments before dripped from one of the boxes onto the floor of the wagon. How could there be so much blood? She began to shake.

"Don't look," Scoot said.

But she couldn't stop looking. Jerrod was sprawled sideways on his back near the front of the wagon bed, arms thrown wildly over the boxes underneath him. She reached out and lifted his right hand. It had the same feel of death that her father's had after the heart attack the year before. She dropped the limp fingers and fell back onto the seat of the wagon, stifling her shriek of grief to avoid attracting any more of Rafe's ruthlessness.

Jerrod was dead.

The wagon kept bumping over rocks and brush as she slumped next to Scoot, struggling to think. But her mind was lost in the grief-stricken shrieking of her heart.

As the bumpy ride continued, she decided she'd rather die trying to escape than however Rafe chose later. He was going to kill her eventually—if she let him. He'd killed Jerrod as if it was as routine as yawning. To escape, she had to stop thinking about Jerrod. She willed herself to do that and worked at remembering the "unbecoming things" her Poppa had taught her on their hunting and camping trips. Mrs. Dayton, the headmistress at Dayton School for Fine Ladies had called it an abomination when she learned he'd been involving Edwina in masculine adventures, but right now, his prowess in the outdoors beat knowing how to fold a napkin.

From what she could see slumped on the seat, they'd come about a half mile from the road and were heading for a wooded area. The two who'd been the look-outs were riding ahead. Scoot was in the wagon next to her. That left Rafe. She listened for hoof beats but heard none.

After counting to a hundred and hearing only the sounds of the wagon the whole time, she decided he must have gone a different way. Convinced she could make it to a thick stand of trees on the right before the two riding in front could reach her, she rolled off the seat.

"Goddamn, missy. Why the hell did ya do that?" Scoot yelled as she hit the ground and threw herself into a roll that took her away from the wagon.

She rolled wildly with the momentum of the fall, then jumped up dizzily and ran toward the forested hillside. The trees grew close enough together that the riders would have to dismount to follow her if she could get to them. She was within fifty feet of the woods when she heard a horse coming fast from behind her. She knew it was Rafe even before a glance over her shoulder confirmed it. She began to zigzag, hoping to make his horse stumble, but it was useless.

Rafe barely slowed as he grabbed her by the hair and pulled her up on his horse. The pain from having her hair pulled again felt like her scalp had been sliced open with a hunting knife.

He threw her face first in front of him. She landed hard across the saddle horn. He pushed a hand down on the small of her back. The saddle horn rammed into her midsection. She struggled not to faint from the pain.

He reined in the horse and walked it slowly back toward the wagon. "You'll have to do better than that to get past Rafe Pettibone."

Rafe Pettibone. The monster didn't deserve a name, but she'd remember it all the same. Rafe Pettibone. Up to now, she'd thought only of getting away. Now she saw more. Once she escaped—and she was going to escape—she would see Rafe Pettibone hanged.

"She stays with me," Rafe said to Scoot, "since you can't seem to keep her where she belongs." Rafe clicked his horse into motion. She would be riding wherever they were going in front of him, upside-down and rammed into the saddle horn. As they made their way up the hill, her father's advice rang in her ears. "Courage doesn't come wrapped with a pretty bow, Eddie girl. Find your gumption however you can and get on with what you have to do."

By the time they stopped, she'd calmed herself and had begun to really think. She didn't struggle when Rafe took her off his horse, standing meekly while he tied her hands. At least, she was looking at things right side up.

The other three men took off their masks. Edwina was surprised at how ordinary they looked. In fact, Scoot reminded her of one of her father's drivers. Both were squat, dark-haired men who smelled of tobacco and axle grease, and neither seemed able to think beyond what they were told. When he noticed her looking at him, he nodded politely. If Scoot were smarter, he'd have made a good ally. But she sensed he had a blind faith in the monster that it wasn't wise to test.

The other two were taller and leaner than Scoot but not as big as Rafe. They seemed intelligent, but neither one would look at her. No help there either, she decided. But how far would they go to stop her?

The red-haired one was fairly muscular. He wore buckskins, which made him look like he belonged in the first half of the century. But his revolver and the rifle he carried were both the latest models. She was amazed to find herself thinking how impressed her father would have been with his choice of weapons. Poppa always got excited about a good gun.

The other man had to be Rafe's kin. He was a lot thinner but had the same greasy blonde hair, narrow face, and sharp nose. Brothers, she guessed, but with a big difference in age. The smaller man seemed barely out of his teens. His young face was smooth and didn't hold the scars—or the hatred—so deeply etched in Rafe's.

From the few words the men exchanged, she grasped that they'd stopped to hide the wagon. Good, she told herself. If they hid it while she was with them, it would be easier to find once she escaped.

The three followers pointed and argued as they stood in the rocky clearing where they'd stopped. Then they all nodded in agreement. Scoot climbed back onto the wagon seat, grabbed the reins, and urged the mules forward, slowly moving the wagon farther up the hill.

She panicked again as Scoot took Jerrod away. She pulled her tied hands to her mouth to stifle the shriek rising in her throat. She'd come back for him. Period.

She began to catalog every detail of the landscape to help her identify the place later. They were halfway up one of the pine-covered slopes in an area that had fewer trees and more of the huge rocks like the ones on the road where they'd been ambushed. She could see where they'd left the road, near a cluster of aspens that included one that had been scarred by lightning.

The area where Scoot stopped again didn't seem big enough to hide a wagon, but when she shifted her weight to her left leg and leaned slightly, she could see an opening in the tumble of house-sized rocks. He maneuvered the wagon into a small clearing in the center. Rocks rose up in twenty-foot walls on three sides. She was memorizing the shape of a gnarled little pine tree that stood on the fourth side of the little clearing when they kicked at it until it fell over and then dragged it across the opening of the hiding place. She switched to studying the shape of a rock outcrop farther up the hill.

A few minutes later the three returned to where they'd left her and Rafe.

"That'll give him some time to lose his looks." Rafe nodded toward the wagon where Jerrod's body still lay. "No need helpin' John Law figure it out."

Clyde—the name she'd heard them call his brother—coughed and nodded to Rafe to move away from the group. They strode to the top of the small ridge and stopped, both gesturing in what seemed to be an argument. The only word that came back to Edwina was "bury" in a voice she hadn't heard before.

Pretending to be shifting her feet, she looked slowly at the lay of things in each direction, memorizing the terrain. The wilderness adventures had been socially unacceptable play with her father. Now they meant survival. The ache of missing him mixed with the horror of losing Jerrod and tears welled in her eyes.

Scoot and the fourth man started to argue.

"Come on, Al. We can take 'em with us."

So the red-haired one was "Al."

"Don't be a damn fool. We don't have enough feed back at camp." He slapped the dust off his jeans. "Besides, it's five miles to the cabin and they'll slow us down."

Five miles, Edwina noted. She could do that on foot.

Al continued. "We don't need mules."

"Ya can't just leave them there to starve," Scoot said. "They didn't do nothin' to deserve that."

"Just let 'em loose. There's plenty to graze on around here," Al said. "Some prospector'll find 'em before the snow flies."

Scoot looked at the mules, then at the grass, then at the wagon, then at Al. "Fair enough," he said. He marched back to the small clearing inside the rocks and began unhitching the mules. He yelled back to Al. "We don't need this if we don't need the mules, right?" He held up a harness.

Al hesitated a second. "Right."

Scoot tossed the tack into the wagon on top of Jerrod's body. Edwina tried to console herself that it might deter scavengers until she could get back to bury him.

Rafe and his brother came back, still clearly angry with each other. When they remounted, Rafe flopped her in front of him over the saddle, again impaling her on the saddle horn.

As they rode away, she strained to keep the wagon in her sight. But soon it was gone—along with her dream of a new life with the man she loved in the freedom of the Colorado mountains. In place of her dreams, fear and confusion swirled in her head. The only thing she was sure of was that she was going to see Rafe Pettibone brought to justice. And that to do that, she had to get away.

When they stopped again, they were in a clearing in the middle of a pine forest. From where the sun now was in the sky, it seemed it had taken them about two hours of steady riding to get there. A small cabin at the back of the open area stood for-lornly in the gathering shadows of late afternoon. The hideout, she assumed.

The outlaws rode into the yard without any yells of greeting.

Good. There were only the four.

They went around to the corral behind the cabin. Rafe dis-mounted, then yanked her off the horse. Edwina glared at him. He pushed her to the ground. She fell at his feet, landing in fresh horse dung.

When she succeeded in standing back up, he let out another bone-chilling laugh. "I'll whip you every way I want, honey." He ran his tongue back and forth over his lower lip, surveying her silently. "But I'm going to savor the prospect for a while first." He nodded toward the cabin and gave her a shove.

As they came around to the front of the cabin, she walked meekly, again taking in everything possible of her surround-ings. To one side, a massive rock outcrop fortified the place. To the other side and in front of the clearing was pine forest—with trees so close together a horse couldn't pass.

As tight as a fort, Edwina told herself dejectedly, no walls but perfect protection. She'd never make it to help if she left on foot. The country was too vast to even know where to start to look for a route back to Florissant on foot. The only way to cover enough ground was on horseback. The only way out on horse-back was down the trail they'd come in on and the outlaws were already discussing who would take what shift guarding it.

Rafe pushed her into the cabin.

Old newspapers, tobacco cans, and other debris were strewn everywhere. The odor of long-worn, unwashed clothing was over-powering. Edwina put her hand over her nose to stifle the stench, which was even stronger than the horse dung on her dress.

"Not your cup o' tea, heh?" Scoot was standing in front of a battered dry sink, watching Rafe and Edwina. He began to giggle. "It sure ain't mine." He danced around like a little girl. "No more women's work," he sing-songed over and over as he hopped. His grin widened. "I ain't gonna cook *no* more."

Rafe looked at him with disgust. "That'll be a blessing for all of us." He turned to Edwina. "Make us something to eat." His look told her she was less than human. "And clean this place up." He turned without another word and tramped out onto the porch.

She breathed a sigh of relief as he left. At least he wasn't looking at her anymore.

But he stomped back in and marched up to her, glaring fiercely. He grabbed her chin and made her look up into his face. His weak gray eyes held no emotion at all as he said slowly, "I'll be ready for you later." He jerked her chin. "And I'll have you 'til I'm tired of you." He let go of her and strode back out to the porch.

The prospect of having Rafe Pettibone that near addled her brain. She could barely think enough to read the labels on the containers on the shelf. Her hands shook. Remembering Jerrod lying dead in the wagon miles away made it even harder to make her brain work. She had to survive—she had to do more than survive. But she couldn't figure out how.

She managed to find enough food to make the meal Rafe had demanded. The flour, lard, and baking soda were enough for biscuits. The bacon that had been sitting on the cold stove had fried up into a whole plateful. With the three cans of plums she'd discovered behind half a sack of dried beans, it was enough to feed the four men. She couldn't have made herself eat even if they'd told her she could, which they didn't. They'd piled every morsel onto their own plates in less than a minute.

Rafe gulped his food standing up in the doorway, then shoved the plate at Edwina and stomped outside. Within minutes, he came from the corral on his horse, carrying a rifle and heading toward the trail. Edwina let her shoulders drop in relief. Rafe was taking the first watch. She had three hours to come up with a plan.

The other three had taken their food to the porch to eat. Edwina listened to them talk as she worked on the rubble inside.

"Hey, Clyde." It sounded like Al's voice. "Ain't it nice to have food you can actually chew?"

Somebody chuckled, then Clyde said, "Scoot did the best he could." He called to Edwina. "Tomorrow you need to make us an apple pie."

"And fried chicken," Scoot added.

Edwina moved to the doorway and shook her head. "Apple pies take apples. And to fry chicken, we need to *have* a chicken." She hoped the bravado hid the rising flood of fear she was about to drown in.

"Yes, ma'am," the three said together as she turned away from the door.

"Reckon we do need supplies," Scoot said. "Maybe Rafe will let us head into Florissant tomorrow."

At the mention of the town, she stepped behind the door to listen. Florrisant was where she and Jerrod had started from in the wagon. Could it have been only this morning?

They didn't say any more about the town.

She picked up the litter in the cabin and took the smelly clothes outside where the air could at least get to them. Once she'd removed the trash, she surveyed the contents of the one room that was "the cabin." In addition to the dilapidated dry sink and rusty cook stove, there was a battered table with three mismatched chairs in various stages of disrepair and an iron bed with a pine needle mattress. She shivered as she looked at the bed. She still didn't have an escape plan that had half a chance of working.

She began to go through the supplies on the wall shelf next to the dry sink, hoping to find something that might help. It was getting dark and the lantern gave barely enough light to figure out what was in all the tins and sacks. She found every-thing from cigarette papers to lantern oil but very little food and nothing that made her see a way to escape.

On the far end of the shelf, she came to a large package in brown wrapper. She put the lantern on the table and lifted the package off the shelf. It sloshed as she carried it to the table. She pulled a bottle from the brown paper and held it in the lantern light. Whiskey.

It was a start.

She put the bottle back in the paper wrapping and set it on the shelf where it had been, moving the oatmeal in front of it for the time being. The night had become very quiet, she real-ized with a jolt. What had happened to the three outlaws swap-ping lies on the porch? She heard a horse and she looked out the window. Clyde was riding down the trail. He had to be go-ing to relieve Rafe. She was running out of time.

The outline of the other two men, rolled into their bedrolls fifty feet to the right of the cabin, gave her a glimmer of hope. The gate to the corral was on the left. If she could get to the corral, she might be able to get a horse away from the hideout without waking them up. But first she had to deal with Rafe. Finally, a plan began to come together in her head.

She took the cast iron frying pan from the oven where she'd stored it and placed it carefully under the bed on the side nearest the wall. Then she got up on the bed and leaned toward the pan to see if she could reach it without getting off the bed. Barely.

She moved the pan to where she could reach it—which left the tip of the handle peeking out from under the bed. Better the risk he might see it than the risk she couldn't reach it if she got far enough to use it, she decided. She set a glass she'd cleaned on the table, got the whiskey down, removed the brown wrap-per and set the bottle conspicuously next to the glass. Then she moved the lantern so both the bottle and the glass would be visible when Rafe walked in the door.

She re-pinned her hair the way she'd often done to tease Jerrod. By pulling one pin, it would fall loosely around her shoulders. She took off her petticoats and hid them under the bed. It was her only hope. If Rafe didn't have the appetites she was assuming he had, she was worse than dead.

Rafe was thinking about his plans for the rest of the evening when Clyde rode up. The lookout post was beyond the pine forest and up a ridge, about a mile from the cabin. The site offered a clear view of the trail into the trees as well as the panorama of the valley and the road between Florissant and Cripple Creek.

"Thought you'd never get here, little brother," Rafe said amiably.

Clyde shrugged. "That's what I get for showing up ten minutes early."

Rafe took out his pocket watch, lit a match and squinted at the dial. "You're right. You are early. Now why the hell did you do that?" He slapped his younger brother on the leg as a gesture of affection. "I'm never gonna break you of those Sunday school habits Ma taught you."

Rafe knew they looked like brothers. They both had the Pettibone face and eyes. But Rafe liked it that—besides being ten years older—he was taller than Clyde by three inches and outweighed him by forty pounds. And his brother's smooth-skinned face still reflected the inexperience of a kid. He looked at his younger brother with the closest feeling to love he knew—pride.

"Why *did* you come early, anyway?"

Clyde dismounted and walked toward the small campfire. He cleared his throat, but hesitated. "Actually, I wanted to talk to you before you went in, Rafe."

Rafe grinned. "Lookin' for some advice from big brother? Want a little of your own time with that tart later maybe?" Rafe had noticed Clyde didn't seem too interested in catting around.

Maybe he needed a captured opportunity.

Clyde didn't smile back. He took off his hat, ran his fingers through his hair, and put the hat back on. Then he coughed self-consciously.

"Well, what the hell is it? I ain't gonna sit out here all night waiting for you to get up enough guts to talk." Rafe winked. "I been at this three hours, man. I got other things to do."

"That's what I want to talk to you about," Clyde finally said.

"What?" Rafe asked impatiently.

"The woman." Clyde looked straight into his brother's eyes. "Don't do that to her, Rafe."

"She got it coming, dammit. She tried to get away. Besides, I *like* the tall ones."

"She's a lady, Rafe. And she said she was sorry. It ain't right to do that."

"Stop trying to tell me what's 'right,'" Rafe growled. "And quit bein' such a sissy. If you was leader of this gang, we'd spend all our time fixin' things up. Before ya know it, we'd be plantin' petunias in front of the jail."

Sometimes Rafe resented the age difference between them. He was so much older he wasn't sure Clyde would ever grow up enough to be worth being around. They were the only boys of six children. Rafe was the oldest. He'd been almost convinced that Clyde, who was the youngest, had been permanently sissified from so much time with four sisters and their ma. Rafe had been downright delighted when Clyde joined the gang two months ago, but sometimes he wondered if the kid would ever understand. The real law of the land favored the man with the most guts and the quickest gun. The glory belonged to the ones the rest feared. And Rafe planned to have his share of glory. Clyde, however, always worried about "right" and "nice."

Clyde cleared his throat again, a habit Rafe decided he would need to break him of.

"Pa says if you do that to a woman, you can't never come home."

Clyde's sincerity made Rafe laugh. "Why the hell would I want to go home?" Rafe wanted to forget the parched ground east of Denver City. To him, it was a place of hard work and disappointment, where every day was filled with orders from his demanding father and his future was a gaggle of mouths to feed once the old man was gone. "All that's there is a hateful old man, a bunch of ugly biddies, and a lot of dried grass."

"The Pettibone women are a fine lot," Clyde said.

"You stayed on that place so long your brain fried," Rafe said. "I'll make my way out here." He leveled his gaze on his brother and spoke slowly. "You ain't gonna find anything worth doing on that damn prairie."

Rafe took two steps, as if to distance himself from the topic, then swept his head toward the surrounding countryside. "Hasn't been anything out of the ordinary," he said. "Did you get any sleep before you came out?"

"Didn't feel much like sleeping. I'll be all right."

Rafe looked at his brother sternly. "Don't fall asleep. Even with the help in Florissant, we gotta be careful no one finds this place." He climbed on his horse. "Necktie parties ain't fun for the guests of honor."

Clyde moved toward Rafe. "Ma misses you," he said quietly.

Rafe gathered his reins, readying to leave. "Well, Ma's just gonna to have to miss me a whole lot more."

He clicked the horse into motion. As he passed his brother, he stopped and gave him a hard look. "I am going to have that woman." He took a deep breath and exhaled slowly. "And tomorrow night, it'll be your turn with her, and I'm going to make damn sure you do, too."

CHAPTER 2

EDWINA SAT RAMROD straight at the table in the cabin, exactly as she'd been taught at Mrs. Dayton's school. Only her hands, clasped so tightly the knuckles were white, belied her appearance of calm. She reminded herself again that trying to get away before Rafe returned was foolish. He'd caught her so quickly the last time that even her own skill on a horse would never be enough.

To be successful, she had to incapacitate him. Otherwise, she'd never have enough time to get down the trail, make it past the look-out, and find the road to Florissant. She blushed as she reviewed the plan she'd finally devised. Her school friends would have fainted just hearing what she had in mind. But then, they weren't the ones dealing with Rafe Pettibone.

Her skin crawled at the idea of having to get that close to him. But it was the only way—at least the only way she'd been able to come up with. "I can do this," she told herself out loud. She clenched her fists and drew in a deep breath. *Find your gumption, girl, and get on with what you have to do.*

The dreaded sound of hoof beats materialized in the darkness. She stood automatically and listened as Rafe went around to the corral. The gate squeaked open and shut.

She glanced at her reflection in the cracked mirror on the wall and was dismayed. Her face looked like it belonged in a coffin. The deep green of her eyes had disappeared into black hollows of fear and her brown hair only made the pallor of her skin more sickly. She pinched her lips together to make them color and slapped her cheeks lightly to bring out some pink.

The few last minutes she expected while he unsaddled his horse evaporated when the gate squeaked open and shut again immediately. She tried one last sultry pout in the mirror. As Rafe was striding across the porch, she checked the table to be sure she had things arranged as best she could. Pushing a stray wisp of hair away from her face, she moved beside the table and grasped the back of the chair. Her knuckles turned white again as she clung to it.

Rafe threw the door open and looked around the room, surveying the now-clean cabin.

Before he could speak, Edwina said, "Oh, Rafe, I'm so glad you're here." She wanted to vomit uttering the words but made herself continue. "I've been waiting for you to get back." The low purring sounds she managed to include with the words amazed her.

Rafe gaped at her. Finally he gulped. "You were?" His eyes didn't leave her face.

"I was afraid one of the others might—"

"They do what I say," Rafe said. "And I *said* I got ya first."

"Oh, Rafe," Edwina said, trying to flutter her eyelashes. "I don't mind cookin' and cleanin' for everybody, but please, can't it only be you I bed with? I only want *you*." The request tasted vile in her mouth, but she got it out without faltering.

She wanted to run past him and into the night more than she had ever wanted anything in her whole life. Instead, she went on.

"I found that bottle while I was cleaning up," she said sweetly, nodding toward the table. "Thought you might like a little."

"I'll be damned," he said. "Where'd you get that?"

Her thoughts raced. Please lord… Oh no! Maybe he didn't drink! "Don't you like whiskey, Rafe, honey?" She almost gagged on the last word.

"Sure do." His eyes moved back and forth between the bottle and Edwina, as if he was trying to decide which to address first.

"Would you like me to pour you a glass?"

Rafe's expression changed suddenly, and he exploded in fury. "You trying to poison me?"

Edwina stepped back at the outburst. "No! I just found it on the shelf and thought you might like it." Her heart pounded in her ears. Her mouth was so dry her tongue tasted like paper. It would have been nice if there had actually been poison available.

Rafe's eyes narrowed. "Then you take a drink first." Just as well that there hadn't been any poison.

She poured a swallow of whiskey into the glass and gulped the contents before she could think about it. When the fiery liquid hit her throat, she coughed so hard most of the whiskey sprayed into the air.

Rafe burst into laughter. As she struggled to stop coughing, he watched her carefully without saying anything. After a full minute of silence, he said hoarsely, "Gimme that. No sense wasting it."

She poured the glass half full of the whiskey and handed it to him silently.

"Fill it."

She filled it to the rim, and handed it to him again.

He held the glass in the lantern light, eyeing it appreciatively. "Mighty nice of Scoot." He took a slow sip. "Maybe with a woman around to do the cookin' now, Scoot won't need to be so stingy with what he keeps to fortify himself." He lifted the glass a bit higher and glared at her. "To my evening's delight." He emptied the entire water glass in a three huge gulps.

He set it on the table with a bang. "More."

She filled the glass again, and he drained it even more quickly. The half bottle she'd started with wasn't likely to make him pass out, but with each swallow, she felt she was gaining more of an advantage.

The glass wasn't quite full the third time before the bottle was empty. Rafe downed the whiskey so fast he couldn't have tasted it. "Looks like I took care of that," he said with a satisfied grunt. He wiped his mouth on his sleeve and glared at her. "Come here."

It felt like her feet had grown roots through the cabin floor.

"I *said*, come here."

She reemphasized the pout that had faded with his command and let go of the back of the chair.

"Come *here*," Rafe repeated, louder. She took a step, but he was already moving.

As he came around the table, Edwina struggled again to project the disgusting facade of being pleased to be alone with him. In the most seductive tone she could manage, she moved toward him. "No need to rush. It'll be nicer if we take a little time." At least she didn't retch.

She'd removed most of her undergarments earlier in the evening. Now her life depended on what she did with the rest of her clothes. Her hands trembled as she slowly undid the buttons on her high collared blouse, stopping once her throat and part of her breasts were exposed. Her face burned with shame. She hoped he would think it was excitement. Then she decided he wouldn't care either way.

Rafe stared stupidly. "Jeshus," he mumbled. Edwina looked at the chair next to him, and Rafe sat down. He took each breath slowly, never moving his eyes from her front.

His easy read of what she wanted him to do and his willing compliance startled her. Would he stay this docile long enough for her to finish the game? She could only hope.

She stooped before him, making sure she'd provided him an excellent view of her cleavage. When she put her hand on his boot, he obediently lifted his foot. The odor of his unwashed foot and sweat-crusted sock made her eyes sting as she removed the boot. She kept going, pulling off the second boot, then rose to stand in front of him.

Rafe's eyes stayed glued to her chest the entire time.

She unbuttoned her skirt and stepped out of it, maintaining the seductive pout as best she could the whole time. She let the skirt fall to the floor. She could do it, she kept telling herself. She *had* to do it.

Keeping her eyes locked with his, she finished unbuttoning

the top, took it off, and let it fall, too. She stood before him in a shift of lightweight muslin, wishing for all the world that she was wearing her father's fur hunting coat and three layers of heavy wool underwear.

The full-length mirror in her bedroom at home had told her many times that the thin fabric of the shift hid very little. She prayed her plan would work well enough that she could at least keep that on.

Rafe continued to watch her quietly, his breathing so heavy she wondered if something was physically wrong. Then he stood up and leaned toward her.

Edwina pulled the strategic pin from her hair and let the mass of brown curls cascade over her almost bare shoulders.

Rafe sucked in a deep breath as he stared.

Her mind screamed a thousand warnings as she moved close to him, reached up, and stroked his cheek lightly. Sheer willpower kept her stomach bile where it belonged. She caressed down the unscarred side of his jawbone to his neck, reminding herself again that her unforgivable behavior held her only hope. Her hands began to shake, and she clenched them tightly to make them stop. She *had* to keep going.

She unbuttoned his shirt carefully, pulled it from his shoulders, and laid it neatly on the back of a chair. The next step was where she expected him to explode in angry protest. But when she reached for his gun belt, Rafe knew what she wanted and became almost gallant.

"I'll get that," he said thickly and undid the holster. He dumped his gun, still holstered, on the table without taking his eyes off her.

Edwina put her arms around his waist and began to caress the small of his back. Disgust joined the shame burning on her face as she hid it in his chest. He pushed her away and panic reclaimed her. He wasn't buying it and there was nothing else she could think of to try.

But instead of hurting her again, Rafe undid the buttons on his pants, let them drop to the floor, and stepped out of them clumsily—never taking his eyes of her as he did it.

She picked up his pants and laid them carefully over the chair with the shirt, before she looked at him. It had never occurred to her that he might not wear underwear. All he had on were his socks. She tried to disguise her gasp of terror as one of delight. He was even uglier naked.

She frantically tried to remind herself of the next step in the plan. She stared at a small scar on his torso, trying to think, as Rafe moved toward her. Finally she took his hand and drew him toward the bed.

He followed like a puppy.

She crawled onto the bed, and he crawled up after her.

"Let me rub your back a bit," she cooed.

"Don't need no back rub," he said. He grabbed her legs.

"Sure you do. You just don't know how nice it will feel." She wiggled out of his grasp and gently pushed him over on his stomach, then lifted herself over him and off the side of the bed nearest the wall. Fighting the unquenchable urge to choke him now that she was in a position to do it, she began to knead his shoulders. As she gently worked the muscles, Rafe began to settle into the bed. She hoped briefly that he might just fall asleep. But within a minute, he was grunting loudly.

As she worked his back with both hands, she used her right foot to ease the frying pan farther out from under the bed. Singing softly in his ear to distract him from any betraying sound, she pushed the skillet to where she was sure she could reach it. Then she leaned over him and began to rub her breasts in circles on his back to free her hands. Her gratitude for the thin film of separation that the muslin shift provided between her skin and his was profound. She felt the cold iron of the pan handle against her palm.

"Oh, darlin'" Rafe groaned.

Just as he raised up to turn toward her, Edwina hit him from behind with a two-handed swing of the frying pan.

His head flopped onto the mattress soundlessly.

She checked quickly—he was still breathing—and thought about shooting him. There was no need to do that. They weren't on the frontier—Jerrod had assured her of that many times before they'd left St. Louis. Any lawman in the area would be ready to deal with the likes of Rafe Pettibone. This was the 1890's for heaven's sake. Law-abiding citizens didn't have to shoot anyone. Besides, the sound of a gun would wake the others.

She grabbed Rafe's clothes and gun and kicked his boots under the bed as she rushed by the table. As she reached the door, she scooped up her own shoes. By the time she reached the corral, she had the shirt partially buttoned and the pants on. She didn't let herself think about who had been wearing them only moments before.

She shoved her shoes in the saddle bag, then wrapped the gun belt around her waist and pulled it to the tightest notch, having no idea if she'd remember her father's lessons on how to use a revolver.

After wedging the gate open long enough to get to Rafe's horse and lead her out, she purposely let the gate squeak shut. If the two men sleeping in the yard did distinguish the noise from their dreams, they would assume it was Rafe, gone to unsaddle his horse.

She walked the chestnut mare very slowly across the clearing as far away from the sleeping men as she could get. The pine needles muffled the sound more than she expected, and she began to breathe again—and to hope. A few hundred yards down the trail, she turned to be sure things were still quiet in the camp. She mounted. In minutes, she had the horse at a gallop, intent on finding the road to Florissant and the Law before the look-out could stop her.

Clyde heard the hoof beats and checked his watch. It was only an hour into his shift. He crouched in the rocks at the top of the ridge and waited for the rider to come into the moonlit view. At first glance, he thought it was Rafe. It was Rafe's horse, and it was Rafe's clothes. But something wasn't right. As the form passed beyond the lookout post without stopping or even waving, Clyde realized the shape on the horse was too small to be Rafe. Once out of the trees and racing through the moonlight, he could see her long hair flying wildly behind her as she rode.

Clyde raised the Winchester, put his finger to the trigger, and followed her as she sped down the trail. Hitting her would be easy, but he knew he wouldn't fire.

When she was out of range, he set the rifle down wearily. He sat down on a nearby rock and let his head fall into his hands. Pa had always taught him it was wrong to harm anyone else. Rafe thought of killing as roughly akin to sawing wood. Pa said you had to work hard to get what you wanted in life. Rafe believed you could just demand it from people who were weaker than you. Pa believed in giving. Rafe believed in taking. When he'd joined the gang, he'd hoped he could talk Rafe into coming home. But if his older brother had taken that woman as he'd planned, Pa was never going to allow him back anyway. Clyde's stomach threatened to reject his fine supper as the conflicting dictates of his father and brother battled in his head.

Finally, he picked up the rifle Rafe had bought him when he joined the gang and laid it against a boulder where the others could find it. He could still see the dust of the woman's horse, but he looked away even as he realized he might still be able to catch her. Slowly he walked to his horse, mounted, and headed toward the road and the opposite direction to where she had gone, never once looking back toward the hideout.

Edwina didn't know where the lookout was located and thought she had yet to pass Clyde when she found herself on the main road. Grateful for the luck, she turned toward Florissant, which she guessed was about ten miles west. She and Jerrod had bought the wagon there the night before and had loaded their belongings into it with giddy excitement. Now she saw the recent memories as some long ago dream. Maybe even a fairy tale.

She did recall she'd seen a man wearing a badge when they'd left the livery the previous night. It was only a matter of finding that man and telling him what had happened. Then Rafe and his ruffians would be in jail, and she could bury Jerrod. And then? She would think about that later.

She was surprised at the quality of the horse she was on. Riding was easy on the road and even with side trips into the hills to watch to be sure they weren't pursuing her, she arrived just as dawn was lighting the brief main street and the ramshackle collection of buildings the locals called a town.

At the first of the buildings, she dismounted and found a water trough. Resting her foot on the trough while the horse drank, she rolled up her pants legs so she could walk without stepping on them. She gathered her hair back up on her head and re-buttoned the shirt so it was properly aligned. She put on her shoes. After unbuckling the holster, she wrapped the belt around the gun and stuffed the whole bundle into one of Rafe's saddlebags. As a final adjustment, she pulled the extra cloth of the pants into a tuck and rolled the waistband to be sure they wouldn't fall down. Then she sat down on the edge of the trough to wait for the town to come to life.

As the sun's rays spread onto the muddy street, she thought she could make out bars on the windows of a small building at the other end of town. When the sun was up, she lifted the reins from the saddle horn, nudged the horse away from the trough, and walked slowly toward the building.

It looked too flimsy to hold an outlaw, but the sign on the front did say "Jail." She walked the horse past it and the remaining few buildings in town, then perched on a fence to watch the jail and wait for someone to show up.

A rooster crowed, and donkeys brayed behind one of the shops. The sounds of people starting their day played on her ears—people yanking wood from woodpiles and drawing water from their pumps, outhouse doors squeaking open and shut.

Finally, a little man came scurrying toward the jailhouse. If he was the marshal, how many others would he take with him to apprehend Rafe and his gang? There was so little of him he would probably evaporate on a hot day.

She waited a few minutes before she started toward the jail. Once in front of it, she tied Rafe's mare to the hitching post, took the four steps to the door quickly, and knocked.

No answer.

She knocked again, harder.

She noticed a quick flutter of the window curtain.

"Let me in, marshal," she finally hollered. "I need your help."

The door opened a crack, and Edwina pushed her way in.

The little man she was staring at truly did look like a mouse—graying mutton chop whiskers, a thin little face and hardly any jaw. To say he was frail would have been kind. He wore the clothes she'd seen on most of the merchants and townsmen the day before—plain britches and a plain, collarless shirt with a black broadcloth coat.

"Wha...wha...what do you want?" The little man trembled as he looked at her.

"My husband's been killed by bandits."

The little man continued to stare.

"I can take you to the murderers' hideout." She went on, feeling her calm of minutes before dwindle away as she spoke. "It was Rafe Pettibone and his gang."

She stopped talking.

The man hadn't even nodded in sympathy.

"They shot him when he wasn't looking. Killed him in cold blood." Her voice was so shrill she didn't recognize it.

The mousy man's mouth hung open in a stupid gape. He seemed unable to shut it so he could speak.

"Help me!"

Her scream at least loosened his vocal cords. "I'm just lightin' the marshal's stove ma'am. I can't help."

Edwina was deciding what to do next when the door opened behind her.

A tall man with a paunch walked in—and he was wearing a badge.

"Where's Rafe? His horse is at the rail. I thought he'd be here." The larger man looked around the room.

Edwina felt her legs buckle as he turned to look at her.

"You come with Rafe?"

Edwina's eyes widened as she struggled to say something intelligible. "No...no...I didn't."

He was as tall and as heavy as Rafe, except his weight was around his middle rather than in the shoulders. Poppa would have concluded he hadn't done a lick of physical work in his life—his hands were too soft and his skin was too smooth. But what bothered Edwina most were the rings he wore on three fingers of each hand. What kind of man wore that many rings?

The marshal looked out the window and stared at Rafe's horse. "Well I'll be dipped. Wonder why he left his horse here." He moved to the doorway and surveyed the street.

"I came on his horse," Edwina said, finally. "I rode it to escape."

The marshal turned toward her. She watched his eyes narrow.

"Rafe Pettibone killed my husband," she said, dredging up every spare bit of confidence she'd ever stored. "The gang robbed us. Rafe shot and killed my husband—Jerrod Sinclair."

The marshal laughed. "Rafe Pettibone? Nope."

"It *was* Rafe Pettibone. He even *said* so."

The lawman, who'd sat down behind his desk and was leaning back on his chair, came forward with a resounding thump on the floor. "You'd best be careful what you're saying, girl. Rafe Pettibone's held in good repute."

"He's a thief and a murderer!" Edwina felt the rage she'd suppressed for the last twenty hours welling in her throat. "He stole everything. He killed my husband. He was going to..." She couldn't utter the word "rape."

The marshal looked at her coolly, saying nothing for what seemed like an hour. Eventually, he nodded toward Edwina, "Looks to me like that's Rafe's shirt you have on."

Edwina looked down at the faded, worn fabric of the shirt.

"And that's his horse out front, right?"

"I had to take them to get away," she said, her voice again rising into shrillness. "He was going to..." Her words trailed off lamely.

"Now lookee here, you hussy..." The marshal moved in front of her and waved his finger in her face for emphasis.

She collapsed in the chair directly behind her.

The marshal stood above her, still jabbing his finger at her. "Looks to me like you're the thief. Pretty nervy comin' in here on a stolen horse and in someone else's duds saying you was robbed. If there's anybody to arrest, it would be you." He looked her over from head to foot. "You're just a harlot trying to get a piece of a man's hide for spite. Rafe's only crime is he needs to have better sense with women."

Edwina's head swam with confusion and lack of sleep. Either she made her mind work or she'd be the one behind bars.

The marshal stepped behind his desk, opened the top drawer, and rummaged in it. "Edmond, where are the keys to the cell?"

As he focused on the drawer, Edwina jumped from the chair and bolted past him and out the door. She was onto the horse before he realized she was moving. She raced down the short main street of town without thinking about the best direction to go, unconsciously returning to where her life had ended.

When Rafe came to, he struggled to recall what he could have done to make his head hurt so bad. He saw the empty bottle on the table and decided whiskey was the culprit. But the throbbing was in the wrong place for that. And it wasn't one of those other headaches that had gotten more frequent lately. This was different.

He tried to get off the bed, but he couldn't keep his head lifted for more than a few seconds at a time. Finally, he gave up and fell back asleep.

The sun was fully up when Rafe heard the commotion of someone riding frantically into camp. Within seconds, Al burst into the cabin without knocking. "Clyde's missing!"

Rafe managed to turn his head toward the door but was still laying face down and naked on the bed.

"What the hell's the matter with you?"

Rafe groaned.

"Where's the woman?" Al glared at Rafe as if he'd lost a whole herd of Angus. "If she heads for Cripple Creek and Marshal Gruen, we're as good as dead."

Rafe forced himself to sit up. The situation was coming back in bits and pieces, but he was having a hard time following what Al was worried about. "Who?"

"The woman, Rafe," Al said with exasperation. "Remember? The one you insisted on bringing back here with us? The one you took after first watch last night?"

Rafe was still struggling, but he was beginning to remember a naughty pout and seductive green eyes in a face framed with soft brown curls. "Was she here?"

Al rolled his eyes. "What the hell did she do to you?"

Rafe tried to stand, but his head hurt too much and he sat back down on the bed.

Al tried again. "Where's your brother?"

Rafe smiled. At least he knew the answer to that one. "He relieved me on watch at midnight."

"Well, he wasn't there when I went to relieve him at six."

Rafe looked at the red-haired Kentuckian. Again all he could manage was, "Huh?"

"He's gone, Rafe. Scoot's covering now, but Clyde ain't around." Al waited for Rafe to respond, but Rafe just looked at him. "Near as I can tell, he lit out northeast. Do you think he took the woman with him?"

"No," Rafe answered slowly. "She was here with me..." Then he stopped, struggling to remember more.

Al began moving around the room. "She won't go far without these." He held up her blouse and skirt.

Rafe stood up again and grabbed the back of his head. "She must've hit me with a shovel or somethin'."

Al moved around to the other side of the bed and pulled the frying pan from near the wall where Edwina had left it. He began to snicker. "Rafe Pettibone, put out of commission with a fryin' pan."

The snickers turned into laughter and the laughter into guffaws. Al was holding his sides trying to stop, tears running down his cheeks. "The great Rafe Pettibone bested with a skillet!"

Rafe glared at him. "Just shut up, Al," he growled. "And help me find my clothes."

"Why the hell did you take 'em off?" Al began to laugh all over again. "That little witch! I'll bet she had you eating out of her hand."

"Shut up, Al." Rafe had no patience under ordinary circumstances. When it came to being made a fool of, he had even less than that.

Al pulled Edwina's petticoats from under the bed and in the

process, dragged out Rafe's boots. "Maybe we can work our way up," he said dryly as he handed the boots to Rafe.

"She put my pants right here," Rafe said, staring at the back of the empty chair. "Right on top of my shirt." After a moment it sunk in. "Son of a bitch! She took my clothes." He looked at Al, who was doing his best not to start laughing again. "And my gun!"

"Get me some clothes from that stuff on the porch," Rafe ordered. "And tell me if Bandit's in the corral."

Al moved through the cabin door, not laughing again until he got outside. Rafe wanted to break his neck for laughing at all, but when a shirt and pants sailed through the door, he decided not to beat the shit out of him. At least not yet.

Rafe put on the shirt but fumbled with the buttons. His vision was still hazy, and images were double, sometimes triple, when he looked at things.

Al reappeared. "Your horse is gone, too." He looked truly apologetic at having to provide the news. "How'd she get her saddled without us hearing anything?"

Rafe didn't answer.

"Some outlaw leader," Al muttered as he walked out the door.

"I'll get her!" Rafe's scream sounded like a crazy man, but he didn't care. "She'll be sorry she messed with Rafe Pettibone." He collapsed on the bed again, the pain throbbing in his head with the force of a locomotive.

Although Edwina left Florissant at a full gallop, she slowed to an easy trot after she was sure the marshal hadn't come after her. Riding too fast would only attract the attention of anyone on the road. A few miles from town, she dismounted and walked the horse up into some rocks in the hills near the road. If the marshal was in belated pursuit, she needed to know it.

She tied the mare a few paces down the opposite slope, then stretched out on the ground behind a rock above the road and watched. There was no one coming from Florissant. There wasn't anyone on the road at all.

When she decided she wasn't being chased, she took time to rest and think. What had just happened didn't make sense. How could a lawman be so wrong about Rafe Pettibone? Did the whole mining district think the same way?

A talkative stranger across from them on the train had babbled on about county sheriffs and town marshals and marshals in the mining camps, but she hadn't listened, preferring to watch the scenery and dream about the house they'd have in Cripple Creek. Now she wished she'd paid more attention. Who would help her get Rafe Pettibone arrested? Did they *all* think he was a "reputable man?"

The road remained deserted, except for three young riders coming toward Florissant. She knew it was as safe to leave as to continue to hide, but she stayed behind the rock anyway, thinking. Getting Rafe arrested didn't guarantee anything, she decided. A jury of people like that marshal would just set him free again. Maybe it was going to take more than a lawman and a jury to set things right.

She went back through all the lessons her father had taught her, trying to figure out what to do next. Nothing helped. Too much ached to think clearly. Her body ached with fatigue, her mind ached with trying to find a solution, and her heart ached for Jerrod. Without intending to, she fell asleep.

Distant thunder woke her hours later. Late afternoon, she guessed—the mountains usually had thunderstorms late in the afternoon. The chestnut was still grazing on the back slope. Edwina knew she'd been lucky—no one had found her, and the horse hadn't wandered off. The perversity of that luck in the middle of her dilemma made her laugh out loud. The sound startled her.

She checked the road, listening hard to be sure she didn't miss someone approaching. The unintended nap had been exactly what she needed. Once she fell asleep, her mind had relaxed enough to come up with at least part of a plan.

First, she had to bury Jerrod. Then she'd save what she could of the wagon, its contents, and the mules. Then she'd deal with Rafe Pettibone.

After fetching the horse and brushing her tracks, she started back toward the road. Squinting to see because of the glare of the sun, she realized she hadn't yet addressed a more pressing need—finding a place to spend the night.

CHAPTER 3

NOT EVEN THE scent of pine and the crisp beauty of the mountains sparkling in the sun could cheer Edwina the following morning. She sat under the rock overhang where she'd spent the night and let herself sob. Each time she stopped the flow of tears, they began again as soon as she took a breath. The realization that she would never again feel Jerrod beside her was too overpowering to do anything else.

She knew she had to bury him, to be sure he was at least respectfully put to rest. But the finality of that good-bye kept her from executing the plan she'd lain awake half the night perfecting. She cried for most of the morning, sobbing herself into fitful naps and then waking to the reality of the loss over and over.

The sun was high in the sky when her reservoir of grief was finally empty. Once she could breathe without breaking into tears yet again, she went to the creek she'd found the evening before and splashed cold water on her face.

Her eyes ached when she moved out into the sunlight. They felt puffy and full of sand. She probably wouldn't recognize herself if she had a mirror to look in, she told herself numbly.

When she began to saddle Rafe's horse, Edwina started to come back to life. She was surprised at how the mare cooperated on what needed to get done. The personality of the animal was a sharp contrast to the grotesque nature of the man who'd owned her.

"Let's give you a name," she said after she threw the saddle on. "You're too beautiful to be 'Rafe's horse.'" She tightened the cinch.

"How about 'Jewel'?" She asked the question as if she expected the animal to answer. Then she patted the horse's neck. "Jewel. That'll work." She finished her preparations and mounted.

But in spite of her pleasant disposition, "Jewel" had made a glaring mess of the surrounding ground. Itchy with dried sweat and at last freed of the saddle she'd carried for too long, she'd rolled wildly in the dirt. Even a novice tracker would notice.

Edwina got off the horse. Grasping a bushy pine branch and twisting until it broke off the tree, she methodically brushed the ground where Jewel had rolled. Once the dirt was level, she sprinkled pine needles over it until it blended with the rest of the area. Then she got back on the horse and headed toward the road to Cripple Creek.

When she reached the spot where the bandits had stopped them, she followed the wheel tracks into the meadow, then the landmarks she'd tried to memorize up into the hills. Perhaps her morning's cry had improved the plan, she decided. Because of the delay, she was returning at same time of day as when they'd covered the ground two days before. The landmarks wore the same shadows and splashes of sunlight.

Instead of riding directly to the wagon, she left the horse downwind a half-mile in an isolated stand of pines. Then she circled back on foot and climbed the outcrop. As she worked her way up the rocks, the sickening smell became stronger. Two buzzards circled overhead. The combined evidence made her climb faster. *No! Not that!* screamed in her head. She heard no small scavengers and hoped that was a good sign. But a stern voice deep inside told her how unlikely it was that Jerrod's body was still in one piece.

Once she reached the top of the rocks, she peered over the edge at the scene below. Scoot was sitting in the opening of the clearing, whittling a stick. The presence of the man explained the lack of crows and magpies. But he hadn't been there the whole time. The birds had had their chance.

A saddled horse grazed beyond the enclosure where the wagon was hidden. Scoot's rifle was propped against a tree stump near where he was sitting. It wasn't going to be as easy as she'd hoped.

From her vantage, she could also see down into the rig. She rammed her fist in her mouth to stifle the shriek of horror that registered once she realized the mangled mess scattered in the wagon bed was Jerrod's body.

Slowly, she moved back off the edge of the outcrop. She let herself sit for a few numb minutes while the shock subsided, then worked her way down to the ground. There was nothing she could do up in the rocks but look and that was too painful to endure.

She scouted the outer perimeter of the rocks to see if there was another way to get in—and out of—the enclosure. No. Then she remembered the mules.

She returned to the horse and cut two lengths from a rope she'd found in Rafe's saddle bag, then looped the pieces over her shoulder. Starting at the far side of the outcrop, where the sound was least likely to alert Scoot if the mules noticed her, she worked on foot in widening concentric circles, just as Poppa had taught her, looking for the animals. But the effort netted nothing. They hadn't even left droppings.

She watched the sky, which was darkening, and listened for riders as she continued to search. Once she was several hundred yards away from Scoot, she chanced circling in front of him as she made her sweep. On the third pass, about a quarter of a mile downhill and hidden from the enclosure, she noticed a grassy area that sloped off to the south. The mules were grazing on the lush grass at the far end. The vegetation in the meadow was unusually thick and green. She mentally filed away the beauty of the place without really thinking about it and moved toward the mules.

What was it Jerrod had told her about the names? She was still so numb she could barely repeat her own name, much less remember some mule's. "They'll come if you use their names," she remembered Jerrod saying. But what were their names?

She approached the first mule. "Easy, easy," she said in her best grooming voice. The charcoal-gray mare with the white marking on her forehead looked at Edwina but didn't move— or bray. Then Edwina remembered the star. "Alice is a star in Wonderland." She and Jerrod had made up the phrase to remind them the one with the mark was Alice. She patted the mule's neck. "Easy, Alice." Edwina tied the rope around Alice's neck and tethered her to a tree at the edge of the meadow. Then she went back for the other mule.

The second one, also charcoal-gray, but a gelding, also stayed quiet when she approached him. "Easy. Easy," she said in the same soothing tone. "That means you're ..." What was it? Phil? Otis? Orville. That was it. "Good, Orville, good," she whispered, patting him confidently. She got the rope around his neck easily and he followed her on command.

She led the mules to the grove where she'd tethered Jewel and tied the lead ropes so the mules could graze but not wander. Thunder rolled in the distance. Maybe it wouldn't really rain so early, she told herself.

She climbed back up to the vantage above the enclosure. Scoot was still working with his jackknife, but he seemed more occupied with waiting than whittling. He kept checking the trail in the direction away from the enclosure. The sun broke through the clouds as a rider crested the nearest hill.

Al brought his horse to a halt in front of Scoot. "See anything?"

Edwina was surprised at how well sound carried.

"Nothin'," Scoot answered. "I think he just wants us out of camp so we don't laugh anymore."

Al took off his hat and ran his fingers through his hair. He shook his head. "How can anyone be that damn gullible?"

"Yeah. And she found my whiskey, too."

Al dismounted and picked up one of the sticks Scoot had been working on—sharp-ended stakes with rounded heads and a notch on one side of the shank. "What are these for?"

"Nothin'. It's just a thing we used a lot on the farm." Scoot sounded embarrassed. "Pa always said to do somethin' useful whenever you had to wait."

Al dropped the stick. "Let's go back in. That gal's probably halfway to Kansas by now." He scanned the forest, as if trying to gain confirmation from the trees. "Rafe said we only had to stay out 'til sundown." The mid-afternoon sun streamed through the branches. "If we take it slow, we can get back to camp about sundown." He leaned toward Scoot. "In fact, we could go into town. Then we'd get back well *after* sundown."

They both laughed. Scoot dumped the stake he'd been whittling on the pile and grabbed his rifle. Then they both mounted and headed toward the road.

Edwina strained to hear their conversation, but once they disappeared down the hill, their voices were gone, too.

Good, she thought as she hurried down the rocks. Rafe would think the wagon was still being guarded. That gave her time—at least if Al and Scoot didn't have a change of heart. If they came back while she was in the middle of what she had to do, it was over. She ran to where she'd left the horse and mules.

Getting all three animals to the wagon took only a few minutes. The stench was overwhelming. Breathing through her mouth didn't help. And the place was noisy now. Magpies and crows had swooped into the wagon bed as soon as Scoot had left.

Before going closer, Edwina clamped her hand over her mouth to assure she wouldn't scream. She crept up behind the nearest crow and shooed it as it pecked at a piece of flesh. The bird flew to a pine bough and cawed at her angrily. There were too many. She shooed them as she worked, hoping their noise wouldn't summon the men who'd just left.

The vultures continued to circle overhead, too. Fine, she told herself. As long as they kept sailing in circles, the human beasts responsible for their meal would think nothing had changed.

There was no wind to move the sickening odor. Now aware of the extent of the scavenging, she wasn't sure she was up to what she had to do.

She found the tarpaulin they'd planned to use as a ground cloth for the tent still folded neatly and wedged behind a large box at the back of the wagon where Jerrod had placed it. She pulled it out and unfolded it, ready to cover Jerrod's body. Then she climbed into the wagon bed.

Her hands shook as she tried to pick up the tack without disturbing Jerrod's body. "Oh, Jerrod.". Tears streamed down her face but she didn't stop to brush them away. How could this be the man she loved? How could this be her? She made herself keep working. Methodically, she threw the tack off the wagon, then moved what the scavengers had left in the wagon bed of Jerrod gently into the folded tarp.

The visual impact of the desecration was unspeakable, but the smell was worse. She couldn't hold a cloth over her nose because she needed both hands to work. With each breath, she fought back nausea. Once she'd dealt with what was still in the wagon, she walked the ground, picking up every scrap of flesh and bone she could find and reverently placing them inside the folded tarp. She couldn't keep from asking herself painful questions. Would his mother's heart melt with regret for her rejection, knowing how he had died? Would she care that he was a good man, his own man? Worse, would he still be alive if she had been more subservient to Rafe?

Edwina told herself she couldn't dwell on the heartbreaking thoughts. She had to get his body to a place where she could dig a grave. The area where the wagon stood now was solid granite.

Staggering through the nightmare, she somehow got the tack on the mules. Once harnessed, she led them to the tree the outlaws had used to block the entrance and rigged the harness to the tree. She worked the team, moving the trunk a little this way and then a little that until they could pull it out of the enclosure. Poppa's indulgence in unladylike pastimes for her was never more appreciated. When her mother died when she was eight, "ladylike" was no longer a requirement. He let her do whatever she was interested in and that had included learning to drive the freight wagons he used in his business. After hitching the mules to the tree one last time, she gave them full head. They pulled the tree out of the gap and then off to the side.

Brushing sweat from her forehead and feeling the tears that had caked on her cheeks, she hitched the mules to the wagon. When she got up in the wagon seat to drive, the horror hit her yet again. She sat, paralyzed and fighting tears. After a few minutes, she lifted the reins.

She got the rig to face the opening. All she had to do was drive it out. But rather than leaving, she got down from the wagon and walked the ground again, picking up more tiny pieces of Jerrod and putting them under the tarp.

Poppa had told her stories of cultures that believed a spirit had to wander the earth until its body was properly buried. Would Jerrod's spirit wander because his body had been scattered? Not if she could help it. She shook herself back to reality. If she dallied too long, she wouldn't be around to bury any of Jerrod. She climbed onto the wagon seat, grabbed the reins, and clicked the mules forward.

Her destination was the beautiful meadow where the mules had been grazing. It was the best place she could think of—other than next to his father in St. James cemetery back in St. Louis. Maybe she could arrange that later.

For now, she chose a spot in the center of the clearing where the rocky dirt looked deeper. Pine trees rimmed the meadow on all four sides, and the clearing was alive with the whites, pinks, and yellows of early summer wildflowers. In the distance were the snowy tops of the high mountains. Jerrod would like it, she decided. She pulled a shovel from the mining equipment at the back of the wagon.

Even in the loose, gravelly soil in the middle of the meadow, digging was difficult. She scooped shovel after shovel full of dirt, and the hole she was trying to dig seemed to get no deeper. When she was finally down about two feet, she hit bed rock. A two foot grave would have to do. She didn't have the strength to start over where the soil might be deeper.

Working the mules patiently, she got the wagon positioned within inches of the grave. As reverently as if she were touching the Holy Shroud, she wrapped the tarp around Jerrod's body and tied it securely in five different places. With the shovel and some tent poles as levers, she eased the precious bundle onto the boxes on the side of the wagon next to the grave. From there, her only option was to push it over the edge and let it fall on the ground. She hated the thought.

As a compromise between her heart, which was demanding total reverence, and her brain, which was screaming warnings about taking too long, she jumped down from the wagon and carried five armloads of fresh pine needles and scattered them next to the wagon where the body might fall. Then she levered the body off the boxes.

It fell with a muffled thud, but the sound left her as weak as if it had been cannon shot. She felt tears streaming down her face again. Clenching her jaw to keep from sobbing, she pulled the body into the shallow grave and began to shovel dirt over it.

Tears were still streaming down her cheeks as she sifted the last shovelful of dirt over the grave. "Good-bye, darling. Say hello to Poppa."

Her emptiness felt larger than the sky.

She covered the grave with rocks to keep the scavengers away. Then she spread pine needles over the grave and the rest of the area, softening the outline of the mound and hiding her tracks. As the sun set, she rolled a beautiful piece of white rock into the clearing and placed it as a natural, but discernible, marker.

"I will always love you, Jerrod Sinclair," she said softly. Her eyes hardened. "And I will do my best to get you justice. Rafe Pettibone *will* pay." She didn't know how, but she would see that it happened.

After driving the mules and wagon to a rocky ledge a mile away, she returned on horseback in the twilight to wipe out the wagon tracks. On the way back to where she'd left the wagon, she sorted through her options for settling the score with Rafe. The Law hadn't meant much in Florissant. But even if the stories she'd read in the newspapers back home about the untamed West were true, there was a way. There had to be a way.

Returning to St. Louis and trying to take care of things from there crossed her mind. But St. Louis held nothing for her—and no one who cared. Her eyes widened as she realized how totally alone she was.

Rafe Pettibone had killed the only person alive that she cared about—and who cared about her. She had to do something. Jerrod deserved justice. Poppa had taught her never to shirk her responsibility, and this responsibility was hers.

But more than justice for Jerrod was at stake. Rafe Pettibone had ended her own life as well. The monster would pay somehow—both for her husband's death and the fact that she had to go on living without him. The act was too fiendishly wrong to "just accept it as the will of God" as the women in her mother's church had insisted when her father died.

The meek behavior expected of "women of breeding" left a bitter taste in her mouth now. She'd tried so hard to do what she'd been taught at Mrs. Dayton's. She'd been completely devoted to meeting Mother Sinclair's standards. After more Mission Society meetings and Ladies Club teas than she wanted to count, she had nothing. And no one.

Being a "proper young woman" was cowardly, she decided suddenly. If she'd gone to her father and expressed her fury about his unscrupulous partner, maybe he wouldn't have died. If she'd been more outspoken with Mother Sinclair, maybe the woman would have reconsidered her behavior toward her youngest son.

Edwina shook her head fiercely to stop the useless thoughts. She couldn't change all the things she'd been too docile to do anything about before. All she could change was what she did next. *She had to deal with Rafe Pettibone.* Herself.

How?

Was there a marshal in Cripple Creek who would help? She dismissed that thought instantly. She'd already tried one version of Colorado law, with disastrous results. She'd be a fool to trust her luck to another. He might be even quicker to put her in jail for stealing Rafe's horse.

No, she had to find a way to handle Rafe Pettibone on her own.

If she could earn some money, maybe she could hire someone. There were men in the West who killed for a living—at least in the dime novels she'd read on the sly at finishing school. But was that what she wanted—to have someone kill Rafe *for* her? Did she really even want him dead? Or was it that she wanted Jerrod's killing and her own loss to be acknowledged and repented of?

The questions multiplied mercilessly as she rode. Running back to St. Louis certainly wasn't the answer. That was the timid behavior everyone expected. If she fled to St. Louis without doing anything, Rafe beat her again, reducing her life to a shadowy nothingness where all she had to live on was the memories of the man she'd lost.

No. If she was really going to live some kind of life ever again, she had to take a stand. She had to *do something*. She had to find a way to deal with Rafe. Not just a little way either—something strong. Something that Poppa would be proud of and that had the magnitude of Jerrod's death reflected in it. She had to kill him. She had the whole rest of her life to figure out how. But she did need to figure out where to start.

After she got the wagon taken care of, she would go to Cripple Creek. The town was bigger than Florissant, and its marshal wouldn't recognize her. It was growing—that's what had made Jerrod so sure that it was at the center of their future. Maybe once she saw Cripple Creek, she'd be able to come up with the right plan for handling Rafe.

As she climbed into the wagon, she also concluded that, for the moment, she had to take her thoughts off dealing with Rafe and put them on her own survival. Although it was June, nights in the mountains were cold. She needed shelter—and food. Getting the wagon to a new hiding place and finding something to eat and a place to sleep before it got dark had to take priority. She clicked the mules, and the wagon creaked forward.

With each turn of the wagon's big wheels, she warmed more to the idea of taking revenge on Rafe by her own hand. She was good with a gun—Poppa had taught her well. And good with a horse—thanks to the same teacher. She felt a chill down her spine as she realized she *did* want Rafe dead. More than anything. And she wanted him to know why he was dying.

It wouldn't be a case of simply shoving a gun in Rafe's belly and pulling the trigger at the first opportunity. She had to come up with brilliant plan and execute it perfectly. Rafe Pettibone was going to pay with even more than he knew he had to lose.

She stopped the freight wagon in a cluster of rocks about a half mile away from the road and five miles closer to Cripple Creek than where she'd buried Jerrod. The secluded spot where she'd decided to spend the night was cloaked in darkness by the time she'd unharnessed the mules.

By feel, she worked through the wagon until she found a heavy blanket and the lantern. She found matches under the driver's seat—right where Jerrod had shown her he'd put them—and lit the lantern. Working quickly in the flickering light, she found the box of canned goods and took out a can of peaches. She kept the lantern lit only long enough to open the can. Then she snuffed the flame and ate the peaches in the dark, not allowing herself the risk of either the lantern's light or a campfire.

Once she'd eaten, she crawled under the wagon, dragging the blanket in with her. She wondered if she'd be able to even close her eyes with all the horrible things she'd gone through that day. But the emotional drain of burying Jerrod and the physical demands of moving the wagon and digging the grave had taken their toll. She was asleep as soon as she'd pulled the blanket over her.

Florissant had two saloons, one of which Rafe and his gang had been told to stay out of. That left them The Elephant. The "building" was actually more of a tent, with wood bracing and rough boards nailed vertically on the lower half of the sides. The floor was dirt—which turned to mud when the beer got to flowing too freely and fellas got sloppy with their elbows. Rafe was sitting at the rough-hewn plank that served as the bar, on a hunk of log—The Elephant's version of a chair.

He would have much preferred to be in one of Cripple Creek's fine drinking establishments. He cursed Marshal Hugh Gruen yet again.

But The Elephant sold whiskey and that was what Rafe needed. He picked up the glass of liquor in front of him and tossed the contents down his throat, then banged the glass on the plank. "More."

The bartender hurried to oblige, smiling a sickening fake smile that made Rafe want to smash his face.

Rafe and his gang were the only people in the place, which was usually the case. Rafe liked that. He felt important having the entire place to himself.

"She's gone, Rafe." Al swirled his glass of whiskey next to Rafe at the bar. "I don't wanna waste any more time wandering around the countryside looking for her." He glared at Rafe.

Rafe banged his fist on the plank bar, making the freshly filled glass in front of him jump. "We gotta find her. That she-demon made a fool o' me. We're gonna find her if it takes the rest of my life."

"Well, let it take yours," Al said. "I ain't interested in chasin' down some scrawny bitch."

Rafe's face softened as he recalled Edwina in the shift. "Naw, Al. She ain't scrawny at all."

"Dammit, Rafe. She's still got a hold of you." Al stood up in disgust. "If you want to rob people, or even a bank, count me in. But I ain't chasin' after no woman just 'cuz she got the best of ya on a bed."

Rafe turned to Scoot, who was sipping his whiskey on the other side of him at the bar. "How 'bout you?"

Scoot lowered his eyes.

"You telling me you won't look either?"

Scoot didn't answer.

Rafe waited, getting more furious with each passing second.

"Tell you what," Al said, ending the silence a second before Rafe knew he would have exploded and hit one of them. "Why don't you go sit at the wagon and wait for her, and Scoot and I'll go into Cripple Creek for a while to see if she's there."

"Yeah, Rafe. That might work," Scoot said with more enthusiasm than Rafe liked. "That marshal didn't tell *us* we had to stay out of town for a month."

Rafe wasn't sure which made him madder—Al's refusal to look for the woman or Scoot's mention of Marshal Gruen's orders to Rafe because of a bar fight he hadn't even started. But he wanted to find the woman. Maybe having them in Cripple Creek was a good idea. She wasn't in Florissant. Compton, the marshal there, had already told Rafe the gal had come to him for help. In fact, he'd raised the ante on their protection to ten dollars a week because of it.

He had to get that whore. Nothing less would be worthy of Rafe Pettibone. But he couldn't imagine having to do it alone. He was the *leader*. The gang was supposed to do as he said. He would send them to Cripple Creek to look for her.

"How ya gonna look for her?"

Scoot started to snicker. "We'll find somethin', boss," he finally managed to say. "Maybe she's taken up at one of the bawdy houses."

"Sure as hell sounds like she's got the talent," Al said under his breath.

Rafe focused on what he could gain rather than clobbering Al. "How ya gonna figure out where she is?"

"We'll hang around, Rafe. Just like we do when we're sizing up a prospect," Al said. "How come you don't trust *us*? It's your brother that run off."

Rafe really did want to hit him for that one. Clyde's desertion at the worst possible moment hurt more than he wanted to admit. He'd counted on kin for the toughest watch, and kin had let him down. He'd been right—Clyde was a permanent sissy. And now, because of it, he had to take crap from his own gang.

Maybe it was better to send them off for a while. He was tired of the jibes and the laughter. "Check in at the hideout by the end of the week. That's four days, ya hear?"

"Right, boss," Al and Scoot said in unison.

Edwina was up at dawn and already busy in the wagon by the time the sun actually rose. Sorting things in the sunshine was almost fun compared to her tasks of the day before.

In Jerrod's field notebook, she carefully listed the contents of each box and bundle, working her way systematically from the front to the back of the wagon. By noon, everything was neatly accounted for in her ledger.

The camping equipment and canned food they'd packed would go with her somehow. The mining tools, assay equipment and books she would hide where she could come back for them when she needed them. She had no idea what she'd do with them, but they'd been Jerrod's pride. She intended to keep them forever.

The blood on the boxes and bundles was a problem, and not just because of the emotional torment it caused her. The scavengers might notice and begin to tear at things once she'd hidden the wagon if she didn't do something. She thought about trying to wash it off, but gave up the idea. There wasn't enough water in the creek. And she couldn't bear the idea of just washing more of Jerrod away.

Using a bolt of oiled cloth he'd included, she wrapped the stained boxes. He'd thought of so much when he'd bought supplies. It was like he was taking care of her even now. She stopped to brush the first tear from her cheek and willed herself not to cry. Later, she told herself. After she'd taken care of things.

Her biggest challenge was to hide the supply-laden wagon. She drove it down into the center of an elongated depression and unhitched the mules, but left them teamed in the harness. For the next three hours she worked them, hauling fresh pine boughs and dead fall to the little gulch. By the last trip, the area looked like a tangle of brush that had naturally collected because of gravity and seed pods. It would probably take a month or more for the green boughs to turn brown. By then, Rafe would be dead, and she'd be able to come back for the wagon.

Once the brush hauling was finished, she slipped out of the pants and shirt she'd stolen from Rafe. Standing next to the tiny stream in the slanting rays of the late afternoon sun, she quickly shed her shift and splashed water over herself. As she lathered with the soap she'd found in the supplies, she was sure she'd never appreciated soap and water more.

Before she redressed, she tore one of her spare petticoats into long strips and wound them tightly around her chest. It wasn't as uncomfortable as a corset, she decided. She sighed at the irony. Before, she'd put hours of effort into looking like a lady every day. Now, if she was going to succeed, she had to hide it.

She put on one of Jerrod's union suits and the work clothes he'd packed—the most worn pair of trousers she could find in his things and a nondescript shirt. It all fit well enough to pass as hers. That reality almost brought her to tears. Jerrod had been so accepting of the fact that they were the same height.

The feel of men's britches had been hard to get used to at first, maybe because she'd had to wear Rafe's. Now she was beginning to appreciate the advantages. Men's clothes were much easier to work in. And not having to wear a corset was so enjoyable she wasn't sure she'd ever be willing to wear one again.

She'd teased Jerrod about trying on his clothes for fun back in St. Louis and he'd told her there was a law against it. Usually he gave her anything she asked for. Was there really a law that said women couldn't wear men's trousers? If there was, it was one more thing she'd have to risk. And one more reason to steer clear of a marshal, whenever she saw one.

She decided she had to burn Rafe's clothes to be sure no one found them. She lit the disgusting pile on fire under an overhang, hoping the smoke would dissipate enough before it escaped that no one could notice it. When she struck the match, she felt almost like a witch. "Burn!" she said as the old cloth leaped into flame. She wanted to stomp on it even as it was burning, to beat out whatever life there could possibly be in it.

"Get hold of yourself, Edwina Sinclair," she said firmly out loud. "You are not going to get anything done if you go crazy." She watched the clothing until it had burned completely, then stomped the ashes to satisfy her earlier urge.

As she packed the remaining supplies on Alice and Orville,

she noted she had only enough food to keep her for a couple of weeks. If she hunted rabbits and small birds, she might be able to stretch it to a month. She wasn't sure how much time she'd need to handle Rafe, maybe a week, maybe a month. But she knew she'd better plan on being able to buy supplies, which meant she needed money. And that meant she had to find a job.

CHAPTER 4

WHEN SHE STOPPED for the night, Edwina guessed she was within a few miles of Cripple Creek. Traveling without the wagon had been faster, which meant that now she could take her time finding a good campsite. Wherever she chose was going to be home for a while, and it needed to be at least functional.

She decided on a spot nestled between three clusters of trees, both because they would protect her from the wind and because they would help hide her camp. A small creek down the hill had enough water for her and the animals. After she'd checked the backside of yet another outcrop of huge boulders on the hill above the site, she was comfortable that they offered additional protection. The opposite side was too steep for someone to climb and spy on her—or worse. She unsaddled the horse and unloaded the mules, then put up the tent, hurrying to beat sunset.

Once that was done, she took time to look around again. As she stared at the pink hues the departing sun laid on the hillside across from her, she smiled at how very pretty the place was. Then she gasped in horror. How could she be enjoying the scenery with Jerrod dead?

She forked a peach from the can she'd opened and took a small bite from it. She was glad to see the return of the night. Darkness made the emptiness she felt more familiar. In the dark, she understood Jerrod was gone. And the dark helped her think.

She watched the valley as the last light of day disappeared and the black of night wrapped around her. The pine scent intensified in the cool evening air, and the dark seemed to almost caress her. In the starry blackness, a few solitary lights—campfires—winked across the valley. A few more sparkled nearer to where she thought Cripple Creek lay. She was surprised she was not the only one camped in the hills. Then she gave a half-hearted laugh. Jerrod had mentioned that many chose to live in tents when they first got to the area.

She let out a long slow sigh. It was time to get on with her plan.

She lit the kerosene lamp, carefully blocking its light with her body, then took the lamp into the tent where she put it behind a small wooden crate to diffuse the light. After sitting herself cross-legged on the bedroll she'd laid out, she picked up the hunting knife she'd found in the supplies. She stroked the knife edge against a sharpening stone that had also been among the things in the wagon, grateful both for Jerrod's foresight and the fact her father had taught her how to sharpen a knife.

She undid her hair. The soft brown curls fell silently on her shoulders. She let herself think briefly of earlier times—when her mother had brushed it every night and told her how pretty she was.

She put her hand mirror on the bedroll in the light and picked up the knife. Leaning over, she grasped a shock of hair and cut if off at ear level with the knife. After several more swipes, she had what she hoped would pass for the haircut of an adolescent boy.

She tried to make the hair look tousled, but it insisted on falling neatly to each side of her face. Exasperated, she finally got up and rummaged through the bundle of Jerrod's clothes she'd brought from the wagon until she pulled out the dilapidated felt hat he'd worn on field excursions. She jammed it on her head.

When she surveyed the results in the little mirror she realized the hat offered a second benefit. Her clear skin, which had been the envy of her friends at finishing school, was now a liability. The hat—and maybe a little dirt—would make her a lot more convincing as a boy.

For almost an hour, she tried different ways of using dirt to make her face look rougher. Eventually fatigue washed over her with an almost paralyzing effect. She snuffed out the lamp without washing the dirt from her face and pulled the quilt around her on the bedroll. The yip of a coyote was the last thing she heard as she fell asleep. She wondered where it lived. And if it was alone, too.

The next morning, she spent more time trying to figure out what to do with her hair and face, but the old hat and a handful of dirt still seemed to be the solution. She added some lamp soot on her lower face and neck, wearing her skin almost raw with all the rubbing. Then she mashed the hat down on her head again.

Edwina, I dub thee "Eddie."

The only person who'd ever called her "Eddie" was Poppa, and then only after they'd made a pact that she would not tell her mother. But from all she'd heard and read about the West, she knew it would be much easier to survive—and find a job— as a male. The disguise would make it a lot easier to look for Rafe Pettibone, too. Eddie it would be.

She ran through the rest of her plan for her trip into Cripple Creek. Taking the least conspicuous animal was essential. Even though she was easier to ride, Jewel might be recognized, and Alice had the star which might draw attention. Orville's plain, uninspired hide was her best hope of looking ordinary. But would he carry her?

She knew enough not to try the saddle. She'd seen her cousin land in the bean patch when one of her father's mules had thrown both the saddle and the cousin right over its head in a fit of stubbornness. Today she'd ride bareback. If that worked, she'd figure a way to rig the saddle so he'd keep it on later.

She grabbed the mule's halter and swung herself up on his back. Orville reared, but she stayed with him. After a few minutes of bucking and twisting, he settled down and accepted her as the boss. She nudged him forward and started down the hill.

In the distance, Pikes Peak, which she and Jerrod had first

seen from the train a week earlier, loomed in barren brownness against the solid blue of the sky. The top still had a bit of snow. The locals in Florissant had assured them it would be gone by the Fourth of July—less than a month away. Pine trees covered the lower slopes nearer the road, and stands of a different kind of tree that she'd never seen in Missouri—"aspens" Jerrod had called them—sporadically interrupted the expanse of meadow where the road wound.

The sunlight seemed to fade the colors of things closer to her. The dirt was a brownish pink rather than red, and the spring green of the meadow grass was muted by the tan of last year's growth. But the sunlight hadn't subdued the sky. It was such an intense blue that it was hard to believe it was real.

By the time she reached the bottom of the draw, where it met the road, Eddie had concluded it was best to try out her new identity a little at a time. Traffic on the road would hopefully be sparse, but she expected to see at least a few riders, maybe even the stage, before she got all the way to town. Instead of staying on the road, she rode parallel to it in the meadow, about a hundred yards distant. The strategy worked well for the broader stretches, especially since she was in meadows with the wildflowers that made her smile. But when the terrain got steeper, the rutted road was the only way through. On those parts, she had to use it.

As she was starting onto one of those narrow sections, she heard hoof beats. Looking behind her, she could see just enough to make out three riders, coming from the direction of Florissant. She caught the glint of what was probably a lawman's badge on the one in the lead.

She swallowed hard, trying to get the fear out of her mouth as they came closer. Maybe it was the marshal from Florissant. Maybe it was Rafe. Maybe the disguise would be less convincing than her mirror had suggested. "Maybes" whirled in her head like a flock of blackbirds chased from a farmer's field.

When the three riders were within a hundred yards of her, she reined the mule to a stop at the side of the road. Stopping seemed the least suspicious thing to do as they passed her, she decided. But then she realized she wasn't any good at deciding what was "suspicious." Her panic was in full bloom.

The horsemen were almost abreast of where she had stopped. She swallowed hard again.

"Mornin'," the lead man said as he passed. He did wear a badge, but didn't look anything like the Florissant marshal. This man was taller. And younger. And didn't have the paunch. But he was probably every bit as casual about the law, she warned herself.

The other two riders merely nodded as they overtook her and rode past. She didn't recognize them either. And they hadn't seemed to find anything wrong with her. Within minutes, the three were dust on the horizon.

"So far so good," she said to the mule. "I can fool 'em from mule back at fifteen feet." She knew she'd have to do better than that before she would be comfortable around other people. She was already desperately lonely. She *wanted* to be around people. Nice people.

She decided she must be getting close to Cripple Creek an hour later. Sure enough, after rounding the next long curve, she found herself on the crest of a hill, looking down into a high valley where the town was nestled.

It looked like it had been squashed. The whole community seemed to be a jumble of small, squat, colorless boxes. No tall buildings. No church steeples. Certainly no monuments. Not even any trees, at least not in the town itself. Cripple Creek spread over the valley for blocks in weary sameness—rough, gray, unpainted buildings, uninspired and uninspiring. The only color Eddie noticed was the sky—still that intense blue.

At least it was a lot bigger than Florissant. Five thousand people, she remembered Jerrod saying. Florissant had only had a handful. Usually a town of a few hundred had at least one building that stood out as an architectural statement of the town's personality. Not Cripple Creek. Its statement was its lack of one. At least not one you could see from a mile above town. What kind of people lived in such a dreary place?

She pulled her hat down over her face and urged the mule down the steep grade toward the Cripple Creek version of "civilization."

As she approached the outskirts of the boomtown, she consoled herself it didn't have to look beautiful. Just the sounds of people—wagons moving on the street, dogs barking, children yelling as they played—would make it beautiful regardless of what the place looked like. At least she'd have someone to talk to. She wouldn't have to feel quite so alone. If her disguise worked.

Eddie rode the mule slowly into the fringe of the town. When she saw the houses up close, she decided Cripple Creek probably didn't even use the word "civilized"—or "pretty" or "quaint" or even "homey." The town was too raw for any of those words. Everything she saw was rough, from the rutted street to the dead-gray color of the slab lumber haphazardly nailed on the sides of the houses. The almost painful ruggedness seemed to taunt her as she moved down the street.

Gather your gumption, girl. You're going to need every ounce you can find.

The houses seemed downright inhospitable. Rows of one and two room shacks made of rough sawn, unpainted lumber with tar paper roofs lined both sides of the street. Some of them had newspaper sticking out of the gaps between the boards. Could this really be a *town*? In 1893? She considered pinching herself to see if it was just a dream but already knew it wasn't.

The streets to either side of the one she was on seemed to have the same kind of houses. Although some looked cared for, none had yards. Each had a ten or fifteen-foot swath of barren ground in front of it where the garbage was thrown. Burros moved from lot to lot, eating what people had pitched out the door.

She was about four blocks into town when she noticed a little girl standing by the side of the road. The child, about five years old, wore a threadbare dress, but had on a brand new straw bonnet with a blue ribbon and silk daisies around the brim. Long blue streamers hung from the back of the hatband and mingled with the little girl's copper-colored hair. The hat and the little girl's hair were delightful splashes of color in the dreary scene. Eddie smiled at her.

Before the little girl could smile back, a gust of wind tore the hat from her head. With a shriek, she strained for the bonnet, but it was already swirling in the air, high above her grasp. The wind brought the hat toward Eddie, and Orville spooked because of the strange object flying at him. She forgot the headgear and focused on getting the mule back under control as he reared and twisted.

Once she'd calmed the mule, Eddie dismounted and retrieved the hat, which had landed on the far side of the road from the little girl. After inspecting the hat to confirm what she expected to be there, Eddie approached the little girl.

Her father had struck a vein, Eddie guessed, and had bought the hat for his daughter to celebrate. "Pretty hat," Eddie said. She smiled. "Your pa buy it for you?"

The little girl's huge blue eyes were solemn as she nodded.

Eddie pulled a loop of ribbon from inside the brim. She put the hat back on the youngster's head and tucked the ribbon under her chin. "Now the wind won't steal it again," she said gently.

She got back on the mule and headed down the street. When she looked back, the little girl was still staring after her.

In a few more blocks, Eddie was in the middle of "town." She'd never seen anything like it. The hodgepodge of log, false-front, and half canvas-half lumber structures was bewildering. What could they be for? What was all the bustle about?

The buildings were finer than the ones in Florissant, though, and there were a lot more of them. Many actually did have two stories—even though she hadn't been able to tell that from her first glimpse of town. When she was right in front of them, they didn't look as drab either. They had lots of signage and colorful goods in the windows.

But she couldn't help thinking of them more as sheds than places of business. They certainly were nothing like her father's offices back in St. Louis. Still they proclaimed "grocer" and "real estate" and "clothing" on their fronts. Stacks of merchandise and canvas banners boasting special offerings were everywhere. And the dusty street was full of men and women hurrying in and out of the buildings and children darting from the alleys and chasing each other in the street.

Eddie wiped her forehead and pulled the hat down over her face again. How could she start to make sense of the chaotic scene? She'd wanted the town to be big enough to find a job and keep it without being noticed. But she'd also wanted the town to be small enough for her to feel safe. She'd hoped Cripple Creek would be both. Now that she'd seen it, she wasn't sure it would be either. And she wasn't at all sure she wanted to find out.

Her stomach growled advice on where to begin. The change from the bottom of her handbag would be enough for a meal. And that would be a good way to try out her disguise the first time. She surveyed the buildings from the middle of the street and chose the Tea Cup Cafe, one of the sturdier, cleaner-looking "sheds."

She looped the reins over the hitching post outside the building. As she reached the door of the restaurant, she pulled her hat even lower over her face. She opened the door and walked in—to the tantalizing aroma of beef stew.

The room was about the size of her father's parlor, but much plainer, though clean. She could hear someone clanking pans in the back which she assumed was the kitchen. An older woman with a huge behind was clearing a table on the far side of the room. "Howdy," she said as she looked up. She nodded toward

WIDOW BOY | **67**

the table nearest Eddie as she wiped her hands on her faded gingham apron.

Eddie sat down, choosing a place at the table where she could see the door but was not directly facing it. She was the only customer in the restaurant. Probably too early for lunch, she realized. But she was hungry—and ready to eat something besides canned peaches. Her stomach growled again in confirmation.

The woman waddled across the room to the table. After a few heaving breaths to recover from the exertion, she asked, "What can I get you?"

Eddie concentrated on making her voice sound deep. "Stew done yet?"

"Close enough it's fit to eat. Want that?"

"Uh huh." Eddie was hungry enough for two orders. "Do I get bread with it?"

"Penny extra."

"Bread, too. Got milk?"

"Fresh this morning from our cow."

"How much?

"Two cents."

"That too, then. The milk, not the cow."

The woman chuckled and shuffled off to get the order.

Maybe this masquerade would work, Eddie told herself with a glimmer of confidence. She looked around the café. The walls were just the other side of the exterior planks, with muslin glued over them. A merchandiser's calendar with a gaudy picture of a bouquet of flowers was hung at eye-level between the front door and one of the two front windows. On the side walls, nothing broke the monotony of the cloth-covered planks.

She counted six tables, each with four chairs around it. A small table next to the kitchen door held extra eating utensils and glasses. The windows were framed in and had calico curtains. Everything was clean, and the tablecloths were freshly ironed. The inside could have been a lot worse after what the street had looked like.

The woman bustled from the kitchen and placed a bowl of stew in front of Eddie. The delicious smell of beef and gravy and vegetables made her stomach growl in anticipation, and the woman laughed. "Eat up, boy," she said, laughing again. "You need some meat on your bones." She set the bread on the table and went back to the kitchen.

Eddie picked up her fork. The stew looked even better than it smelled— chunks of browned meat, carrots, onions and potatoes all swimming in gravy that was a deep rich brown. She wondered if anyone had ever spruced up a town by painting the buildings with gravy.

She took a dainty bite, carefully chewing the wonderful mouthful. Then she tore off a small piece of the bread and ate that, just as properly. Within a few bites she stopped eating in mid-chew. How foolish!

A boy wouldn't eat that way.

When the woman returned with the milk, Eddie was stuffing so much in her mouth that she could barely swallow. She hated it that she couldn't even taste the food, but she was afraid she wouldn't look like a boy if she ate less at a time.

"Slow down," the woman said. "It ain't goin' anywhere without you. Take the time to taste it."

The embarrassment of being chided for her table manners made Eddie blush so deeply she could feel the heat all the way down her neck. But at least the reprimand gave her the chance to enjoy her food. She took a middle-sized mouthful and chewed slowly, smiling up at the waitress. "Yes, ma'am," she said once she'd swallowed.

As she ate, she wished she'd paid more attention to the stable boys back in St. Louis. If she was going to pretend she was a boy, she had to know how they behaved.

She was finishing off the last of the bread, sloshing it down with the rest of her milk, when a tall, dark-haired man with a genial expression came through the door.

"Howdy, Mabel. How's the beefsteak today?" The man turned away before "Mabel" had a chance to answer and looked straight at Eddie. "Ain't seen you around these parts, son."

Eddie noticed a metal star with the word "Marshal" on it pinned on his shirt pocket. When she dared to look at his face, she was surprised to find she recognized him. He was the first of the men who'd passed her on the road. She cleared her throat, again concentrating on making her voice stay deep. "Just got here, sir. Saw you on the road from Florissant."

She pulled her hat down over her face again, trying to hide behind the brim. When she realized she had her hat on at the table, an offense for which Poppa would have thrown a boy out of the house, her hand flew to the brim. Should she take the hat off? She was too frightened to do it. What if the marshal told her she had to? Oh come now. Cripple Creek certainly didn't seem like the kind of town where you got thrown in jail for wearing your hat at the table.

"Come with your parents?"

In rising panic, she realized she hadn't provided her new persona with any background.

"Let the kid finish his milk, Hugh," Mabel said. "He's been right polite. And he's already paid."

The marshal's face took on a hint of pink. "Sorry," he said. "Sometimes we get those damn troublemakers from Denver City. Sit down and eat with no intention of paying." He squinted at Eddie. "You run away from home?"

She looked up at him. "No, sir. My mama's been dead a long time. And Poppa died last year." That was all the truth, she thought with empty gratitude. Being an orphan, even at the age of twenty-one, was not a happy experience. But telling this man a straight-out lie would have been very difficult. Just the set of his jaw told her he brooked no nonsense.

A soft gray shadow crossed the marshal's face. "Sorry about

your folks, son." His eyes took on some warmth. "Maybe you can find a job here in the Creek. It's a growin' town."

"Thank you, sir. I hope to." She got up from the table. "That was a fine meal, ma'am," she said, smiling at the woman. She moved past the marshal, trying hard not to look like she was running away as she hurried out the door.

After she had gotten back on Orville and moved farther down the street, she leaned forward and patted the mule on the neck. "Scarier than I expected, but we did it." She smiled at the fullness in her stomach, too. The hot stew and the cold milk had tasted better than anything she'd ever eaten in St. Louis. Maybe being in Cripple Creek was going to turn out all right.

With enough change for only one more meal in town, Eddie moved her thinking to the next matter of importance—finding work. She rode slowly down the busiest street, which had a crude sign proclaiming it as "Bennett Avenue." Even though they seemed drab, the buildings she was passing held all kinds of businesses. Many of them offered "gold properties" for sale. She wondered how much money you needed to buy a "gold property"— and what you had once you bought it. The bustle spread out around her in all four directions. There had to good possibilities for finding work.

She evaluated each business as she passed it. The groceries and dry goods stores had too much exposure to the general public—including Rafe Pettibone and company. A law office was out—a boy in his mid-teens wouldn't be well suited to work there. A laundry? Not as a boy. Her eyes finally lit on the livery's sign. Perfect. She could handle horses with the best of them. She tied Orville to the hitching post and went inside.

A man was pitching hay from a sunlit loft above her into stalls to her right. His well-tanned muscles glistened with sweat as he worked. He had a thick head of black hair that curled around his ears. When he noticed her, she nodded. He sounded gruff and exasperated when he yelled, "What you need, kid?"

"You the owner?" Eddie had thought through the words before she said them, concentrating to keep her voice deep.

"Yep."

"I was wondering if you could give me a job." She'd never felt her palms sweat before.

"You and a hundred other drifters." He threw the pitchfork into the pile of hay and let himself drop to the floor in front of her. "Everybody who comes into town stops here. Every one of 'em tells me they got a way with horses."

So much for that idea.

"Sorry I bothered you," she said contritely. She looked down at her boots, flustered that she'd handled the meeting so badly.

The man softened. "Oh, that's all right. Guess I'm just tired of pitching hay."

"I'll do it for you," Eddie offered. "It doesn't have to be a regular job, just for today." Even a little money would help.

"Nah, I can't afford it," the man said, now sounding a lot friendlier. "Besides, it does a man good to do a little hard labor himself regular."

"I suppose." Eddie's face drooped. She moved to go, then turned back to the man and tried her best rendition of a boy's smile. "Know of anyone who does have work, sir?"

He started to shake his head, but stopped. Then he spent what seemed like an eternity mulling something and inspecting her up and down—like he was buying cattle—before he spoke. A sly grinned started to form at the edges of his scowl.

He knows, Eddie decided in a panic. Will he tell the marshal?

She did not relax when his whole face transformed into a mischievous grin. He nodded his head thoughtfully. "I bet you could get the best job in camp."

Eddie swallowed her sigh of relief. "Where?" She shifted uncomfortably from one foot to the other as he looked her over from head to toe again. Did he suspect something or not?

"Since the town fathers made the lot of 'em move off Bennett, the ladies of the evening have taken to hiring errand boys." His eyes had a twinkle, even in the dim light of the lower level of the stable.

"Errand boys? Ladies of the evening?" She'd heard of them at a Mission Society meeting. Lost souls who made money pleasing bad men.

"If I could get a job running errands for those beauties, I'd let you run the stable!" He sighed. "But they won't take real men, only boys too young to get frisky with the doves." He looked her over again, peering at her face under the hat brim. "How old are you, son?"

"How old do I have to be to get one of those jobs?"

The burly man let out a robust laugh. "They want a baby. Somebody smart enough to do their bidding but not old enough to want to take out his wages in trade." He walked around Eddie, appraising her yet again. It felt like he could see right through all the clothes she'd put on to look heavier.

"You might be able to do it." He shook his head slowly, savoring a pleasant memory. "If you decide to look, be sure you stop at the Red Velvet. Tess Temany is a fine woman. She runs a damned good house." From the look on his face, Eddie concluded the opinion was born of firsthand experience. And the part about "damned" was probably right on target.

"Myers Avenue is just a block over, but it's a world away. Just take Bennett back to First Avenue, then head down First to Myers."

When she turned onto Myers, the short ride seemed to have taken her to an entirely different town. The buildings were still that tired drab tan-gray, but somehow, they didn't wear it the way the buildings on Bennett did. The place was far more alive.

Even this early in the afternoon, the plink of barroom pianos competed from several dance halls. The babble of men's voices and the clink of glasses wafted into the street from inside the swinging doors of the saloons and gambling houses. The smell of whiskey and beer came at her from every direction. Eddie assessed the raw energy of the rowdy block as she rode slowly up the street, not sure whether to hurry away or keep going.

Without warning, a rumpled man came flying out of a swinging door and sprawled into the street. Another, much larger man appeared in the door behind him. "You know the rules, Henry. You pay before you take the go-round." The wiry man in the street pulled himself up out of the dust and, after a half-hearted attempt to brush himself off, walked calmly into the next saloon.

The street was only a few blocks long, but it seemed to offer help in committing every sin possible within that distance. There seemed to be a bizarre sort of order in the layout, though—the saloons, dance halls, and gambling emporiums all seemed to be on the right side of the street. Residences, some with lace curtains in the windows, occupied the left side. What woman in her right mind would agree to live in such close proximity to so much wickedness? Then, with a shock, she realized they were the parlor houses—where the "ladies" plied their trade. There had to be at least ten of them!

Myers dwindled into a gulch dotted with mine workings and aspen trees in another few blocks. A row of tiny, graying shacks at the mouth of the gulch reminded Eddie she was still in Cripple Creek.

After a few moments of gawking at everything on both sides of the street, Eddie began to survey the houses of ill-repute on her left more carefully. The names made her giggle. "Sunnyrest" certainly wasn't a sanitarium for tuberculosis patients. The "Possum Ranch" most likely didn't raise anything but Cain. And they probably weren't studying botany at the "White Leaf." Still, they looked proper, almost prim, with their lace curtains in the windows. Most had the same rough-hewn exteriors as the buildings on Bennett, but they had flowers in the yards and glass windows in their front doors and porches that suggested a bizarre sort of primitive elegance.

Eddie passed several, noting two with signs for errand boys. She'd just gone by The Old Homestead House—whatever had prompted that as a name?—when she came to the Red Velvet. Larger than most of the others, with a real second story, it, too, had an aura of frontier "refinement"—and a sign in the window advertising for an errand boy.

Eddie dismounted and hitched the mule. She took off her hat, smoothed her hair and replaced the hat. She wanted to grab a fistful of dirt and rub it onto her cheeks, but decided not to risk it. After drawing in and exhaling a slow breath, she squared her shoulders and walked up the steps to the porch.

A large black woman answered Eddie's knock. "Can I help you, son?" The kindness in the woman brimmed over in a huge smile. Eddie like her immediately.

"Come to see about the job," Eddie said, nodding to the sign.

"How old are you?"

"I think I turned fifteen last birthday, but I don't rightly know." Eddie looked at her shoes for effect. "I'm an orphan."

"Fifteen's a little old, but I'll get Miss Tess." The woman smiled that big smile again. "Maybe she's tired of waitin' for the right boy." She motioned Eddie inside.

As the woman labored up the narrow stairway inside the front door, Eddie looked around. The entry included a brass umbrella stand set next to an expertly carved oak hall tree with a beveled mirror. A black feather boa hung from one of the hooks of the hall tree.

After the Tea Cup Café, the parlor walls were mind-boggling—mahogany wainscoting on the lower half and white taffeta between it and the pressed tin ceiling. On the far wall was a Ferrand and Votcy foot bellows organ, just like the one Poppa had given her for her eighteenth birthday. It even held two piano babies like she'd put on hers. What kind of damned woman would haul the little cherub statues all the way to Cripple Creek?

A settee and two armless chairs with red velvet upholstery

were clustered near the front window. Lace-edged linen pillows with "Chicago" embroidered on one and "Cincinnati" on the other were carefully plumped on the ends of the settee. On the table next to the settee was a sculpture—a man with his beautiful daughter on horseback and her youthful beau clinging to her hand as the scowling father rides off. More upholstered chairs and more tables with tasteful knick-knacks lined the other walls. Tiffany wall lamps. A fashionable stove. This wasn't at all the picture the women of the Mission Society had painted of such a place. "Damned" looked rather presentable.

A high-backed, circular bench in the trademark red velvet took up the center of the room. Above it hung another, larger Tiffany lamp. With a start, Eddie realized that a tiny young woman with translucent skin and a frail air of independence was sitting seductively on the bench. She'd been watching Eddie gawk. Eddie smiled self-consciously, and the woman waved.

"Sorry, Kate. He isn't clientele. Can't you see he's still a puppy?" When Eddie turned, she discovered the booming voice belonged to a pleasant looking woman as tall as her but endowed with far more cleavage, half-heartedly hidden behind a swatch of lace.

She had auburn hair—perhaps from God but maybe from henna. Regardless, it was pinned into an attractive mass of curls that cascaded down the creamy skin of the woman's neck. Thirty, at the most, Eddie decided as she tried to guess her age. The woman wasn't the pale, unhappy wretch the ladies of the Mission Society had described. She was beautiful—and she seemed perfectly happy with her damned spiritual state.

"I'm Tess Temany," she said, extending her hand gracefully and smiling. "Irene says you want to be my errand boy."

Eddie shook the delicate hand quickly. "Yes, ma'am."

Now Tess looked Eddie up and down. "You're a bit big. How old are you?"

"Fifteen, I think, ma'am," Eddie said. Hoping again for sympathy, she added, "I'm an orphan so I'm not right sure."

"Orphan or not, the errand boy doesn't mess around with my girls. That's why I sent the last one packing." Tess picked a twig off Eddie's jacket. "Fifteen's a bit old."

Eddie gulped. "I need the job, ma'am."

"Do you like women?" Tess wagged her finger in Eddie's face. "I can't have an errand boy that cuts into business."

"N...n...no, ma'am," Eddie stuttered. "I don't like women." Then she realized that answer could also be wrong. "At least not yet."

Tess allowed herself the hint of a smile. "I need someone six days a week, eight in the morning until half-past five or so. When you aren't running errands, you'll be doing chores for Irene in the kitchen." She surveyed Eddie again, then gave her a stern look. "She's the best cook in camp. Part of your job would be to keep her happy."

Eddie's eyes widened. "What's *that* mean?" She looked past Tess to the kitchen door.

Tess laughed. "Nothing strange." She shrugged. "Keeping Irene happy doesn't take much. Fetch what she needs, do what she asks, and tell her the food's good."

"You mean I'd get meals?"

Tess ignored the question. "And it doesn't hurt to listen to her philosophize every once in a while. Irene likes to have an audience now and again." She stopped, as if just then hearing Eddie's earlier question. "Meals, yes. Room, no. I don't want the errand boy anywhere near my girls with his clothes off, even if he's sleeping."

"I can find a room."

"It won't be much of one. All I'm willing to pay is three dollars a week."

Eddie grimaced. That settled one thing. It would take forever to make enough money to hire someone to kill Rafe. She'd *have* to do it herself.

Tess continued. "If it works out all right and you prove your worth, maybe there'll be more later. If you stay away from the girls. That's the most important thing."

"I can stay away from the girls," Eddie said earnestly. She drew in a breath to slow the excitement in her voice. "When do I start?"

"Tomorrow morning. Be here at eight o'clock. Irene will show you what to do." Tess's instructions were crisp. "I'll be down after noon. We can talk about the other errands then."

Eddie beamed. She had a job.

Tess startled Eddie with a laugh. "If you're going to work for me, it would help to know your name. Or do you just want me to call you Errand Boy?"

Eddie's blush was genuine and, hopefully, effective. "Sorry, ma'am. My name's Eddie Taggert. You can call me Ed if you prefer."

"I prefer Eddie. You sound younger that way. Short for Edward?"

"Edwin...a." The last syllable slipped out automatically. "I mean Edwin. I'm so flustered, I might tell you my name is Maybelle next," Eddie stammered, trying to cover the mistake.

Tess flashed another smile as she led Eddie through the door. "See you tomorrow, Eddie."

Eddie was grinning from ear to ear as she climbed back on the mule. She had a job. With meals. She'd only have to deal with the shopkeepers and the women at the Red Velvet, not the whole town. She headed back to Bennett Avenue. All she had to do now was find a room. Cripple Creek was going to work out fine.

But as she moved up the street, she noticed places offering rooms also had signs in their windows. They all read "No Vacancy." All of the places that called themselves "boarding houses" were full. She'd checked every street. She walked the mule up one street and down the next, looking for a place that didn't have a "no vacancy" sign. At last, she found a ramshackle two-story building with a banner proclaiming "Pease Hotel." She left

Orville at the hitching post and walked in. When she looked past the front desk, she was stunned to realize that most of the "building" was actually a tent.

The desk clerk, a thin blonde man with a droopy mustache and a sour expression, looked up from the dime novel he was reading, impatient at being interrupted. "What do you want?"

"I'm looking for a room." Eddie pulled herself up as tall as she could and spoke in her deepest voice. "I'll need it for a month or two."

"Right. You and all the rest of the drifters. No money and no job. I'm just supposed to let out beds for charity."

"I have a job."

The grumpy man's disposition changed slightly. "It'll cost you two dollars a week and you'd share your area with another fella. If you take the far back, I can give you a nickel-a-day discount. That one's right next to the privy."

Eddie vaguely felt the rough cloth of Jerrod's work trousers against the inside of her thighs as she fought back frustration. "I need a private room."

The skinny clerk started to laugh. "The only place that has those is The Continental. And they charge two dollars a *night*."

Eddie shoved her hands in her jacket pockets and turned to leave. If she was going to live in a tent, it may as well be her own.

"You can't be bashful your whole life," the clerk called after her.

Eddie let the disappointment of not being able to find a room outweigh the euphoria of finding a job as she rode out of town. She really didn't want to live in the tent. Staying in the tent would have been fun with Jerrod. Now it would only be a lonely, necessary shelter until she could devise the right plan and deal with Rafe Pettibone.

She let tears trickle down her face for a while and then sniffed resolutely. "Well, if it's where I'm going to live, I may as well make it the nicest place I can." She rode the rest of the way back to camp thinking of ways to make the tent more livable. "It could be worse," she said forlornly to herself as she unsaddled the mule. "At least up here, I'm among friends." She rubbed Orville down, then checked on Alice and Jewel.

That night as she worked on another can of peaches, she mulled over the situation again. The tent was near a stream, with good grazing for the animals nearby. It was her own, and it meant she could get away from the bustle of town every night. Maybe the tent was a blessing after all. At least she could be Edwina in the darkness of the hills. And her tears at missing Jerrod would fall unnoticed on her bedroll. She could live in the tent for a month, particularly since she'd be spending her days at the Red Velvet.

But something was wrong. It kept gnawing at her from a little corner in the back of her mind. She hadn't done something it was important to do. As she was falling off to sleep, it came to her. She might be camped on a mining claim! That would make her a claim jumper. Jerrod had gone on and on about how it was one of the most despicable of all possible acts in a mining camp.

She tried to remember what he'd told her about mining claims, wishing she'd brought some of his mining books along rather than leaving them all hidden with the wagon. The only thing she could recall was that prospectors usually put a record of the claim in a tobacco can inside a pile of rocks—a cairn. She hadn't looked for cairns, much less tobacco cans. She fell asleep thinking about them.

CHAPTER 5

THE NEXT DAY, Eddie was up at dawn, crisscrossing her camp on foot, looking for a pile of rocks that would make her a claim jumper. She searched almost a half mile radius before she relaxed. Nothing suggested she was on a claim. Smoke from five different spots on the hills south of Cripple Creek told her she was probably outside the pay zone of the mining district, but she decided to look again that evening when she got back from town anyway.

As she dressed, taking extra care to be certain the bindings under her rough shirt were smooth, she smiled about what she'd just done. Jerrod had been a fanatic about claim jumping. When he'd covered the subject in his school work, he'd ranted for hours every night about how unscrupulous someone would have to be to take another man's claim. Now the situation didn't seem as clear-cut as he'd led her to believe.

She worked on her face for almost twenty minutes, rubbing in dirt and some charcoal from last night's campfire. Her reflection in the hand mirror in the early morning light was encouraging. Maybe she'd be able to do without the hat for a short time if she had to. She checked the camp, and after assuring things were as secure as possible, she headed for town bareback on Orville.

"Mornin', Irene," she said as the cook opened the front door.

"Who's tellin' you my name is Irene?" The woman looked at her with the hint of a grin.

Eddie was flustered. "Sorry, ma'am. Don't recall your last name. Tess called you Irene."

"Only white ladies is called 'ma'am' in this house. And you

better call the madam 'Miss Tess' if you want to keep the job. Me, you can call Aunt Irene." She broke into a broad grin. "Course, you can call me Irene, too. Most everybody does."

Irene seemed to be a genuinely happy soul. Her smooth dark skin made her seem timeless, but somehow, she had a grandmotherly look. "Come on in the kitchen, child, and I'll get you some breakfast." With that she bustled down the hall toward the back of the house.

The kitchen was large and gave the impression important work was done there. Irene placed fresh biscuits and milk in front of Eddie.

Eddie inhaled the delightful smell of the biscuits and the coffee that was brewing on the stove. "What kind of cooking do you do, Irene? Just meals for Tess—Miss Tess—and the girls?"

"Lord, no! This is a house of pleasure. Eatin' goes hand in hand with the other enjoyments menfolks come here for." Irene wiped her hands on a dish towel as she talked. "Some nights we'll have more 'n twenty people at the table. A lot of them are guests of the big mining men in town. I've heard it said more than one mine's funding flowed easy after the investors spent a night at the Red Velvet."

Everything intertwines, Eddie thought, amazed at her own naiveté. "How often do you have to cook that way?" Irene's job seemed to go well beyond simple domestic chores.

"I cook big every night, but I only cook special once or twice a week. It's too hard to get in smoked oysters and the other fancy stuff more often than that."

Eddie was flabbergasted. Who in this rough town would even know what smoked oysters were?

"Good biscuits."

Irene beamed. "That's the kind of stuff I *like* to cook. Home food. The kind that makes chillun and a good man happy."

"You have a family?"

Irene's thoughts seemed to drift far way. "Nah. Not anymore.

All dead now." Her look brightened. "But they was a handful when they was around."

Eddie wondered what had happened to Irene's kin but was unwilling to ask. She finished the milk and took the dishes to the wash stand. "What do you want me to start with? Tess—Miss Tess—said you'd keep me busy until she came down around noon."

"I'll do that. Why don't I start you with kneading this bread dough? Tires me out to keep shoving at it, but it needs a good long working to turn out right."

Eddie rolled up her sleeves as she moved to the table, but detoured to the wash basin and scrubbed her hands.

Irene nodded her approval.

Eddie began kneading the mound of dough, punching it in the middle, pulling the top over and punching it again.

Irene watched with interest. "Boy, where'd you learn to knead bread like that?"

Boys didn't knead bread. Eddie scrambled for an explanation. "I used to watch the cook at the orphanage. She let me try it once in a while," she said after a second. "Once, I thought I'd become a great chef."

"What changed your mind?"

Eddie's mind was whirling. Oblivion was her best friend. She couldn't afford too much of a past for others to scrutinize. "Me and some folks didn't agree on what I was going to do for them."

Irene's eyebrows arched, but she didn't say anything.

They worked in silence for a while. Irene moved about the kitchen from this to that as field marshal for the evening's feast. Eddie punched and pulled the dough. The rhythmic process was relaxing.

But the silence somehow didn't befit the kitchen, and it bothered Eddie. Finally, she asked, "How many ladies are there in the house?"

"Ladies? Depends on how you define the word." Irene boomed

a big laugh at her own joke.

"Well, then, how many women are there at the Red Velvet?" Two can play this game, Eddie told herself.

"That depends, too. Some of those females in the parlor are still girls."

This time, they both laughed.

Eddie cleared her throat, attempting to sound very official. "Tell me, Miss Aunt Irene, how many *females* are there at the Red Velvet?"

With equally false pomp, Irene replied, "Twelve...nine girls, a chambermaid, me, and Miss Tess."

And one more who's pretending otherwise, Eddie added in her head.

Tess entered the kitchen just after eleven. By then, Eddie had peeled enough apples to make pies for the entire town.

"Mornin', ma'am," Eddie and Irene said, almost in unison.

Tess looked worn in spite of her deep red silk wrapper. "Could I have coffee, Irene?" Her voice was flat. Clearly morning, even the little bit that was left of it, wasn't her best time. With red eyes and a complete lack of expression, Tess turned to Eddie. "You're here. Good."

Irene handed Tess a small tray with a fancy cup and saucer, a serving pot of coffee, and one biscuit.

Tess took it and made her way back upstairs.

"Glad I didn't try to talk to her yesterday morning," Eddie said under her breath.

"Don't be saying things like that out loud if you want this job," Irene clucked. "Miss Tess works in the evening. Remember that. At eleven in the morning she looks like church ladies look at sun up."

"Besides," Irene said, "I wouldn't have *let* you talk to her yesterday morning. What we see in the kitchen is a different version of Miss Tess Temany than the rest of the world ever sees." She smiled with self-satisfaction. "Miss Tess says this here kitchen is the happiest place ever for her. She likes to come down here sometimes, even before she's dressed—just 'cuz it feels good. Like today." Her voice became somber. "And we don't talk to *nobody* about what she looks like when she does. Understand, boy?"

Eddie nodded.

They went back to the cooking chores. Irene was making soup for lunch as well as preparing for the evening's festivities. "The girls don't eat much during the day. Just enough to get them to dinner," Irene confided as she pushed chopped onions and carrots from the cutting board into the soup pot. "They all worry too much about their figures. God never intended them to look like scarecrows."

She patted Eddie on the shoulder. "Don't you worry though. I won't feed you like a pigeon. You'll get plenty to eat around here."

Lunch proved Irene was true to her word. In addition to the vegetable soup, she plunked down a loaf of bread along with butter and jam. Then she carved them each a thick slice of ham. Eddie felt she would burst from all the food, but it sure beat canned peaches.

They were just finishing lunch when Tess returned to the kitchen. Eddie stared at the transformation. She was back to the Tess she'd met the day before—auburn hair piled intricately on top of her head, creamy skin with gently rouged cheeks, and an elegant day dress. Again the mismatch of the town and the house jostled Eddie's thoughts. The irony of her own dilemma also crossed her mind. A year ago, she would have been wearing a dress every bit as fashionable. Now here she was, hiding in Jerrod's work clothes.

Tess smiled as she walked across the kitchen. "Now, I'm ready for the day." She turned to Eddie. "There are some errands you'll need to run every afternoon, Eddie. Let's get you started on them."

Eddie obligingly wiped her hands on her trouser legs in preparation for the new duties.

"First, wash your hands like a civilized person, Edwin."

Embarrassment flooded her face as Eddie sloshed water over her hands and worked the bar of soap into them. They'd been in more water that morning than in three months. As she wiped them, she relaxed. She'd inadvertently done just what she needed to do to be convincing as "Edwin." Maybe the whole masquerade would become automatic after a while.

"Do you know where Oberlander's Drugstore is?"

Eddie shook her head.

"It's on Bennett, about four blocks up on the other side of the street. I need you to take this to Mister Oberlander." She handed Eddie a playing card, the jack of spades.

Eddie looked at her quizzically.

"He'll know what it means."

"I don't have any money to pay him."

"We have an account there. I pay at the end of the month." Her voice took on a playful wickedness. "I doubt the dear druggist would deny me, since I never deny him."

Barter isn't a bad approach, Eddie told herself as she took her jacket from a peg and prepared to leave.

Tess called her back. "Edwin, there is one habit I simply won't abide." She put her hands on her hips and looked at Eddie, tapping her foot as if she were the schoolmarm. "Neither men nor boys wear hats in my house."

"Yes, ma'am," Eddie said, removing the hat as she moved through the kitchen door to the porch at the rear of the house, then quickly putting the hat back on once she was outside.

Eddie used the walk to think about how to make her face more believable so she could work without the hat. While she was waiting for the druggist to finish with another customer, she studied the names on the bottles behind the counter.

"Yes, son?"

"Mister Oberlander, Miss Tess sent me with this." Eddie

handed him the playing card. "She said to put it on the bill."

The meek little man took the playing card and sighed, seeming to recall something pleasant. "I'll need to fetch this from the back."

The curtain didn't close completely when he went into the back room, so Eddie watched as he threw the cover off a small table to the side of his storage shelves and opened a safe hidden underneath. Working the dial quickly, he opened the safe, removed a vial, and closed the heavy door, all in less than a minute. He put the tiny bottle in a brown paper sack and returned to the front of the store.

"Here you are, son."

"I'd also like some of that black shoe polish, please." Eddie caught herself in her "Saint Louis elite" politeness and added gruffly, "I'll pay for that myself." Why did she feel so dishonest? Would Jerrod have condoned the ruse she was trying to pull off? She wasn't sure.

Maybe there weren't laws about women wearing pants. But she was sure he would have laughed at the idea of trying to make herself look like a boy by rubbing shoe black on her chin.

"That'll be two cents."

She dutifully handed Mr. Oberlander the coins.

Jamming the shoe polish in her pocket, she began to think about how to experiment with it. She needed something more durable—and less abrasive—than grit and soot. Tess might make her wash her face next.

Eddie was still mulling over the best way to apply the shoe polish when she reached the Double X Saloon. As she was passing the noisy, smoke-filled place, a surly patron came staggering out. He lurched through the door and lost his balance. As he flung out his well-muscled arm to steady himself, he sent Eddie sprawling into the street.

She could smell the whiskey as he mumbled, "Shorry, kid." Then he turned and tottered back into the saloon without helping her get up.

Eddie waited until the man was inside the neighboring saloon. When she stood, her jellied knees were unwilling to support her. She grasped a porch post and tried to steady her nerves.

Without a doubt, the drunk had been Scoot. Why hadn't she considered that they might be in Cripple Creek? The four of them weren't likely to just sit out at that disgusting cabin all day, every day.

The close call made her realize a disastrous flaw in her plan. As an errand boy, it would be hard to explain a gun. If she found Rafe in Cripple Creek, she'd have to kill him some other way. She remembered the knife she'd used for her haircut and decided to begin carrying it in her boot.

But if Rafe was in town, she wanted to know it. Once her legs were solid again, she walked slowly to the door of the Pig's Eye, out of which Scoot had staggered, and looked in. Through the smoke, she could see Scoot and the one who'd been in the discussion about the mules. She was pretty sure his name was Al,. Where were the other two? More specifically, where was *Rafe*?

She hurried the rest of the way to the Red Velvet, furtively glancing at the swinging door to the Pig's Eye again and again, expecting Scoot to come charging after her any second. Once she reached the Red Velvet, she went straight to the kitchen, removing her hat as she came through the back door. No one was there. She moved toward voices she heard in the front part of the house.

"It looks lovely, Irene. Mister Burnleigh and his guests will be so impressed." Tess was obviously pleased with Irene's handiwork, whatever it was.

Eddie found them in the dining room, which was being prepared for the evening meal, still five hours off. The table sparkled with crystal and silver. Irene had even gathered fresh wildflowers for a centerpiece. Eddie savored the scents as she walked into the room. The smell of silver polish and starched table linen was like being home.

She handed Tess the package, holding her breath as the madam scrutinized her without the wide-brimmed hat. "You're better looking than I thought," Tess said after the inspection. "But then you're so young you could as much be a girl as a fella."

Terror kept Eddie from even attempting a response.

Tess scowled, "You keep that dreadful hat off inside, hear me?"

"Yes, ma'am." Eddie reminded herself to breathe and made herself stand still, waiting for further direction.

Tess and Irene kept fussing with the flower arrangement.

Finally, Eddie cleared her throat to get Tess's attention. "Is there something else you want me to do?"

Tess looked up. "Have you fetched the papers yet?"

Eddie looked at her blankly.

"Each afternoon, you must get the Denver and Colorado Springs newspapers when they come in on the Wells Fargo Express wagon." Tess pulled a deep-blue columbine from the lead crystal vase and repositioned it on the other side of the bouquet. "Then go to the Crusher office for the local news. The Express gets in around three." She looked up from the floral work to send Eddie on her way. "If you do it just as I described, you'll be able to get them all without waiting."

"Do I need to pay for them?"

"No, the subscriptions are all paid in advance."

Of course, Eddie thought as she headed out the back door. And probably in trade.

Rafe hated waiting. And at the moment, he hated it more than ever before. It was past noon on the Saturday Al and Scoot were supposed to check in, and he still hadn't seen them. He'd been a damn fool to let them go to Cripple Creek without him. But if he went in after them, that sissy-pants marshal would put him in jail.

He'd waited too damn long for word on whether that conniving woman was still around. For four days he'd scoured the hills looking for her. The only thing he'd learned was that she'd found the wagon and buried her wood-pussy husband. Damn. His plans were working out all wrong, and he hated it. He was the man who gave the orders. Why was he sitting here waiting for the rest of the gang?

He checked his watch for the eighth time, noting only ten minutes had passed since he'd checked it at noon. Disgusted, he shoved the timepiece back in his pocket. The sound of horses brought him to his feet.

Grabbing his rifle, he headed for the trees. He wanted it to be Al and Scoot, but he was smart enough to realize it could be anyone. From a lookout position in the tight stand of pines near the huge rock on the perimeter of the yard, he watched as the horses came into view.

He let out a sigh of satisfaction. His followers were coming to report, as ordered. But he stayed hidden until they dismounted, and he was sure it was really them.

"Rafe?"

Scoot's call was the nicest sound Rafe had heard in four days. "Over here," Rafe said gruffly as he came out of the trees. "You two sure took your good sweet time." A scowl hid his pleasure at seeing them.

"It ain't close to dark yet, Rafe," Al said. "Ya said to report on Saturday, and we got plenty o' Saturday left."

"A man with a backbone handles his job early in the day," Rafe growled. That was the way they taught you in the Army. What kind of loafers was he working with anyway?

"Suit yourself," Al said, shrugging.

"Aw, cut the crap," Rafe said irritably. "See her?"

The two gang members shook their heads and said nothing.

"Not a sign?" Rafe wasn't pleased with the news.

"I think she's probably took the train back East," Al said.

"In a man's clothes, with no money, and totin' a gun?" Rafe's voice was rising with his growing impatience. "I don't think so."

"Wagon still there?"

"Gone when I got there at sunup the next day." Rafe's eyes narrowed as he looked at the two men. Then his glare settled on Scoot. "That had to be a miracle since you were out there 'til sundown."

Scoot kept his eyes down and said nothing.

"So it don't seem likely she just hopped on the train, now does it?" Rafe was getting more angry with every word.

"Where'd she take the rig?" Al didn't seem too concerned about the situation.

That bothered Rafe, too. "Don't know." His frustration at being outwitted by a woman was hard to hide. "Lost her once she took it over the rocks." He slammed his fist into the other palm. "Brushed the tracks." He shook his head angrily and glared at the two of them. "What the hell kind of woman would know to do that? I've looked for four damn days and can't find a sign of that wagon."

"Shit." Al's comment was echoed by Scoot a half second later.

"How we gonna find her?" Scoot's question was almost a wail.

"That's what I thought you two were supposed to be doing in Cripple Creek."

Al and Scoot squirmed beneath Rafe's gaze.

"She wasn't there, Rafe," Al said finally.

"Where'd you check?" Rafe's voice was taking on volume. He made himself stop. They were the only ones he could count on to find her if she was in Cripple Creek. If he showed his face in town before the Fourth of July, the high and mighty Marshal Hugh Gruen would have his ass in jail before he made it down Bennett Avenue.

"Look harder," he said in a rational voice.

"You mean you want us to go back?" Scoot's tone betrayed his delight at the prospect.

"Yes. Only this time, use your heads and look where she's likely to be." He fixed his gaze on Scoot. "And it ain't in the bottom of a bottle o' whiskey at the Double X."

On Sunday, her day off, Eddie moved camp again. She'd found a better meadow, hidden by a wooded area and closer to town. Before she even pulled a stake from the tent to move it, she walked the new ground, methodically checking for cairns. She didn't think she was on anyone's claim.

The new site had enough grass for the animals to graze for months. A decent-sized creek meandered close by. Just as Poppa had advised, she pitched her tent on high ground away from the stream. As a precaution, she smeared mud on the tent fabric to make it look different. She didn't want anyone to start putting pieces of information together—especially Rafe and his gang.

Once the canvas was up and sturdy, she partitioned the inside into a sleeping area and a living area, and put her writing materials out on the small box she had designated as her desk. Write? To whom, she asked herself. No one.

Poppa was gone and he'd been her only living kin. Her mother-in-law had made it clear that she and Jerrod were no longer a part of the family. And Mother Sinclair had made sure Jerrod's brothers understood they, too, would be left penniless if they dared to cross her. Since Jerrod's father had died, Mother Sinclair's heart had slowly shriveled to dust inside her money bags.

Eddie wondered if she would evaporate emotionally like her mother-in-law had now that Jerrod was gone. Being dead would be better, she decided.

She tried again to take stock of her situation. The aching numbness was still an almost constant feeling when she wasn't at the Red Velvet. When she closed her eyes, she could see Jerrod's face far off in a soft mist. Then she would see Rafe, snarling behind him. She could rid herself of her nightmares about Rafe—after she'd gotten justice, she'd be able to forget the awful man. But would Jerrod's face also dim as the days passed?

To get Rafe, she needed a plan—and she had to have access to the bastard. Working in Cripple Creek was a risk, but Cripple Creek was the best hope she had. She needed money and information. Both were available in town. The encounter with Scoot had confirmed the second fact, but it had also made her aware of the danger she'd placed herself in to get the funds and facts she needed.

But what information did she really need? She already knew how to find the hideout. She knew that he had no feelings on which she could play. At least not beyond hate and anger. What she didn't know was the life he lived day-to-day. She needed to know more about when and how he was vulnerable. "Why not find out?" she said out loud. It was still before noon. If she rode Jewel, she had time to find out then and there. But taking his horse meant she'd have to be really careful.

She took the road to Florissant as far as she felt was safe, galloping to make the most of the remaining daylight. A few hundred yards before the turn to the hide-out, she led the horse off the road and as far as she could through the thickening stand of pines. Then she tied her in an area with thick underbrush and hurried through the trees on foot.

She came up over the rock outcrop on the far side of the cabin, surprised at the easy access to the top from that side. Lying flat on her stomach, she watched the clearing in front of the cabin. No one seemed to be there, but she heard a strange squawking from the other side of the building.

A couple minutes later Rafe appeared, clutching a magpie by the legs. She wondered how he'd captured a bird, particularly a magpie. The bird fluttered, settled on the outlaw's hand, then fluttered again, as if trying to fly but unable to. Rafe walked with the bird to the far side of the clearing and tied something to a small, gnarled tree stump. The magpie flapped its wings again, then perched on top of the four-foot stump.

Rafe took out his revolver and fired a shot at the bird. The bird flew up in a panic, stopped from escape by a tether. Rafe aimed again. After three more shots, he stopped. He threw back his head and laughed like one of the lunatics Eddie had seen at the asylum in St. Louis on a tour given for the Mission Society ladies.

Rafe began shooting again. The frightened magpie flapped wildly, beating its wings while bullet-clipped feather fragments fluttered in the air. Rafe reloaded and repeated the process. On the twelfth shot, he killed the bird. Then he walked to the stump, still laughing, and recovered the tether.

Eddie shuddered. Rafe Pettibone's heartlessness went well beyond necessity or the consequences of a hard life. Cruelty was his entertainment.

She waited until he went into the cabin to move off the rock. Then she ran silently to where the horse was grazing. She mounted quickly and raced down the road in the darkening shadows, anxious to put distance between her and the ruthlessness she had just witnessed.

Back in camp, she reconsidered what she had thought would work. She would not give Rafe the pleasure of making her his next magpie. To deal with his version of evil, the plan had to be more elaborate than what she'd come up with. And it had to be foolproof.

CHAPTER 6

IT WAS A bright Monday in late June, with an intense blue mountain sky and a soft breeze. Eddie whistled as she rode down Myers Avenue that morning. Whistling was something else her father had taught her—and was thoroughly unacceptable for a lady, Mrs. Dayton had insisted. Her new life was bearable when she was with people, especially with Tess and Irene. Sometimes, the Red Velvet felt almost like home. The ache from missing Jerrod would never go away. But every day brought something new and interesting.

Eddie tied the mule at the back door and walked into the kitchen. Even with her back to the door, Eddie could sense something was wrong with Irene. She was almost afraid to say good morning.

As if to resolve the difficulty, Irene turned around. Her left eye was swollen shut.

"My God, Irene. What happened?"

"Ain't nothin'," Irene said sullenly. "Just a problem."

"Problem?"

"Some white men think all colored women are whores—"

"Who did this to you?"

"Don't matter."

"Did he—" Eddie paused trying to be delicate. "Did he get what he wanted?"

Irene broke into a reluctant grin. "Got a mouthful of his own teeth." Now she looked truly worried. "I hope Miss Tess don't fire me. He just come in the kitchen, drunk as a skunk, while I was cleaning up last night."

"How could Tess be angry with *you*?" Eddie was indignant. "If I was you, I'd just quit and leave here."

"And where'd I go then?" The look Irene gave her made Eddie feel like she was twelve. "To the next camp? His kind don't just live in Cripple Creek." Irene shook her head slowly, her mouth compressed into a resigned line. "I got to have food and a roof, child. I ain't got nowhere to go 'cept another place just like this."

Eddie understood. Tess was fair. Irene could be a lot worse off if that weren't the case. "I understand. But it's just not right."

Irene took a long slow breath and looked straight and deep into Eddie's eyes. "Maybe we should talk about some other things that ain't right. Like women pretending to be errand boys in houses of ill repute."

Eddie went rigid, too stunned to say anything for what felt like a whole lifetime. Finally, she looked pleadingly into Irene's eyes. "I have to."

Irene raised her eyebrows, asking for more.

"I have no choice—"

"No choice about what?" Tess entered the kitchen in her dressing gown, remnants of her question in the look on her face. Then she saw Irene. "God almighty, Irene! I hope the other guy looks worse than you do."

"I'm afraid so, ma'am. He spit teeth."

"Sounds like he got what he deserved. Bet he won't hang around your door anymore."

"It wasn't Irene's door he was hanging around," Eddie blurted. "The damn fool was at the Red Velvet last night and came looking for more in the kitchen."

Tess turned a stony white. "A customer did this?"

Irene shot Eddie an angry look. "Now you're gonna make me lose this job. I told you to shush." She turned her back on both of them and busily tidied things that didn't need it.

"Irene, I hired you to cook. You shouldn't have to put up with that." Tess was in grand form, hands on her hips, head raised in righteous indignation, foot tapping the floor precisely. "Why would I fire the best cook in Colorado?"

Irene sagged in relief.

Tess moved closer to examine the swollen eye. "Put some beefsteak on it. The prize fighters claim that brings down the swelling." She picked up her breakfast tray. As she moved through the doorway, she turned to Eddie. "Start your errands now, please. I have a special job for you this afternoon." As she took the first step of the stairs, she added "You'll have to pick up the newspapers later, but do the druggist and sundries now."

Eddie went out the back door wondering if her unfinished conversation with Irene would mean she didn't have job when she got back. She ran through the errand routine in a fog, not even caring that she was picking up laudanum from Mr. Oberlander for the fourth time in less than a week. She churned through her options for trying to patch her disguise back together well enough to fool Irene. It was useless. Irene knew.

There wasn't time for any more discussion with Irene when she got back to the Red Velvet. "Miss Tess wants you in her sitting room," Irene said as Eddie entered the kitchen.

Eddie gave Irene a perplexed expression.

Irene answered the unasked question. "She didn't say what for, and I didn't ask."

Eddie's eyes pleaded.

"Don't worry. I ain't gonna tell nobody nothin'. Least of all Miss Tess." But the look in Irene's eyes told Eddie she still had some explaining to do.

Eddie climbed the polished stairway and knocked at the door of the sitting room. At Tess's response, she entered a room similar to the front parlor, but with a distinct business air—in spite of its rose water sprinkler and crystal whiskey decanter. Eddie felt Tess watching her.

"Do you like what's in this room, Eddie?"

Eddie held her breath. "I don't know what you mean, ma'am." She did, but she had to play this well. Not fooling Irene might be workable. Not fooling Tess was unthinkable.

"Would you like to spend time in this room with me? Or in one like it with one of the girls?"

Eddie tried to force herself to blush. "I'm sorry, ma'am," she said, twisting her hat in her hands for effect. "I ain't ready for that kind of thing. I...I...just don't think I can do that." She was mumbling something about not wanting to disgrace dead parents when Tess broke into a hearty laugh.

"You made the grade again, Eddie boy. Before I trust you with the kind of work I want you to do next, I needed to be sure you were going to be around." She looked at Eddie with a business-like coolness. "And if you mess with my girls, you *aren't* going to be around."

Eddie fidgeted from one foot to the other. "I understand, ma'am." Maybe this whole idea was the wrong way to go about getting to Rafe Pettibone. Tess would be furious when she found out. But now was not the time to change plans. That would be even more impossible than the mess she'd gotten into.

"You said you needed me to do something different, ma'am?" Eddie prayed the inquiry would get them past the embarrassing discussion.

"Yes. Something no one else in the house knows about. I need you to swear you will not say anything." Tess looked at her intently.

"You're my employer, ma'am. I'll do whatever you say." She was sincere and hoped she sounded like she was. And she hoped what Tess wanted of her was legal.

"Good." Tess dragged a heavy canvas bag from under the big desk that took up the corner of the room by the window. "I need you to learn to deal with Clarence Billingsley for me."

Eddie stared at her dumbly.

"He's the assayer over on Fifth near Bennett."

Eddie still didn't understand.

Tess pulled a chunk of dull gray rock out of the sack and handed it to Eddie. "He specializes in high grade."

"You mean gold ore?" What Tess had just handed her looked like plain old rock.

Eddie tried to remember what Jerrod had explained about "high grade." Something about taking the best ore, she thought he had told her. He'd been angry about that practice, too—called it stealing. "You want me to steal gold ore?"

"No, I want you to help me get a fair price for my ore. A few of the prospectors pay with stuff from their diggings. I get it fair, but...." Her face hardened into the businesslike coolness again. "Billingsley's not fair with me."

"What do you want me to do?"

"Help me figure out how much it's worth so I know what to demand from Billingsley when I sell it to him." She leaned toward Eddie earnestly. "I want you to find a way to assay my gold ore in Clarence Billingsley's shop without him knowing it's mine."

"What?" Maybe what Tess had in mind was legal, but doable was something else.

"Billingsley uses some of the boys in town to do his heavy work. He doesn't pay them except in what they learn." Tess grinned. "Bet it doesn't take you a week to figure out what I need you to know."

"Why can't we just take it to someone else?" As she asked the question, Eddie realized with a jolt that Jerrod would have been the "somebody else." Her evenings-and-Sunday heartache made a rare workday appearance.

"No one else buys the small amounts," Tess said with a sigh. "I've rat-holed eleven bags of this stuff trying to figure out how to get a fair price for it, and there's still not enough to go to anyone but Billingsley." Then the twinkle returned to the corners of her eyes. "Besides, it's so much more fun to beat a rat at his own game."

"True," Eddie said. True. True. True.

Hanging around the assayer's office was more difficult than Eddie expected. The marshal strolled by at least once every afternoon, always managing to put on a very stern look when he caught her eye. Each day, she pulled the hat further over her face, straining harder and harder in the resulting lack of light to see what the unsuspecting assayer was pointing out.

The first day, Billingsley had only let her sweep the floor and load the rock into the little crusher next to his work bench. She liked the little "chipmunk" crusher, but the work was boring. She'd wished she were back at the Red Velvet or out running errands.

But by the fourth day Billingsley was delightedly explaining the process to her as he worked up a sample. "See here?" He rubbed the crushed rock in his hand between his fingers. "Has to be as fine as talcum powder before you start." He dumped the fistful back on the flat metal surface Eddie had learned the day before to call a "buckboard" and began to crush it further by rocking a long-handled grinding tool over it again and again.

"How long does it take to crush a batch?" Eddie was surprised to find she was really interested.

"Depends on your arm," Billingsley said. "Here, work it a bit and see."

Eddie grabbed the heavy crushing tool and rocked it back and forth on the buckboard. She pushed hard, and Billingsley beamed.

"You're a quick study, kid. Maybe you can become my apprentice if you keep learning this fast."

Eddie offered a triumphant smile, hoping to convey that was exactly what she wanted, and went on crushing the rock.

The next day Billingsley showed her how to measure the right amount of rock powder into the crucible and how much to add of the salt, lead oxide, flour, borax, and baking soda to get the metal to separate in the assay oven. It seemed like they were baking a bad-tasting cake.

Later in the afternoon, Eddie watched in awe as he broke a conical button of metal away from the slag that had formed when the crucible was heated.

He pounded the button into a cube and put it back in the oven on a little round dish made of bone that he called a "cupel."

When he pulled the cupel out later, he gave Eddie a broad smile. "This is where Mother Nature tells the truth."

Strange choice of words, given how he treated Tess, she decided.

He weighed the silvery button that had remained on the little dish once it had cooled. His eyes sparkled. "Good, good." He wrote some numbers on a piece of scrap paper.

Then he showed Eddie the arithmetic to calculate combined gold and silver per ton and how to mark the resulting number on the job slip he would return to the customer. But when he actually wrote it up, the number was an ounce per ton less than what they had calculated. Eddie noticed that Billingsley had marked "to be purchased by the assay office" on the slip.

Eddie boiled inside, straining not to let him know what she thought of such dishonesty. Instead of the tirade, she let out a long slow breath. She'd been so absorbed in the work, she'd forgotten why she was there. The realization made her shiver.

"It's gettin' late, Mister Billingsley. I gotta go." She flashed what she hoped was a curious-boy grin and asked, "Can I try to do a sample all by myself?"

Billingsley beamed again. "Sure, son." Then he became serious. "But find a few hunks of ore you can practice on."

"Yes, sir," Eddie said. She smiled as she started for the door.

She was a hard worker and that endeared her to Billingsley. While she hauled bags of ore, fed the little crusher and worked the buckboard, he told her more than she ever expected to learn about the ore in the area. She learned what was worthless and what, with a certain hue, was likely to run a thousand dollars a ton. He showed her what the rock looked like when it weathered on the surface or lay loose in the coarse soil of the area. 'Float' the prospectors called it. And he showed her samples of the richest ore in the District. It looked just like Tess's "high grade."

He uncovered the large scale that he kept in the back room for his purchasing activities and showed her how to calculate the value of a bag of by determining the value per ton and working backward to the value of the bag. But most important, on Thursday and Friday, he let her run assays on her own samples—which had come from the eleven bags of high grade Tess had accumulated.

"Looks like a good vein," Eddie said as she showed Billingsley the second assay of her "practice ore."

Billingsley looked at the numbers and whistled. "I thought you made a mistake yesterday," he said, sounding almost like a doting father. "But you got the same number again today with a different sample. That's pretty convincing assay work." His beady little eyes glistened. "Where'd you get that sample, son? Fourteen dollars a pound is mighty sweet."

"A friend let me have it," she said. It was the truth.

"Does your friend have any more?"

"I'm not sure, sir," she said innocently. "Do you want me to ask?"

"Yes," Billingsley said, slowly nodding as he said the word. "Yes. Why don't you do that. But—" He winked at Eddie conspiratorially, "—don't say anything about the assay value. That's our secret. Right, boy?"

"Yes, sir." She swallowed hard after she turned to leave. "See you next Monday," she said over her shoulder as she walked out into the twilight.

Eddie went directly from Billingsley's to the Red Velvet. Tess was in the kitchen, talking with Irene and nibbling baked pastry scraps when Eddie came through the back door.

Eddie took off her hat, grinning. "You were right." She handed Tess the job slip she'd made out for practice that afternoon.

Tess looked at the slip. "Come upstairs," she said tersely.

Eddie dutifully followed her to her sitting room.

"Fourteen dollars a pound?" Tess's eyes were wide with disbelief. "That's got to be the richest ore in Cripple Creek!"

"Probably, ma'am. Looks like the stuff Billingsley showed me from the Independence."

Tess waved her hand above her head. "We must have two hundred pounds at least." She shook her head as if she was still trying to convince herself the value was that high. "That Stratton fella sure fooled me. I thought I was doing *him* the favor taking his rock!"

"That fits," Eddie said, pleased she recognized the name. "He owns the Independence."

"Well, I'll be." Tess seemed totally astonished by the news. She popped up and began pacing the room. "Fourteen dollars a pound," she muttered. Then she sat down at the desk.

Eddie smiled and gave her the best part of the news. "He wants to 'talk' to the friend who gave me the samples."

"When?'

"Monday." Eddie smiled at Tess, then offered something else she felt was important. "We'd better go together. Once he finds out he's been tricked into being fair, he won't be happy." She nodded as if approving her own thinking. "Two of us would be safer."

"But I wanted so to confront him all by myself." Tess's mouth verged on a pout. "The last time I took in some of Stratton's ore, Billingsley gave me fifty cents a pound."

Eddie remembered the marshal's interest in the assay office. "Two of us would be harder to argue with, Miss Tess." And it would leave one of us to run for the marshal if it gets ugly, she added to herself.

"All right," Tess said with a sigh. Then she brightened. "Either way, I get to see the look on his face."

Rafe stared at the half-light as dawn pushed through the tattered flour sack that was tacked over the window. He was trying to figure out how he could get out of paying Norma for the night. Either he'd had a lot more whiskey than he remembered or the headaches had made him take total leave of his senses. There was no other way he would have ended up at Norma's.

The trip to Florissant had seemed completely logical when he'd thought of it the day before. He'd searched for three more days after sending Al and Scoot back to Cripple Creek. He'd gone damn near crazy trying to find something that wasn't there—the woman. He'd needed supplies. He'd needed to chat with Compton, that pansy excuse for a marshal, to see if he'd found anything. He'd needed someone to make him feel important. But most of all, he'd needed something to do.

He would not have needed Norma, not in his right mind. Norma had the shape of a pregnant sow. Her skin was slack and wrinkled. The gap between her front teeth was wide enough to push a quarter through, and her breath was so bad it made your eyes water. How had he ended up at her shack? His plan had been to relieve his boredom for a few hours in Florissant, not to spend the night in Norma's flea-infested bed.

She moaned in her sleep and reached for him. He slid out of bed quietly before she found him, but her eyes popped open as he stood.

"Gotta be goin'," he said.

"I promised ya breakfast." Her stringy blonde hair stuck out at odd angles, making her head look more like a bird's nest than a part of a human body.

Rafe looked around the room. There wasn't anything remotely like food in the place. "Outta what?"

She grinned and pulled a half a bottle of whiskey from under the bed. She poured a shot into a glass crusted with brown. She saluted him and downed the whiskey in one huge gulp. Taking a grimy wrapper from a chair, she pulled it around herself as she stood up. When she tied it in front, it left a space where the cloth couldn't reach over her full body. She adjusted her bosom so that her breasts were well positioned in that space.

"Come on, Rafe, honey. I'll give you a little dessert before you go." She waltzed toward him, working her heavy hips in a comical slinking motion. "Come here, honey pot."

Rafe got into his pants and pulled on his boots. "Nah, Norma. I gotta go." He was sober and it was morning, for God's sake. There wasn't an animal in the barnyard that didn't look more appealing than Norma in the light of day.

As he grabbed his shirt, the now familiar pain began to take hold. His eyes lost focus, and he clutched the table next to him for support. The pain in his head was like someone was taking a knife and slowly slicing away the flesh behind his eyes.

"What's the matter, honey?" Norma was at his side instantly, holding his arm and walking him back to the bed. "Can you see?"

The room swam in a blur of dim colors and vague shapes, then went black. He shook his head hard, feeling the pain grind behind his eyes even more intensely. Then his vision cleared. "Yeah. I can see," he growled to Norma, as if there had not been a five minute break between her question and his answer.

"Honey, you gotta see a doctor." Norma's voice was soft.

"Nah, it's just a bump I got a while back. It'll go away."

"There's good doctors down in Colorado Springs," Norma said.

"Nah."

"But it could be something real bad, Rafe—"

"I said no!" Rafe yanked the door open and left, his shirt still in his hand.

The pain had subsided almost completely by the time he reached the hideout. Maybe Norma was right. Maybe he needed to see a doctor. "No," he said out loud as he pulled the saddle blanket off his horse. "I don't need a sawbones." A taste as bitter as vinegar filled his mouth, and his eyes narrowed. "I need to get that bitch. Ain't nobody gonna make a fool o' me the way she done." He trudged to the lonely cabin. "She ain't got the best o' me, and she ain't gonna get the best o' me." But in his heart he was afraid the damn woman had already robbed him of both his pride and his mind.

Eddie told herself she couldn't kill Rafe until after she finished the work with Billingsley for Tess. That meant she had Sunday to herself without having to worry about furthering "her plan." She used it to wander in the hills and enjoy what the magazines back in St. Louis often gushed about in travel articles—springtime in the Rockies. The glorious blue sky and limitless panorama, the bright green of the new foliage, and the antics of the ground squirrels when she stopped to rest all proved to be soothing distractions.

She was fully relaxed when she set out for work Monday morning, viewing everything with a rose tint.

She noticed the doctor's buggy in front of the Red Velvet from a block away and kicked Orville into a trot. Leaving the mule saddled for the moment, she hurried in the back door. Irene was cutting out biscuits in the kitchen.

"Who's sick?"

Irene didn't turn to greet her.

Eddie said louder, "Irene, what's going on?"

"Miss Candace," Irene said without looking up from her work. She briskly cut out more biscuits, as if she had to make enough to feed the cavalry. "I don't know why those girls do such foolish things," she said finally.

"What foolish things?"

"Opium, laudanum. Don't make no difference."

"Candace accidentally took too much of something?" It was like trying to pull information from under a big rock.

"Kind of." Irene moved over to the stove and carefully pushed a full pan of biscuits into the hot oven.

"She did it on purpose?" Eddie was horrified at the thought.

Irene nodded.

"Is she...? Is she going to be all right?"

"Doctor says maybe. She didn't have enough to kill her quick, but she's still bad." Irene patted the flour off her hands and came over to Eddie. She put her hands on Eddie's shoulders.

"You come talk to me 'fore you ever do something fool like that. Understand?"

Eddie nodded solemnly, not at all sure of what Irene meant.

"I know you got your reasons, girl."

Eddie returned Irene's gaze, panic lacing her thoughts as she looked into the innocent brown eyes of her friend.

"You can talk to me," Irene said.

Eddie pulled her eyes away. "I don't know what you're talking about, Irene."

"Hog swill," Irene said softly.

Tess bustled into the kitchen, still wearing her evening finery. "I need some strong coffee for me and Doc Fillmore. I can't expect him to watch her by himself."

"Pot's already made." Irene poured coffee from the pot into a silver server. "I'll send Eddie up with some biscuits soon as they're out of the oven."

Tess raised her eyebrows. "The boy stays out of the girls' quarters," she said firmly.

Irene began wiping her hands distractedly on her apron. "Yes, ma'am. I forgot. I'll bring them up myself."

After Tess left, Eddie took the offensive. "You're going to get me in trouble."

Irene looked at her. "All right, 'boy,' do it your way."

After Irene delivered the biscuits, she and Eddie sat down for their own breakfast. Irene offered Eddie a bowl of wild strawberries with fresh cream. Peace treaty, Eddie thought. They ate quietly, each afraid of the topics the other might bring up.

"Why did she want to kill herself?"

"Who?" Irene was more flustered than Eddie had realized.

"Candace. Why did she want to die?"

"It's a rough life, Eddie." Irene rearranged the food on her plate. "Near as I can tell, she'd set her cap for some fella Tess chased off yesterday. Guess Candace followed him here from Leadville hoping he'd ask her to marry him." Irene drew designs in the jam she'd spooned onto her plate.

"How old is she?" Eddie began to trace circles in her own jam.

"Nineteen."

"Why that's two years younger than me! She's got—" Eddie looked at Irene in horror. "I mean...I...It's just...I mean...."

"You mean just what you said, child." Irene put her hand on Eddie's forearm and squeezed it gently.

CHAPTER 7

CANDACE DIED AT ten that morning.

Eddie struggled not to fall apart. She wanted to run. She wanted to hide. She wanted to be safe in the big leather chair back home in the library, waiting eagerly for her father to come in from the office to spend the evening with her. Instead, she went about her work as if it was just any weekday morning.

Tess was hard to read about it. "We're either going to go on with life or I'm going to cry for a week," she told Eddie when she announced they would see Billingsley that afternoon. "I can't afford to cry for a week." But Eddie knew Tess hurt a lot more than she was letting on.

Candace's death made Eddie feel the Billingsley project was doomed before it went any further. She'd gone over the plan with Tess five times, but the whole thing suddenly didn't feel right. Tess planned to take a derringer, just in case, and Eddie had the knife in her boot. But neither gave them much protection if Billingsley got ugly fast. Stop it, Eddie told herself for the hundredth time as she ran the morning's errands. How was she ever going to kill Rafe Pettibone if she was too cowardly to confront a crooked assayer about a fair price?

When Eddie got back to the Red Velvet from her errands, the burly man from the livery stable was leaving. He looked at Eddie as if he ought to know her but didn't make the connection.

"Thanks, Artemis," Tess said sweetly as the man backed down the walk, his hat in his hands. "We'll have your wagon back to you before dark."

"That'll be fine, ma'am." He put on his hat but kept walking backwards, his eyes glued on Tess. "That'll be fine." He finally turned around before he fell over anything.

"Everything ready?" Eddie decided not to admit her sense of doom.

"Going like clockwork." Tess had already managed to have the ore bags loaded on the wagon. She climbed up onto the rough seat. "You gonna drive or not?"

Eddie boosted herself onto the driver's seat and sat down. "That's the plan, isn't it?"

She took up the lines and clucked at the mules. The wagon moved forward.

"You know how to do this." Tess seemed amazed. "How'd an orphan boy learn to drive a wagon?"

"Hired us out at harvest sometimes," Eddie said matter-of-factly, grateful to Poppa for letting her practice on the rigs at his business when the drivers had gone for lunch.

They worked their way toward Billingsley's office, moving with the rest of the traffic and taking their time. That had been discussed, too. No need to attract attention. Tess had even toned down her attire. In a plain gray cape with a hood, she managed to look fairly ordinary until you got close.

They pulled into the alley next to the assay office and stopped where Eddie knew the ore wagons parked. She took a deep breath as she set the brake.

"Go get 'em. Eddie boy," Tess said with a smirk. "I'll be right here waiting." She smiled as Eddie got down from the wagon.

Eddie went around to the front of the office and walked in. No one was there. "Mister Billingsley?" Her call brought a series of shuffles. Billingsley's head appeared in the door from the back room. "Ah, Eddie." His face became serious. "Did you talk to your friend?"

"Yes, sir." Eddie tried to believe her voice didn't sound suspicious.

"And?"

"All the ore is outside in a wagon."

"A wagon!" The greed on Billingsley's face made it shiny with sweat.

"Yes, sir."

"Well, let's go see." As Billingsley hurried out the door and turned toward the alley, he leaned over to Eddie who was next to him. "You didn't say nothin' about the assay, did you, kid?"

"Of course, he didn't, Clarence," Tess boomed from her seat in the wagon. "He didn't say nothin' at all about that being mighty fine high grade you stole from me at fifty cents a pound last time."

Eddie watched the street out of the corner of her eye. This was not the time she wanted the marshal to come by with another stony reproof for hanging around the assay office.

"Now see here, Tess Temany, I'm an honest man—"

"And I just joined the Sisters of Saint Francis." Tess got down from the wagon. She had color in her cheeks well beyond the rouge.

For a moment, Eddie was afraid the two might get into a fist fight.

But then the tone of Tess's voice changed amazingly. "Well, now, Clarence, honey. We all know it's buyer beware." She batted her eyelashes at him.

That wasn't a part of the plan they'd written down, but it worked pretty well. Billingsley was listening.

"Let's not fret about what happened before. Let's figure out what's fair to do now." She smiled her sweetest smile. "I mean, a single man in this town doesn't want the ladies of the Row to think he's crooked." She coughed demurely. "It could get mighty lonely of a Saturday night."

Tess's coquettish behavior seemed to be helping. Eddie knew that Billingsley usually reddened quickly when he was angry, but at the moment his flabby skin was still a sallow white. "I imagine we can come up with something fair," he said in tones of strained gentility.

Tess raised her eyebrows, then waited.

"Ten dollars a pound." Eddie could see sweat on Billingsley's forehead.

"Clarence, this little paper says it's worth fourteen," Tess said sweetly. She batted her eyelashes some more.

Billingsley ground his teeth. "How do I know it's all that rich?" His growl told Eddie they were still safe. Billingsley growled most of the time, but not when he was ready to explode.

"I cut the sample just like you taught me, Mister Billingsley," Eddie offered. "I took rocks from each bag and crushed them all, then mixed 'em good before I took the sample."

Billingsley let out a huff.

"Quick learner, isn't he, Clarence?" Tess was enjoying the joke.

Eddie wished she wouldn't rub it in so hard. More enemies was the last thing Eddie needed in Cripple Creek. And Clarence Billingsley would be an awful enemy.

"Eleven-fifty, and that's my last offer," he said, sweat running in a little line down the side of his face.

"Make it twelve, and I won't tell all of Myers Avenue what a crook you are."

"All right," Billingsley said, mopping his neck with his handkerchief. "Bring it inside, and we'll weigh it." He opened a side door that led directly into the back room and the big Toledo scale.

As usual, the scale reminded Eddie of her father's cartage business, and she felt a twinge of sadness. She began to pull the sacks off the wagon, stacking the first six on the scale.

"Fifty eight pounds," Billingsley announced.

Tess looked at Eddie, and Eddie looked at the scale. "That can't be right, sir," Eddie said, confused as to what the problem could be. Each bag weighed at least twenty pounds and some more than that. She knew from just lifting them. Eddie moved toward the scale.

Billingsley began to fidget. "Let's get on with this project," he said, a bit too loud. "I don't have all day for you two."

As Billingsley leaned to remove the first of the "weighed" sacks, Eddie noticed a board wedged under the back side of the base of the scale. "Just a minute, Mister Billingsley. The scale seems to be hung up," she said, telling herself it could have happened by accident. She kicked the board away. "There." She smiled triumphantly. The scale read a hundred and twenty-three pounds.

Now Billingsley's face was getting red. Eddie hurriedly removed the first six bags and laid the remaining five in their place on the scale.

"A hundred twenty-three plus a hundred and two," Tess said. "That makes two hundred and twenty-five total, right, Clarence?" She screwed up her face, doing the arithmetic in her head. "That means you owe me two thousand seven hundred dollars." She smiled sweetly at him. "I assume you'll be paying by bank draft?"

Billingsley was grumbling as they followed him into the front room where he had his office. He opened his desk, seeming to reach for his writing materials. Eddie had bent over to straighten her pant leg, which had caught on her boot. She saw the metal of the gun as his fingers moved toward it. Her knife was in her hand, and pressed into his fleshy middle, before she knew what she was doing. "Just the draft, Mister Billingsley. You don't need the gun."

Billingsley's fingers changed direction, and he took out his pen.

His face was still too red for Eddie's comfort when they left with the draft. So he was angry, Eddie reassured herself. She'd take care of Rafe the following Sunday and then leave—Billingsley wouldn't have a chance to get back at her. She wasn't worried for Tess. The assayer liked Myers Avenue too much to mess with *her*.

Tess broke her own rules about being seen in public and went directly to the bank. She deposited the draft and then requested three hundred dollars in cash. Eddie's eye widened as the teller counted out the money. Tess smiled at Eddie and put the money into her handbag without counting it a second time. Then she walked back to the wagon as if the transaction was nothing out of the ordinary.

When Tess and Eddie returned the wagon to Artemis, he fell all over himself again the whole while Tess talked with him. After delivering the wagon, Tess started back down Bennett Avenue on foot.

Eddie wasn't sure what she was supposed to do and began to lag behind. Where were they going now?

"Come on, Eddie," Tess said as she stopped in front of a building with "James A. McCloud, Undertaker" in sad black letters on the window. "Death is a part of life. You may as well learn about it before you have to bury someone you love."

Eddie bit her lip to make it stop quivering.

As they walked through the door to the place, Tess whispered to Eddie. "Her kin disowned her. We're the only folks she has."

The smells of the undertaker's office triggered an onslaught of memories for Eddie, both of her father, lost and properly buried, and of Jerrod, killed in cold blood and buried without even a minister's blessing. She had trouble focusing as Tess asked her opinion on the various choices they had to make. The taffeta and satin linings, the coffins "in the latest fashion," the Bibles—it all blurred before her as she struggled not to succumb to the shrieking in her head. Here they were, burying a harlot with dignity, while Jerrod—sweet, good Jerrod—rotted in a lonely grave in the hills. She shoved her hand in her mouth and rushed past Tess.

Once outside, she clung to the post that supported the porch roof and gasped for breath.

And now she'd made a complete fool of herself on top of everything else, she realized. After several gulps of fresh air, Eddie steeled herself to go back inside.

But the undertaker was already seeing Tess through the door. "We'll do it all just as you've requested," he said with the mandatory hushed tones of the profession.

Tess took Eddie by the arm. "I'm really sorry, Edwin." Eddie was startled by the softness in her voice. "You're the one who made the money we needed to bury Candace the way I wanted to, and I go and remind you of the folks you've lost."

The funeral was held on Friday. Candace would have been proud.

The next Sunday, Eddie was up just after the sun and saddling the horse. The magical blue sky made her think of how intrigued Jerrod had been with it. "It's almost too blue," he had told her twice in the few hours they'd been in the wagon. With three weeks to get accustomed to it, the ache of missing him was familiar now. She missed him more than it was possible to miss anyone. When she was alone, the emptiness was suffocating. She had to deal with Rafe. Maybe then the ache would melt back into the general pain of being alive and alone.

She loaded both Jerrod's small gun and Rafe's larger revolver and packed extra ammunition for the smaller gun into the saddle bag. This was the day. The plan was simple, but she was sure it would work. She'd been close enough to shoot Rafe when she'd watched him torture the magpie. She'd just climb the rock outcrop and wait until he came into range.

She mounted and headed out. Again, she stayed as far as she could from other travelers. Coming over a knoll, with the dirt road winding in the valley below, she found herself in a meadow ablaze with red wildflowers—Indian paintbrush. They'd been Jerrod's favorite since the first time he'd seen them. She wondered if the clearing where he was buried was as colorful. She looked at the sun, then at the road. There was time for a short detour. Wheeling the horse around, she headed for Jerrod's grave.

Leaving Jewel to graze, Eddie hurried toward the meadow on foot. As she got closer to where the outlaws had hidden the wagon, she moved carefully, going from one hiding place to the next and waiting to listen and look before moving forward.

The site where they had left the wagon was deserted. The sticks Scoot had whittled were still scattered in the same loose pile. From the tracks, Eddie could tell one person had looked the area over thoroughly at least once since she took the wagon. The boot tracks made her guess it had been Rafe.

Once she was sure there was no one else in the area, she moved more quickly. When she stepped into the meadow, she caught her breath. The meadow where Jerrod was buried was a riot of color. The red of the paintbrush danced in the breeze with blues and yellows, whites and pinks of other wildflowers.

"Oh, Jerrod," she gasped. "It's *better* than Saint James." The guilt of not having buried him properly in the cemetery of the church where he had been christened lifted. In its place, the ache she carried permanently became more pronounced.

She moved toward the center of the clearing. The stones on the grave were still in place. The pine needles she had spread still covered most of the area. But her witness was through tears that came unbidden and unstoppable. She crumpled to the ground next to the rock she'd placed as a headstone and began to sob.

She cried longer and harder than she thought her numbness would allow, never shifting from her position at the head of the grave. When she had no more tears to offer, she dozed in the same position.

When she opened her eyes, she was looking into the slanting rays of the late afternoon sun.

Rafe Pettibone would live a little longer.

She put out her hands to push herself up in the lengthening shadows. The change in light offered evidence she had not noticed before. Her eyes widened in fear. In front of her, clearly marked in the soft dirt, was an imprint of the same boot she'd seen earlier near the wagon's hiding place.

The next week, June was gone, and it was the Fourth of July. The entire house had emptied to see the big parade. The Fourth was the one time when Tess let the girls venture into the public's view, provided they remained a discreet distance from the families.

"We don't need to advertise, and the townsfolk don't appreciate it," she'd announced. "If seeing the parade isn't enough, then stay here. I have nothing else to offer you for entertainment."

Eddie had been surprised at Tess's terseness and even more surprised when she'd given Eddie and Irene time off from their chores to watch the parade, too.

As they worked their way through the crowd to the near side of Bennett Avenue, Eddie was astonished at the number of people who had turned out. Where had they all come from? There seemed to be more parade spectators in Cripple Creek than for the Fourth of July parade in St. Louis.

"As many folks as in that Saint Louis you keep talking about, huh?" Irene grinned.

Lately it seemed Irene could read her mind. With so much to hide to keep herself safe, the possibility made Eddie more than a little uncomfortable. She had to get on with killing Rafe so she could put it all behind her.

Eddie and Irene moved onto Bennett Avenue and blended in with the crowd. A block and a half farther down, they found an open spot along the street and claimed it before anyone could step in front of them. Once they had stopped moving, Irene pulled two fat sugared doughnuts from a sack she'd carried from the Red Velvet and held one in each hand. "Happy Fourth o' Joo-lie," she said with a quick bow, handing Eddie one of the doughnuts.

"When did you make these?" Eddie took a big bite. The sugary dough tasted like sweet clouds. "Umm. This is really good."

Irene beamed. "Boys usually like doughnuts the best." Then she raised her eyebrows. "Ain't that so?"

Eddie wasn't ready to get into a discussion about her gender, but she was pretty sure that was where Irene was heading. "Yes, ma'am," she said noncommittally. "This doughnut sure is good."

To avoid Irene's eyes, Eddie looked up the street to see if the parade was coming. She saw no sign of the brightly uniformed bandsmen or decorated carriages she'd been told to expect, but the sidewalk spilled over with people waiting for them to march by. When Irene stopped looking at her and began to study the crowd, Eddie relaxed.

Her mind began to dip in and out of various pools of idle thought. Freedom—this Fourth of July, the concept was confusing. What was freedom anyway? The choice to act? The chance to live? Was she free? Would she be free when Jerrod's death had been avenged?

How about the girls at The Red Velvet? How free were they? She recalled her trips to the drugstore. She'd carried the jack of spades only once. That was morphine. She'd concluded two weeks ago that Tess used it. Mr. Oberlander didn't worry about secrecy anymore. He left the curtain open when he went into the safe, and with each trip Eddie had been able to figure out a little more. Ace of diamonds was opium. Ten of clubs was hashish. And the queen of hearts was laudanum. Eddie was certain that had been for Candace. She hadn't carried the queen of hearts since Candace died.

Eddie decided she had a bizarre freedom in her new identity. No one told her things were too dangerous. Except for her job, no one told her what to do. The tent was adequate, although the nights were cold. On Sundays, she could do as she wanted.

But she wasn't really free. She would not be until Rafe Pettibone was dead. God required that of her before life could hold anything else. She laughed at herself for the thought. She'd stopped believing in a good God when her mother died. Maybe freedom was a myth, too.

She'd been looking at the crowd and not seeing, but suddenly her eyes focused on a group of three men directly across the rutted street from her and Irene. Scoot, Al, and Rafe Pettibone. Her heart stopped beating.

They were punching each other like school boys and ogling Jolene, one of the newest and youngest girls at the Velvet. Eddie thought she could actually see Rafe drool. Her stomach juice crept into her throat.

Thoughts swirled in her head. There were three of them, but this was her chance. She reached down and felt the smooth handle of the knife in her boot. The blade was six inches long. It would pierce his heart if she could get all her weight behind the thrust.

She looked to the left of the three outlaws. A family with two toddlers happily waited for the parade. To the other side, a gaggle of young boys jostled each other. Was this the time? If Rafe was in town now, he might not be at the hideout on the coming Sunday, when she planned to deal with him. But the children didn't deserve to see anyone stabbed. Could she afford to wait? Could she afford not to wait? What if she couldn't get a good enough chance and she didn't kill him when she tried?

Her eyes returned to the bystanders. She would wait.

Jerrod—and Poppa—would have agreed with her decision to wait, she decided. But she refused to ask herself if they would agree with her plan to commit such an act at all.

The sound of a marching band made her look back down the street. The parade had begun. But no matter how hard she tried, she couldn't focus on the musicians or the carriages or the dignitaries on horseback. Like a hungry animal tied out of reach of its food, she watched Rafe. Finally she tugged on Irene's arm. "I need to leave."

"The parade's just started, child," Irene said, with a slight edge of irritation. She took her eyes off the street to look at Eddie. "You're ghost white. What's come over you?"

"I don't know, ma'am," Eddie mumbled. She didn't want to

blame the doughnut. "Maybe it's a touch of something." She glanced across the street involuntarily.

Irene took her by the arm and began to push through the crowd, moving in the direction of the Red Velvet. When they got beyond the spectators, she stopped and wagged her finger in Eddie's face. "You may have good reason, missy, for what you are doin'." She dropped her hand to her side and looked at Eddie. "But it's time you told me what this is all about." She caught Eddie's eyes with her own compassionate brown ones. "Those three ruffians ain't folks you'd notice just for fun."

She took Eddie by the arm again. Instead of heading for the Red Velvet, she walked her down the alley where the coloreds and other outcasts lived. She stopped at a tiny whitewashed shack. "No one will bother us here." She unlatched the door and pushed it open.

Irene's home was as immaculate as the kitchen at the Velvet. Though the furnishings weren't elaborate, the room gave the sense of a life wisely lived. A small jar on the plain kitchen table held a few sprigs of wildflowers. On the other side of the room was a narrow bed, covered neatly with a fraying quilt. A well-worn Bible was on a small table next to the bed. The walls held several sepias, one of a smiling group of dark-skinned people—a man, a young woman with Irene's smile, and four children.

Eddie scrutinized the photographs. "Your family?"

Irene smiled and nodded. Then she stopped. "No you don't," she said, scolding like a worried mother. "We came here to talk about you." She put her hands on her hips as if to emphasize she meant business. "You aren't going to weasel out of this conversation again."

She pulled out a chair at the table. "Sit." Then she walked around to the other side of the table and pulled out the other chair. "Miss Tess won't expect us back from the parade for another hour."

Eddie sat, without any sense that she had another option.

"You can tell me, girl. I've had enough sorrow in my life to be able to carry another's without falling down."

The kind look on Irene's big face made Eddie fight to keep her eyes from brimming with tears. "Irene, don't you ever call me 'girl' again," she said sternly. "My name is Eddie Taggert. That's all you need to know."

"All right, 'Eddie Taggert,' what's going on?" Irene's voice was a mixture of loving mother and commanding general. "A good lookin' woman can't masquerade as a boy forever. I ain't the only one with eyes."

Eddie sat silently. She didn't have any idea how to begin.

"Just start at the beginning and tell me everything."

Irene was reading her mind again, Eddie realized. But she still didn't say anything.

Irene reached across the table and grasped Eddie's arm. "Who are you?"

"Edwina Taggert Sinclair."

"Where're you from?"

"Saint Louis."

"How'd you get to Cripple Creek, Colorado all by yourself?"

"I didn't come by myself."

Irene waited for Eddie to continue.

"My husband and I were going to start a new life here."

"What happened to your old life?"

"It's a long story and not a big part of why I'm here." Eddie sighed. "My father was duped by a business partner and ended up bankrupt and died. Jerrod wanted to be an assayer, and we came West." She shrugged. "Now I have no one."

"Where's your husband—Jerrod?"

"They killed him."

"Who?" Irene's face registered her understanding as she was saying the word. Eddie watched as the compassion in her eyes turned to fury. "Those three across the street?"

Eddie nodded.

"Why didn't you go back to your mother?"

"She died when I was eight."

"And your husband's kin?"

Tears welled in Eddie's eyes. She tried to fight them back. "His mother disowned him when he decided to move to Colorado."

Irene patted Eddie's arm. They were quiet for a while. Eddie wandered absent-mindedly through her own thoughts without really comprehending anything.

Finally, Irene spoke. "That doesn't explain why you're passing yourself off as a boy."

Eddie's tears stopped, and her eyes hardened. She raised her head and thrust her chin out defiantly. "Rafe Pettibone killed Jerrod in cold blood." She felt the fire in her eyes. "I'm going to give him the same treatment."

Irene shook her head in disbelief. "Now just how do you think you're going to do that?"

Eddie's eyes burned brighter. "I have two guns. I practice with them every Sunday." She raised her pants cuff to show Irene the knife in her boot. "If he'd been alone today, he'd be at the undertaker's now."

"You sure you want to do this?" Irene asked, as a grandmother would of a child who'd chosen to run away. Then her eyes went to some other place and time. "Revenge isn't the cure-all it looks like," she said, still lost in her faraway place. "It just brings more unhappiness."

"This is different."

"Oh?"

"Jerrod was a good man. He didn't deserve to die. He's dead for no good reason." The words tumbled over each other as they came out. It was wrong for him to be killed. She knew that. But Eddie couldn't find the words to explain it properly. Finally, tears streaming down her face, she looked at Irene. "I just have to do this. That's all."

And it was all. She had no life beyond killing Rafe Pettibone.

The prospect of dying for her decision was not an issue either. Only the need to do it right was clear—to do it well. To make him pay every bit as dearly as Jerrod had paid.

Eddie and Irene sat at the table without any more talking for what seemed like a long time.

"We gotta get back," Irene said finally. She rose from the chair and came around to Eddie. "Think about it some more, child. Two wrongs ain't never made a right yet." She gripped Eddie's forearm gently. "And killing is always wrong."

CHAPTER 3

THE PEOPLE WHO had watched the parade were dispersing when Irene and Eddie got back to Bennett Avenue.

"Fine parade," a woman in front of them said.

"Sure do like that Elks Band," another responded.

Eddie and Irene fell into the rhythm of the crowd's progress and reached the cross street without much effort. They headed for Myers Avenue with a thinner crowd. A block away from the Velvet, they were alone.

"Promise you won't say anything to Tess," Eddie said once she was sure no one would overhear.

Irene gave her an exasperated look. "What'd you take me for? A skunk?" She wrinkled up her nose. "It's your business, and I won't meddle in it." She gave Eddie a sidelong glance. "I just think you're wrong, that's all." She kept walking. "Don't worry. A secret with me is as safe as in a tomb."

They reached the back yard of the Red Velvet. Eddie muttered, "Thanks," as they went up the steps.

Tess was in the kitchen sipping coffee when they came in. She seemed pleased to see them. "How was it?"

"Fine parade," Eddie answered.

"Sure do like that Elks Band," Irene added.

Tess beamed with vicarious pleasure. "I used to love parades."

"Why didn't you go see it?" Eddie wished the words were back in her mouth.

"Reminds me too much of home."

"Oh." Eddie felt like a clod. "I'm sorry."

"Don't be sorry," Tess said. "I'm the one who chose to leave." But her eyes glistened with tears.

Maybe it was just not a good day for conversation. Eddie

vowed to keep her mouth shut for the remaining two hours of her workday. She moved to the sink and began to pump the water Irene had told her would be needed for preparing the evening meal.

A few minutes later, Irene handed her an ice cream bucket with a crank. "Here," she said. "Why don't you work on this for a while?"

"Can I do it out back?" The weather was too perfect to stay indoors. Besides, Eddie hoped the blue of the sky and the clearness of the air might help her think.

"Guess there's no extra benefit to doing it under my feet," Irene answered. "It's all set. All you have to do is crank."

"Yes, ma'am." Eddie took the container and went out the back door.

From behind her, Irene heard Tess speak.

"Is he out of earshot?"

Irene was surprised to hear the question. She leaned just far enough into the door frame to see Eddie walking to the back of the lot. "Uh huh."

"I need to talk to you about that kid," Tess said. "Something about him just doesn't seem right."

"It's a hard life being an orphan," Irene said, hoping it would be enough.

"No. It's more than that."

Irene scrubbed the skin of the potatoes so hard it looked like she might not need to peel them. Tess had something on her mind. It was clear to Irene she was going to hear it, whether she wanted to or not. It was part of being employed. "How?"

"He's not just shy around women. He ignores them. It's almost as if he feels he's the same as us."

Irene left the potatoes on the drain board. Wiping her hands on a dish towel, she turned to Tess. "What do you think is wrong?" May as well get it out in the open, Irene thought angrily. Eddie was going to think she'd tattled the first chance she got.

Tess squirmed, which Irene had never before seen her do. Then she looked at Irene earnestly. "Do you think maybe Eddie's queer?"

Irene looked at her like a deaf mute, too relieved to say anything.

"You know...ah... like they called it in a magazine I just read: 'homosexual'?"

Irene decided playing stupid might make Tess more comfortable with her conclusion. She looked at Tess as if she had no idea what she was trying to explain.

"Do you think he likes boys instead of girls?"

Now Irene grinned. "Maybe," she said with a casual air of indifference. She was working hard not to burst out laughing. For Eddie's sake, she had to play along. "What difference does it make?"

Tess cocked her head to one side, thinking.

"You're right," she said after a few moments. She flipped the auburn curls as if to confirm her decision. "In fact, it would be downright convenient not to have to train a new errand boy each time the current one discovers what his equipment is for."

Cranking ice cream required no brain until the very end. The person doing the cranking just had to know when to stop. Eddie knew she was still a long way from that decision so she worked with a mindlessness that soothed her. She daydreamed about picnics with her father and mother on the Fourth of July when she was young. She thought of watching last year's fireworks in St. Louis with Jerrod. She tried not to think about freedom, especially the freedom of choice Irene had made her aware she had. It was easier to assume it was her responsibility to kill Rafe. Thinking about the morality of it gave the task an entirely different cast.

She was still avoiding her moral seesaw when she heard yelling from in front of the house. The noise seemed to have the tone of an argument. She moved across the back yard, put the ice cream bucket on the back steps, and hurried up the side yard. As she came around the front corner, a familiar voice made her stop. She jumped back around the side of the house.

"You ain't so fancy, Miss Tess Temany," the loud, awful voice yelled. "You don't have to be so high-falutin. My money buys as much as any other."

"Buy it someplace else, Rafe." Tess's voice was controlled and firm. "I don't want your kind around my girls."

Eddie peeked around the corner of the house. Rafe Pettibone was on the porch, as unwashed and angry as ever.

"I can pay." He waved a wad of money in Tess's face. Eddie wondered which unfortunate travelers had been forced to give it to him.

"It's not the money, Rafe." Tess turned gracefully on her heel and slipped back into the house.

"God damn you, woman," Rafe bellowed into the wood and glass of the door. "I don't take 'no' for an answer. Ever. You'll have me, and you'll know why!"

Eddie couldn't believe it when the front door opened again.

As she peeked around the corner again, she could see Tess move a step beyond the doorway, standing solidly with a shotgun aimed at Rafe's belly.

"Get off my porch, Rafe Pettibone. And don't come back." Tess brought the gun up higher. "Now."

Rafe and Tess stood stock-still, locked in a mutual glare, for what seemed like forever.

Eddie saw Rafe's fingers twitch, but he didn't move for his gun. Finally, he turned and left the porch, stomping back up

Myers and into one of the dance halls.

Pity those girls, Eddie thought.

The exchange had been so intense Eddie didn't realize until ten minutes later that Tess might have killed Rafe before she herself had the chance. A wave of peaceful helplessness washed over her as she considered the possibility of someone else taking care of the problem for her. Then the outrage of being denied her due replaced it. No. She was the one. When Rafe died, she had to be the one pulling the trigger. It was the only way to do it properly for Jerrod.

Rafe looked down on the city of Cripple Creek from the stage road above town. He'd left the dance hall in frustration ten minutes after going in the door. The girls at the dance hall had seemed ugly and stupid compared to what he wanted at the Red Velvet.

He had no doubt he'd have his way with whoever he chose at the whorehouse. He just needed to do some planning to make it happen.

From his perch above the city, the bustling town was small enough to be an anthill. Maybe it was an anthill, he decided. The people sure as hell were like ants—nuisances that bothered him. He'd get Tess Temany. She was second on his list, right after that damn woman who'd hit him with the skillet. And after the two of them came that fancy-pants marshal.

Al and Scoot rode up before he could add to the list.

Al's face was filled with hope. "Private stage?"

Rafe shook his head.

"Freight wagon?" Scoot's eyes were bright with the possibility. "Nah."

"Then why the hell'd ya pull us out of the Creek?" Al's voice had an irritated rasp.

"Tess Temany wouldn't let me into the Red Velvet."

Al and Scoot both looked at him. They waited. After a few seconds, Al asked, "What's that got to do with us?"

"We're gonna get her," Rafe said matter-of-factly. "Right after we find that first bitch."

Al and Scoot looked at each other, then back to Rafe.

Al kicked a loose rock. "Rafe, you ain't been back in town a whole official day yet. What the hell do you wanna do a fool thing like that for? Tess Temany is high class. You'll have the whole town on your—"

Rafe put his hand up to stop the sermon. "I *said* we're gonna get her." He felt his Adam's apple bulge as he strained for more voice. He looked slowly at each of them, his eyes fiery. "I'm still the leader of this outfit, ain't I?" His growl meant to imply there was only one answer.

"Yes, boss," Al and Scoot said in unison.

"That's better." Rafe folded his arms over his chest. "What'd you find out about that other she-devil?"

"Ain't a trace of her, Rafe," Al said.

"We've looked everywhere," Scoot added.

"Why's it so damn hard to find one measly woman?"

Both of the men answered his question with a shrug.

"No one I've asked knows anything about her," Al said. "I've checked restaurants, hotels, grocery stores, boarding houses. Nobody's seen her."

"You boys just don't know how to look." Rafe slowly unfolded a mean grin. "Now that I can move around town without the marshal on my back, *I'll* find her." He took his hunting knife from its sheath. "And when I do, she won't stay in one piece for long."

The next morning, Eddie was whistling again. No one cared if an errand boy whistled, and it made her feel happy. She'd finished the early errands, including making a bank deposit for Tess, and was on her way back to the Red Velvet. At ten o'clock, her stomach was already growling. As she passed the Tea Cup Cafe, where she had first tried out her disguise, Marshal Gruen was heading in the door. She nodded to him and smiled.

"Mornin', Eddie," the lawman said. "How things goin'?"

She automatically assumed her boyish persona. "Pretty good, sir. You?"

"Can't complain." He looked at his watch. "Got time for coffee—and a cinnamon roll?"

Eddie nodded enthusiastically. Maybe he had heard her noisy stomach.

The first time the marshal had invited her to have coffee, Eddie had begged off, afraid of Tess's disapproval. Instead, the wily madam had encouraged Eddie to cultivate the friendship. Tess believed it always helped business to be on good terms with the local law. If that meant letting her errand boy take coffee with the marshal, it was fine with her.

The first few mornings at the Tea Cup, Eddie had gulped fear with her coffee. Spending time with the marshal meant conversation, and she was afraid she'd say something to give herself away. But after a few of their visits, his kind eyes and the pleasure of being able to ask him questions made her forget her fear. He was beginning to seem like the older brother she never had.

She still wasn't sure about him as a lawman—or of any Colorado lawmen, for that matter. Just making sense of the way the law functioned in the West was a challenge. Marshal Gruen had explained it all three times, but it hadn't helped her confidence a bit. According to him, each town had a marshal. But a mining district could also have a marshal—that's what he was. And then there was the county sheriff. As the Cripple Creek marshal, he was also a deputy county sheriff. She was convinced there were too many badges and not enough justice.

Her opinion rested heavily on her experience with the marshal in Florissant. He represented her first encounter with "the Law" in Colorado. She knew his version of justice was all wrong. The rest of them were probably wrong, too—even Marshal Gruen, who told good stories and bought her sweet rolls. As they walked into the restaurant, she reached the same conclusion again: Don't trust your justice to the Law in Colorado.

But Irene's homily about killing gnawed quietly.

They sat down at a table, and Marshal Gruen waved to the waitress. "Two coffees, Mabel. And the biggest cinnamon roll ya got in the pan."

Eddie expressed her gratitude with a smile.

Mabel set the cups of coffee and the roll in front of them, along with two spoons and a pitcher of cream. She nodded toward the sugar bowl, which was already on the table. Every time they came in, she followed exactly the same routine.

Eddie and Marshal Gruen hid their grins by looking down, but Eddie knew they were both amused by Mabel's predictability. The marshal scooped a spoonful of sugar and dumped it in his cup. Eddie stirred cream into hers.

"Tess treating you right?"

"She's a good boss, sir." What had prompted that question?

"How much does she pay you?"

This conversation was going in the wrong direction quickly. "Enough."

The marshal sipped his coffee for a few minutes. "I could get you on at the Independence. They're opening a new level."

"The Independence Mine?" Eddie stirred her coffee. Was this a set-up? Most of the miners stripped to the waist for their shifts. She decided she'd better play along, if only to be sure the marshal didn't know her secret. "What're the wages?"

"Three dollars a day."

"A day! Before Tess gave me a raise, that's what I made in a week." She wished she hadn't said it. She was making six dollars a week now, but why had she blabbed about it at all?

"My brother's father-in-law is a shift boss. Want me to talk to him?"

Eddie stirred her coffee again. Being underground all day sounded awful. How could she dodge this without disappointing the marshal? She smiled. "No, thank you, sir. I'd rather stay out in the sunshine." Still, a mine would give her a place to hide, time to perfect her plan, and more money. Money for what? She would kill Rafe this Sunday. That's all there was.

"You gotta make something of yourself, son," the marshal said, with an intensity that put Eddie further on edge. "You can't run errands for a whorehouse the rest of your life." Marshal Gruen stirred his coffee like it might scorch if he stopped. Round and round the spoon went, creating a miniature whirlpool that matched Eddie's panic.

When he stopped and looked at her, she knew she had to come up with something more convincing to get him off the subject. She thought about using the line she'd used with Irene, about becoming a great chef, but decided against it. Instead, she opted for simplicity. "Yes, sir," she said. "I'll think about that some."

The marshal seemed relieved but not yet relaxed. He started stirring his coffee again. Then he looked up and cleared his throat. "Eddie...?" He went back to stirring his coffee.

Eddie's panic accelerated, and she found herself leaping to ridiculous conclusions. Irene must have told him about her masquerade. She kept her eyes focused on the coffee cup across the table, waiting for the marshal's next words, which she was sure would expose her.

He coughed and tried again. "Eddie, I know you ain't had a pa or a ma to help you, and I was wondering...."

She looked up.

The pink of embarrassment pushed through the marshal's tanned cheeks. "Boy, has anyone talked to you about right and wrong?"

"Pardon?" He'd taught her to say that last week, instead of

"Huh?" which she had perfected on Tess and Irene. She *never* said "Please, repeat," as her mother had taught her.

"You're a good kid. I'd hate to see you get in trouble because you didn't know what it was." The words spilled out of the marshal's mouth.

"What do you mean, sir?"

"Sometimes, things that look right are wrong..." Now the marshal seemed short on words.

"I don't understand what you're trying to tell me." Maybe Irene had snitched on only part of it. Eddie waited for him to tell her killing was wrong.

Instead, he took off his Stetson, ran his fingers through the thick brown hair that hid under it, and replaced the hat. "This is harder than I thought it would be."

"What is, sir?"

"Dammit. I worried about you the whole time you were hanging around that assay office."

Maybe having an older brother was a nuisance, Eddie decided. He leaned back and looked straight at her. "Tess Temany wasn't thinking very well when she asked you to do that. You could have gotten hurt—bad—and still may. Billingsley ain't a good man, even if he's in an honorable profession."

"Yes, sir." As Eddie took another sip from her cup, a tall man entered from the street. She almost spit the coffee out in mid-swallow. The Florissant marshal had just walked into the Tea Cup.

Marshal Gruen followed her gaze, but missed her reaction. When his eyes rested on the newcomer, he scowled. "Now there," he said, his voice low, but clear with dislike, "is an even better example of a bad man in a good job."

The marshal from Florissant noticed the two of them and headed for their table. Marshal Gruen clicked his tongue in disgust.

Eddie's mouth went dry when the Florissant lawman stopped in front of them.

"Mornin', Hugh," he said to Marshal Gruen. Then he looked at Eddie. "Mornin'," he said and nodded. He looked back at Marshal Gruen. "You seen Rafe Pettibone? I was supposed to meet him at the livery at ten." He pulled out his pocket watch to check the time.

Eddie's eyes riveted on the timepiece.

"Ain't seen him," Marshal Gruen said. "But then, he knows I don't hold him in high regard." He moved the spoon in his coffee cup around slowly. "Try the Double X."

The Florissant lawman put the watch back in his pocket. "Good idea. I'll do that."

Eddie heard the screen door slam after the Florissant marshal had walked across the room, but she was afraid to look at Marshal Gruen, sure that what she had just seen would show on her face. Finally, she forced herself to raise her eyes.

"I think I understand what you were trying to tell me, sir," she said. There was only one way the Florissant marshal could have Jerrod's watch.

Twenty minutes later, Eddie was still struggling with a jumble of emotions as she walked back to the Red Velvet. Marshal Gruen's concern was touching. His desire to make her life better seemed genuine. Maybe he was different than the fraud she'd asked for help in Florissant. Maybe Irene could say killing was wrong because Marshal Gruen really was there to protect her. Maybe the law was real. An army of uncertainties tramped over her well-made plans and destroyed her resolution. Maybe killing Rafe was as wrong as she'd been taught.

As Eddie neared the Red Velvet, she noticed Jolene, standing in the yard in her wrapper, looking around as if someone were calling to her. Suddenly, a man grabbed Jolene from behind, put his hand over her mouth, and hauled her kicking noiselessly toward a shack behind The Old Homestead next door.

Instantly, Eddie broke into a run. The man was dragging Jolene into the shack when Eddie flew at him from behind, hitting him at the knees and knocking him over. He lost his grip on Jolene as he fell. As soon as his hand was off her mouth, Jolene screamed.

"Let her alone," Eddie commanded. She circled around in front of him, her fists up, ready to take him on. When she faced him, she froze in terror. Rafe. She raised her hands, still clenched into fists, trying to hide her face, but she knew it was too late.

"You." His mouth stayed half open as the reality sank in. Eddie dashed past him as he grabbed his knife. Jolene stood, screaming, while Rafe pursued Eddie into the backyard of the Red Velvet.

Eddie hoped to get to the mule, but Rafe was too close to try it. She dashed up the back steps and into the kitchen. The room was empty. As she heard the thud of Rafe's boots on the steps, she rushed to latch the screen door. Too late. He yanked the screen door out of her hands and off its hinges.

Eddie looked wildly around the kitchen but couldn't see anything to use to defend herself. All the knives were in their proper places in the drawer on the other side of the room. Even the ubiquitous rolling pin wasn't in sight.

As Rafe lunged at her, she dodged. He fell, hitting his head on the edge of the table. He staggered quickly to his feet and came at her bellowing like an enraged bull. His big hunting knife whisked back and forth in front of her eyes as she backed around the room.

She was afraid to take her eyes off him long enough to get her own knife from in her boot. They circled the kitchen again and again, Eddie walking backward and using her memory of what was where to keep from stumbling, Rafe walking forward and brandishing the knife inches from her face.

"Damned whore! Thought you could fool Rafe Pettibone, did ya?" As they reached the open door to the pantry, he moved to grab her. Eddie ducked but lost her balance. Rafe's grasp missed her as she crashed into the pantry shelves. She tried to pull the knife from her boot as she fell.

Rafe saw the blade and kicked her hand before she had a firm hold on the knife. It clattered noisily onto the kitchen floor. He sheathed his knife. "Now for the fun—"

Eddie kicked him hard in the knee.

"Goddamn!"

As Rafe hopped on his good leg, Eddie jumped up and tried to run past him and back into the kitchen. But he was on her before she could get away, first grabbing her by the arm, then taking a tightening grip around her throat. "You think I'm that stupid, eh?"

Her vision blurred, and her head got light as he squeezed her windpipe. She struggled to scratch his face, but she couldn't get enough air to move any part of her body much. He began to bang her head against the shelf behind her. She made one last feeble attempt to kick as she began to black out. Then she heard a voice from somewhere behind Rafe.

"Let her go this second." When Eddie opened her eyes, Irene was choking Rafe with a loop of twisted dish towel. She held the rolling pin poised above his head in her other hand. A few seconds later, Tess came up behind her—with the shotgun.

Rafe snarled. He had loosened his grip when Irene surprised him, so Eddie had caught her breath somewhat. She stomped as hard as she could on his instep.

"Yow!" Rafe grabbed his foot.

As soon as Rafe let go, Eddie shoved past him and ran into the kitchen. She retrieved her knife, then moved behind Tess. Could she kill him now? Not with the finesse she'd promised herself. She held the knife quietly and waited.

Tess leveled the gun at Rafe. "I told you before to get off my property, Rafe Pettibone." She raised the gun slightly. "I meant all of it—and forever." She motioned with the gun toward the back door. "Now."

Irene turned Rafe toward the back door, holding him by the shirt collar and threatening him with the rolling pin.

Once Irene and Rafe passed Tess, Irene stepped to the side. Tess joined the small parade, pressing the shotgun firmly into the middle of Rafe's back. Resolutely, the two women marched the outlaw to the back door.

"This is the last time, Rafe Pettibone." Tess sounded like a cavalry officer. "It ain't good for business to run to the marshal, but in your case, I'll make an exception if you ever come near my place again."

In a flash of insight, Eddie realized her days at the Red Velvet were over. Rafe would come back as long as she was there. She had to leave. She hurried through the parlor and out the front door before Tess and Irene turned around.

CHAPTER 9

WHEN SHE RAN from the Red Velvet, Eddie's one thought was of escape. Not knowing which way to turn, she'd chosen the first hiding place she'd seen. Only after she'd hidden in the rain barrel on the other side of the front yard at the Old Homestead House did she focus on the fact that she'd just lost her second chance to kill Rafe. And both of the chances she'd had were due to luck, not any well-executed plan of her own.

She felt defeated when she hadn't yet gone to war. Shivering—both from the water in the bottom of the barrel and from another close call—she tried to come up with some idea of what to do next. There had to be a right way to do this.

Come up with a *decent* plan, she chided herself. No more chance encounters. Rafe Pettibone meant to kill her. Either he died or she did. Death had been as close as his rotten breath only moments before. The shivering intensified until she was shaking uncontrollably.

Cramped inside the barrel, she found it impossible to do much but wait. She'd jumped into it as a way to get out of sight quickly. But even in the summer heat, the four inches of water that remained in the bottom of the barrel chilled her. The fact that Rafe was probably still close by didn't help.

Deal with first things first, her father had told her. Her boots were soaked through. First, she needed to find another place to hide.

She poked her head up over the edge of the barrel just as Irene came out the front door of the Red Velvet and stood on the porch.

"Eddie?"

Eddie dropped back into the damp darkness of the barrel. A

sickening sense of loss mixed with her fear. She could never see Irene again.

"Eddie? It's all right, child. You can come out. He's gone."

After a few minutes with no answer, Eddie heard the squeak of the front door. Irene had gone inside.

Eddie wanted to jump out of the barrel and run to the kitchen and Irene's warmth. She wanted to believe she could go to the marshal and that he would deal with Rafe. She wanted peace—for Jerrod and for herself. She wanted to think about things that were soft and gentle and happy. But she could only see one way to be safe from the monster who had ripped through her life like a cannonball. She had to kill Rafe Pettibone.

The front door of the Old Homestead opened. Someone shuffled down the steps, past the rain barrel and toward the side of the lot. Within minutes, the person returned and went into the house. Even if it had been dry, this hiding place wasn't going to work. She had to move.

Eddie raised her head above the rim of the barrel and scanned the area. The backyard seemed deserted but she couldn't see much. Going through the backyards was her best hope. She pulled herself up over the edge of the barrel. Her boots squished as she hit the ground. She dashed into the Old Homestead backyard, then through the next and the next, each soggy step moving her farther from the Red Velvet and the people she loved.

When she reached Bennett Avenue, she stopped and pulled off the jacket she'd been wearing and yanked her hat from her head. Anything that made her look different might help. A few blocks up, she slipped into the alley between the bank and the dry goods store. Empty crates were stacked to one side of the alley. She pushed a space between them and the wall and hurried behind the flimsy fortress.

As she was rolling her hat and jacket into a bundle, she heard Rafe's angry voice on Bennett Avenue. "I'm going to kill that she-devil." The sound of his voice petrified her. She wondered if they would find her days later, curled behind the crates—dead from fear. Finally, she heard no more of the voice. Eddie prayed he'd moved on.

As the shadows lengthened, the tension in her body relaxed, and she began to weave another plan. When the slant of the sun's rays told her the shops were about to close, she started on a critical errand.

After checking both directions on Bennett, she entered Fitzsimmons Dry Goods Store.

"Evenin'," Mr. Fitzsimmons said, coming in behind her with a rack of union suits that had been on display outside.

Eddie nodded. She picked up a bottle of black dye and quickly approached the counter.

"That all you need?"

"And some glue." She reached in her pocket for money.

The portly shopkeeper wrapped the purchases in paper and tied the package with a string. "That'll be eight cents."

Eddie plunked a nickel and a three-cent piece on the counter and picked up the package. "Thanks," she said as she hurried out the door.

Once back in the alley, again safely behind the crates, she waited for dark.

With Big Linda sideways on his lap, Rafe found it easier to stop thinking about Edwina Sinclair. Big Linda wasn't fat, but she was round. And she was tall—Rafe always went for the ones who came up high enough to kiss without stooping. He hated bowing for anyone. He nuzzled his face into Big Linda's big breasts.

"Easy there, boy. You know that's against the rules." She wiggled around on his knees, working her way sideways up his thighs with her ample behind.

He rested his face in her cleavage again. Instantly, he felt a hand firmly grasp his shoulder.

"You know the rules, bub." The huge bouncer was not friendly. "The lady can sit on your lap for as long as the dance. Or the lady will dance with you. But if you want any of the other stuff, go across the street. That's what those girls have beds for."

Big Linda's wicked pout made the sermon even more unbearable. Before Rafe could get her to settle back in, the music stopped. Damn.

Al and Scoot came through the door as Rafe was rummaging in his pocket for another quarter to secure Linda for the next "dance." He shoved the coin back in his pocket and waited for his two companions to cross the dance floor. Once they were within conversation distance, he spoke. "About time."

"We were...ah...busy," Scoot said, looking at the floor.

"You damn well better not be too busy to come when I say." Rafe wanted to belt him right there, but the bouncer would pitch him out of the place if he did. Once they were at the hideout, he would give Scoot a reminder lesson on who was boss.

"Aw, get off it, Rafe." The toothpick Al had been chewing rested in the corner of his mouth.

Too damn cocky, Rafe told himself. Time to teach that boy a lesson, too. He pulled himself up to his full height and looked slightly down at Al. "Why the hell weren't you here an hour ago?"

But Al seemed different than before. A little taller. New boots maybe? Rafe looked at the Kentuckian's feet. His boots were as scuffed as they'd been last week, with what seemed to be the same shit from the corral caking them.

"Scoot told you. We were busy." Al said the words slowly, his eyes locked with Rafe's the whole time.

"You saying your plans are more important than the gang's work?"

Al and Scoot both smiled, as if victory had just been declared and they were a part of it. "You mean we're gonna rob somebody?"

"This gang does more than just rob people."

Scoot looked bewildered. "It does?"

Al got even taller. "Rafe, if you got a bone to pick with another damn hussy, pick it by yourself." He had an angry confidence oozing out of him that Rafe distinctly didn't like.

Rafe tried to stare him down. "This work has got to be done first. Then we'll get back to our usual endeavors."

"What work?" Al and Scoot asked the question in unison.

Rafe slowly unfurled the meanest grin he could manufacture. "I found Edwina Sinclair."

"Shit." Al turned and headed for the door.

"Where you goin'?" Rafe stared at him incredulously. "You gotta help."

Al turned and looked coldly at Rafe. "That ain't what I signed on for. You wanna hunt women, you do it without me."

Rafe couldn't believe this was happening. He was the leader. Al and Scoot had to follow. "Where ya gonna go?"

"Denver City, maybe. Or Omaha. Don't rightly know."

Al's coolness made Rafe's stomach churn. He felt like he was talking to his old man.

"I ain't takin' this bull one more second," Al said and walked out of the dance hall like he owned the whole district.

"Al, wait—" The pain began slicing behind Rafe's eyes, and he stopped mid-sentence, unable to remember what he had planned to say.

In the time before darkness finally came, Eddie decided she had to at least try to retrieve the mule. She'd have to leave the custom-rigged saddle, which she'd left in the shed that morning, behind, but, even bareback, riding the mule meant she could make better time. From the alley, she could hear the plink of the pianos and the laughter of patrons on Myers Avenue. She already missed the excitement and bustle of the short street. Swallowing hard, she made peace with not going back to say goodbye to Irene and Tess. It was safer for them and that's all there was too it.

Once the darkness was complete, she pushed the crates away from the wall and slipped into the alley, then onto Bennett Avenue. People were still walking up and down the street, socializing as they made their way back to homes with cozy beds and doors they could close. Eddie slowed her pace to match the strolling townsfolk, each step an exercise in discipline.

She wanted to run as fast as she could or, better yet, to gallop down the street in a fury once she had the mule. Running fast and far away seemed wisest. But there were people she cared about in dingy, raw Cripple Creek. Irene and Tess, maybe even the marshal, had been the best friends of her whole life—not counting Jerrod.

She'd decided which route she would take with Orville before she even got to Myers, then realized with a jolt that she might not even find him. Tess may have sent him to the livery, where her own horses were kept. Nothing ever got simpler.

After a block and a half of the excruciating stroll, Eddie cut over to Myers where she could run through the backyards of the houses on the Row again. As she came around behind the Red Velvet, she heard a familiar sound—the jingle of Orville's tack as he shook his head in greeting. The dining room window cast enough light for Eddie to see the mule, rubbing himself against the clothesline post, saddled and ready. Irene really could read her mind.

Eddie greeted the mule by leaning her cheek against his face, a habit they'd both come to enjoy. The combined scent of mule hide and saddle leather smelled better than French perfume. She led Orville quietly away from the Red Velvet, past the two-room shacks up Poverty Gulch. Then she mounted and continued into the mountains. Once the lights of Cripple Creek twinkled in the distance, she circled back, working her way through the hills above the city and toward her camp.

That night, she allowed herself neither campfire nor lantern. For the first time since she'd begun to call the tent home, the darkness scared her. She listened, muscles taut and senses sharp, for noises that would tell her Rafe had found her.

But no such noises came. Instead her head filled with the whisperings of her conscience, Irene's advice, and the unanswered question of what was right regarding Rafe Pettibone. In between the bits of sleep her weary body snatched without permission, she revisited the outrage and the emptiness of the life Rafe had left her. And she remembered Irene's admonition: Killing is always wrong. By dawn she had accepted that she had to talk to Marshal Gruen.

She reconverted the saddle so she could use it on the horse, which took a little time. But turning Jewel into a bay by using the black dye on her mane and tail proved a bigger task than anticipated. What she had thought would require less than an hour took most of the morning.

Next, she made herself a mustache from hair she'd trimmed from her head. That took less time than she expected, but was harder to get used to. In the first few minutes she wore the new piece of her disguise, she sneezed four times.

She changed into Jerrod's other jacket. It looked ridiculous with the work pants, but it was green, and the one Rafe had seen was grey. All she needed was enough disguise to get in and out of town safely. She didn't plan to try to fool the marshal any longer about who she was.

But who was she? At the moment, Eddie Taggert seemed far more real than Edwina Sinclair.

By early-afternoon, she was ready. As she pulled the saddle and blanket from the stump where she had put them the night before, a piece of paper fluttered to the ground. She picked it up. The smell of lavender greeted her as she opened the fold.

Eddie,

I made Irene tell me everything. Please don't try to take care of this alone. I don't think they'd hang a woman, but jail is mighty unsavory. Irene and I will help you get to the marshal.

Tess

Eddie wondered if her tears would wash off the mustache. Nothing ever got simpler.

When Eddie looked down on Bennett Avenue from the curve above town an hour later, Cripple Creek looked no different than the day before. She hoped that would be the case. If so, Marshal Gruen would be sitting in his office, reading the mail that had come in on the stage and working on the paperwork he hated. Rafe would be well-established behind a bottle of whiskey and a girl in some dance hall. But what if today *was* different than yesterday?

She didn't want to exclude Tess and Irene. She knew they really cared. But it was wiser to go to the marshal on her own. If Rafe was watching *anywhere*, he would be watching the Red Velvet.

Coming down Carr Street, just the other side of Bennett, she made her way to the back of the jail without mishap. With Jewel hidden safely behind the building, she walked out onto Bennett Avenue.

She pushed hard on the hair on her lip, trying to make it stick more tightly. Instead, a third of the mustache came off on her finger. Frantically, she tried to press it back on, but it fell back into her hand each time she let go of it. Finally, she yanked the rest of it off in frustration. Then she hurried up the steps to the marshal's office. A notice was tacked on the door:

Death in the family. Out of the office until July 19.

H.Gruen, Marshal

Two weeks! How was she going to wait that long?

A yelp made Eddie turn toward the street. A small yellow dog was scurrying around the end of a building, away from the unkindness it had just suffered. A man—lean and scruffy—was working his way methodically up the other side of the street. He looked thoroughly into each alley he passed. With horror, she realized it was Rafe—and that he was looking for her.

She turned back to the door, wishing she could pass through it like a ghost. Instead, she stood, paralyzed by the possibility that her next breath might never come. He was still a hundred yards from her. Quietly, she walked down the steps and into the alley. Once behind the building, she watched from around the corner until Rafe moved past the marshal's office. Then she mounted and headed in the other direction.

To stay behind Rafe, she'd had to leave town in a different direction than usual. Once she was out of town, she realized she was on the road to Victor, heading south and a little east, away from her camp—as well as the hideout, the outlaws, and Rafe Pettibone. She listened for riders but didn't worry about where she was going. She really had no where in mind. For now, she just had to get to where Rafe wasn't.

Once Cripple Creek was no longer in sight, she rode the horse slowly down the dusty, sun-dappled road, absorbed in dark thoughts of Rafe Pettibone. The stink of his clothes, the suffocating rottenness of his breath rolled over her in repulsive repetition.

The braying of a donkey brought her back to reality. Fifteen yards ahead, an old prospector was trying to coax a heavily loaded burro over a treacherous spot in the road. From what Eddie could see, she sided with the donkey. The ground the old man was trying to make it walk over was crumbling away into the gulch. Either of them might end up with a broken leg—or worse—if the ground slipped further while they were on it.

"Move, you disgusting hunk of buzzard bait." The prospector pushed on the animal's rump. The donkey braced her front legs and brayed. He hit her behind the front knees with a stick. "I should have made you into pot roast long ago." The old man pushed on her from behind. "Now get goin', or we'll settle this once and for all." He pulled an old pistol from the rope he used as a belt. "Now, move!"

"Wait!" Eddie jumped off her horse and ran toward them. The shriveled, little prospector leveled the gun at her.

From the closer vantage, Eddie understood the real problem. His cloudy eyes suggested he must be nearly blind .

"Don't shoot her," Eddie commanded, trying to sound cordial.

"I couldn't shoot ol' Sunshine." The prospector patted the donkey.

"Then put away the gun." Eddie moved close enough to put her hand on the barrel of the old pistol. Pushing on it until it pointed toward the ground. The prospector put the gun back in his belt.

Eddie grabbed the donkey's halter on the side opposite the old man. "Maybe we can get her to cooperate if we go a little sideways first," she said, as she maneuvered the animal around the washout. The donkey complied.

Eddie smiled at the old man across the back of the donkey and stuck out her hand. "I'm Eddie Taggert. I'd be pleased to know your name."

"Salt Lick Charlie McGill," he said, not seeing Eddie's extend-ed hand. "But most folks just call me Charlie."

"Pleased to meet you, Charlie. Been prospecting these parts long?" What could he find with his eyesight failing?

"Two years. Not the Independence, but it keeps me in whis-key and bacon."

She grabbed Jewel's reins and walked the horse alongside the donkey. "You're working a claim by yourself?"

Eddie immediately sensed she had insulted him.

"I can handle it." His tone was cross. "You young ones are all alike—no respect for what those older'n you know."

She was starting to recognize the potential in the situation. Working in a small mine might be perfect. But to get in his good graces, she needed to convince him she was worth having around.

"Sorry. I didn't mean no offense." She waited a few seconds. "You probably know more than I could ever learn if I spent the rest of my life at it."

Charlie didn't say anything.

"I know it ain't none of my business, but how can you tell what you got?"

"You're right, kid. It *ain't* none of your business."

Eddie looked at him coolly, trying to come up with a better strategy for getting him to invite her along. Bluntness seemed her best option. "I need work. Why not let me help you?"

"Got enough trouble with claim jumpers without asking one along."

They walked in silence for a few minutes, then Eddie tried again. "I'd be willing to work for you for room and board and three dollars a week." Three dollars a week! She had to be crazy. For all she knew, the tent she lived in was better than what he had.

"I don't need some greenhorn," Charlie said. "How do I know you'd be any good? I ain't even seen you 'til this minute."

"I worked for Clarence Billingsley for a while—know some about the ore in these parts. I could make your life easier." She felt like she was trying to sell snake oil.

"You're a cocky one."

"Sorry, sir." She dropped her head contritely. "But it just makes sense—you could use the help, and I need a job."

His scowl relaxed. "I need some time to think on it." Charlie's tone was still crusty. He couldn't recognize this good fortune any better than he could see a washout in the road.

Then, out of the blue, as if he'd been contemplating if for a week, he said, "Ya got a deal."

CHAPTER 10

THE TERRAIN THEY passed through was all new for Eddie. Evergreens and aspen spread before them like a lumpy crazy quilt. The ruggedness of the topography became more pronounced. Craggy boulders loomed in huge proportion to their surroundings. With the sun sparkling off the surfaces of the giant rocks, the whole scene looked like a fairyland.

For moments at a time, Eddie lost herself in the beauty of it, not thinking at all about where they were going or what she was getting into. She wondered lazily whether she should have packed her camp before they headed south. Then what she'd just done hit her. She had just agreed to live with someone she knew nothing about. He might end up being every bit as evil as Rafe. How could she have been that blind?

The word itself provided some reassurance. *He* was blind or so close to it she would have a big advantage if she needed one. He was also old and crippled with arthritis. And he was shorter and probably weighed less than she did. She shook her head in amazement as she realized she didn't need to *find* her gumption. It was already there.

When they crested another hill, a row of snow-capped peaks appeared on the horizon. "What are those?" she asked, pointing to the glistening mountain range.

Charlie looked where she was pointing. "What are what?"

"Those mountains." She was embarrassed she'd asked the question. How could she expect him to see what was that far away if he couldn't see the particulars of the road?

Charlie squinted hard. "Oh. Them's the Sangre de Cristos. Means 'blood of Christ' in Spanish. The padres claimed that at sunset them mountains turn red as blood."

Eddie thought of more recent blood and sighed.

The road got steeper, and the hillsides seemed to stretch to the sky with outright urgency. Then she and Charlie turned off the road. As they headed up a heavily wooded gulch, Eddie felt the cool rush of evergreen shade. It smelled like Christmas. She was instantly homesick.

Charlie looked over at his new apprentice as the shadows of better times crossed her face. "Regretting this already, ain't ya? It's a long way from town. You can't run in every night for the fun."

"I'm not missing fun," Eddie said matter-of-factly. "I'm missing home."

Charlie's eyes crinkled as he smiled. "Ain't spent much time with anyone since I ran away from home. This'll be the closest thing to 'home' I've had in so long I can't count." His smile faded. "That is if I don't run you off."

"Let's just see how it works out," Eddie said. She'd have a roof over her head, or least that's what she'd assumed.

For some reason Eddie couldn't grasp, Charlie began chattering like a squirrel. "I got just the cabin, and it's small. Been wanting to build on a lean-to for a while anyway. You could sleep there. Won't be as fancy as a room in town, but it's shelter." He stopped abruptly. "Aw, hell." He began to turn the donkey around. "Better head back to town now and get tools for you. No sense in making another trip."

Eddie got wide-eyed at the thought of returning to where Rafe was looking for her. "Why?"

"I only got one set of tools. One singlejack ain't enough for two of us."

"I've got plenty of tools, sir." Too late, Eddie wondered if it was wise to admit her cache. Better than going back into town, she decided.

The old man eyed her suspiciously. "Did ya steal 'em?"

"Nope. Inherited 'em."

Charlie looked at Jewel, who was waiting patiently.. "You ain't even carryin' saddle bags. You ain't got no tools."

"I hid 'em so I wouldn't have to haul 'em around." The answer sounded reasonable to Eddie. Besides, it was true. Her life lately had become more bizarre than most of the stories she'd read, she realized with amazement.

Charlie's eyes narrowed again. "What else did ya hide?"

Eddie sucked in air slowly. If she was going to live on his claim, she had to admit she had the animals. She may as well tell him about the rest. "A freight wagon and two mules."

The prospector broke into a wide grin. "Goddamn!" Charlie started jumping around in the road in his excitement. "Really?" Then the slits returned. "You sure you didn't steal 'em?"

"My brother and I came west to prospect together," Eddie lied. "He died."

Charlie's look softened. "Sorry," he said gruffly. He fiddled with the pack on the donkey for a few minutes. "Where'd ya put all that stuff?"

"Got a camp about a mile west of the Creek. Mules are there. Wagon and tools are hidden a couple miles farther west—along the road to Florissant."

The donkey was still waiting in mid-turn, standing sideways on the path up the gulch. Charlie turned the burro back in the direction they'd been going. "That's too far to fetch it today. We'll go after it in the morning."

Eddie was not at all sure about the "we."

"Come on," Charlie said. "Let's get to camp 'fore the sun's gone."

Eddie held back, suddenly aware that if the camp was too far away to reach, she was also losing her chance to get to Rafe easily.

"Hurry up," he snapped. "We ain't got forever."

"Coming," she said, with more enthusiasm than she felt. Why couldn't she just make a plan and get on with it? She'd been stupid to suggest this.

"You work the claim with me, and I teach you what I can. You get a roof and grub. I get to use your mules and wagon. That was the deal, weren't it?" Charlie seemed to be warming to the arrangement as quickly as she was cooling to it.

"Plus I get three dollars a week," Eddie said. "Remember?" Maybe that would change his mind.

Charlie paused, as if evaluating the bargain they'd already struck all over again.

"Do we have a deal or not?" Eddie hoped they didn't.

"Yep." Charlie urged the donkey forward. "With mules we can really get down to business!" His laugh tinkled in the air.

"How long 'til we get to your camp?"

"The Tin Rooster's a ways up the gulch. Should take us another hour."

Eddie guessed they'd been on the road two hours already. Three hours from Cripple Creek was too far! Then she remembered they'd covered the ground on foot. If she used the horse, she could still deal with Rafe at his hideout in a single day.

She watched the old man's back as they labored up the trail next to the creek. She had to stop second guessing herself. Otherwise, she'd spend each day undoing what she'd done the day before. If she was going to stay with Charlie, she had to decide once and for all to trust him and the location. If she wasn't ready to do that, she had to leave. Now. Without going another step toward his claim.

Patting Jewel's neck, she urged her forward and resumed trekking resolutely behind the old miner.

"Rafe! Rafe! I've found her." Scoot was hollering even before he came through the swinging doors of the Double X.

Rafe moved the lady of the moment off his lap as Scoot stopped in front of him. "Where?"

"In the hills, a mile or so west of town." Scoot was triumphant.

"What was she doing when you found her?" Somehow, Rafe wasn't so sure Scoot had actually seen Edwina Sinclair.

"Well...I didn't really find *her*—"

"Then why all the hollerin' about finding her?" Lately, Rafe admitted, it was too damn easy to lose his temper. Scoot was the only member of the gang left. Snarling wasn't going to keep him around. "Just what did you find?" Rafe said calmly. "Tell me everything."

Scoot cleared his throat to begin. Then he took off his hat and ran his fingers through his hair, preening himself for his grand performance.

"Get on with it," Rafe growled. It would be a whole lot easier not to lose his temper if Scoot weren't so damn good at tempting him.

"I found her camp. I know it's hers."

"How?"

"The mules are there."

Rafe snorted in derision. "She probably sold 'em."

"There's only one person using the tent—"

"You expect me to believe that fine lady is living in a *tent*?" Rafe snorted again.

"Well, it's some lady." Scoot pulled something he'd stuck in the back of his pants. "I got her mirror. See?"

"I'll be dipped. In a tent?" Rafe tried to imagine any one of his four sisters in a tent. "Naw, ain't no woman gonna live in a tent."

"If you're so damn sure this ain't her, maybe you should just find her by yourself."

Rafe put up his hands in a gesture of conciliation. "Her camp, eh?" He gave Scoot a grin—half congratulation, half whiskey. "Maybe we should head out there and wait for her." But first, a toast. He grabbed the bottle of whiskey.

"After dark, Rafe," Scoot said eagerly.. "We could get her tonight." He looked around the room. He leaned over to Rafe and said under his breath, "Then we can get back to real business."

Rafe glanced at the woman who had been on his lap as the pain started to build behind his eyes. "Tonight," he said, nodding with satisfaction. As soon as he could see again. He pulled the bottle toward him as the blackness descended.

An hour later, Rafe wove out the doors of the Double X. "We'll get 'er tonight," he mumbled.

Scoot was waiting at the hitching rail. He grabbed his horse's reins from the hitching post and hurried behind Rafe toward the livery.

"We're gonna get 'er tonight," Rafe said to no one as he wobbled down the street. He felt his gut twist into a loud hiccup.

"Maybe tonight ain't the right time, Rafe," Scoot said, finally catching up. "You know you can't shoot straight when you're full o' whiskey."

"Nah." Rafe staggered into the livery and grabbed his saddle blanket. "We're gettin' that bitch tonight." He threw the blanket over a sorry-looking dun. The blanket landed in a heap on the floor on the other side of the animal.

Scoot retrieved the blanket and placed it properly on the horse. Then he worked on the bridle.

Rafe managed to get the saddle on the horse's back. He pulled on the cinch. "Yes, sirree, we're shure gonna get 'er." After grabbing the reins from Scoot, he led his horse out the livery door.

Once he had the dun in the street, he grasped the saddle horn, put his boot in the stirrup, and heaved himself into the saddle. As he settled on the leather of the saddle, the blanket and saddle slid around and under the horse. Rafe fell on his back in the street with the saddle on top of him.

After a moment of stunned silence, he yelled, "Get this damn thing off me!"

Scoot had lifted the saddle before Rafe even finished the command. He stood staring at Rafe for a full minute, mouthing words without saying anything. Finally he said, "Sleep it off, Rafe. I ain't wandering around in the dark next to a drunk with a gun and a grudge." He dumped the saddle on the ground beside Rafe. "Sometimes, you're worse than a man can put up with."

Rafe watched as Scoot gathered the reins of his own horse but didn't get up. The pain behind his eyes had begun again. A few minutes later, Scoot walked past Rafe, heading back to the hotel. "Get some sleep, Rafe," he muttered, as if *he* were the boss.

But Rafe was glad Scoot hadn't stopped. The black blindness was awful enough as his own secret. He couldn't bear the idea of his gang knowing about it.

He waited until he was sure he was alone, then stood and staggered his way to where he thought the horse was. He found the reins, then the horse's neck. He held onto it in terror.

When he woke in the morning, he was on the hay in the stall with the dun. He didn't know how he had gotten into the stable with the horse or how the saddle had gotten back where it belonged.

He'd find the woman first, and then he'd find a doctor.

Squaw Gulch was the most beautiful place Eddie had ever seen. The trees were thick enough to offer shade and the scent of pine, but sparse enough for wildflowers to bloom between them. The flowers nodded in the breeze as she and Charlie moved up the gulch toward his camp. Even the rocks added to the enchantment as they sparkled in the setting sun. As they approached the claim through the trees, far away mountains could be seen through the crags of the nearer rocks. It was an incredible sight.

The cabin sat against the south side of the gulch with open space on three sides, about twenty feet from a hole in the side of the mountain—what she assumed must be the portal to his mine. To the other side of the clearing, Eddie spotted the low roof of what had to be a spring house. A small stream trickled from beneath the structure. If her guess was right, a cistern inside caught and held fresh water that bubbled out of the ground. When the cistern was full, the water overflowed into the stream—which held more than enough water for the animals. "You didn't tell me you had a spring."

"You didn't tell me you had mules."

They both laughed.

"Where are you planning to put that lean-to? The mine side looks good." Eddie saw numerous possibilities in the way the area could be set up. "We can build a corral for the animals over here. See, there's already enough of a tree barrier here. We'd just have to string wire on three sides."

"Goddamn! You sound like a woman—changing things as soon as you lay eyes on 'em."

Eddie backed away. "Sorry. We'll leave it just the way it is." She looped Jewel's reins around a small fir tree thirty feet from where they had been talking.

After a minute, Charlie followed her. "Nah, you're right. We gotta secure the stock. Ain't no reason why we can't put in a corral." He took a slow breath. "But no wire. What money I got's for giant powder and fuse, not wire. We ain't setting up no ranch."

Eddie turned her head away. A ranch was sort of what she'd been thinking of, she realized with embarrassment.

The cabin was small but better inside than Eddie had steeled herself to expect. It was one oblong room with a fireplace at one end and the door on the other. There was one window on each of the other two sides. To the right of the door—on the far end, near the fireplace—was an iron bed with a jumble of blankets and clothing on it. To the left, just inside the door, was a table, piled high with books and yellowed newspapers, and two chairs. A battered sideboard with a dry sink seemed to have been meant for kitchen chores, but it didn't look like kitchen chores were part of Charlie's routine.

"You can sleep by the fire tonight," Charlie said. "Tomorrow, we'll get your gear and start on that lean-to." He shuffled over to the table. "Right now, we need some supper." He looked at Eddie thoughtfully, then shook his head. "I'll do the cookin'. A kid like you don't know which part of a pan to put over the fire."

Eddie heard him muttering under his breath about "the damn cookin'."

Charlie pulled a slab of bacon from a shelf near the table. The edges of the slab were blue-green with mold. He carved off four slices and threw them in a dirty frying pan without trimming the mold.

Eddie's stomach lurched at the thought of having to eat what he had begun to fry.

He pulled a crusted pot from the edge of the fireplace, then teased the almost dead fire back into flames. He took the lid off the pot and stirred the contents. "Ain't nothin' like camp beans to make a miner happy," Charlie said as he replaced the lid.

The sickening smell of scorched beans reached Eddie's nostrils. Eating Charlie's version of food was going to be a serious challenge, particularly after Irene's cooking.

Somehow, Eddie forced down a plateful of burned beans and moldy-edged, incinerated bacon without gagging. She even managed to say, "Good food, sir."

Charlie beamed. "Ain't ever cooked for somebody else," he said proudly. "Pretty good, huh?" He slopped up the last of his bean juice with his index finger and slurped it into his mouth.

Eddie nodded. Maybe in a day or two she could get him to let her take over the cooking. Otherwise, she was going to starve.

"I'll clean up," she volunteered. She was sure he'd relinquish that duty willingly, that is if he saw the need to do it at all. If so, he'd at least start with a clean pan in the morning.

Charlie broke into a wide grin. "This set-up is gonna work just fine."

As Eddie was wiping the last dish, Charlie threw an old quilt on the part of the table they'd cleared to eat. "Might need this tonight. Gets pretty cold up here."

She'd already resigned herself to having only her horse blanket for bedding. Charlie's offer was a kindness she hadn't expected. "Thank you, sir."

Charlie scowled as he sat down on the edge of the bed. "If we're gonna work this claim together, I can't have you callin' me 'sir.' Makes me think you're talkin' to somebody else." He pulled off a worn-out boot. "Call me Charlie."

"Yes, sir."

His face turned to stone. "You mockin' me?"

"No, sir."

He stood.

"I mean, no, *Charlie*." Eddie sighed with relief when he sat back down.

"And I'll call you—" He looked at her inquisitively. It wasn't just his eyesight that was going.

"Eddie." She smiled. "You can call me Eddie."

"Time for bed, Eddie." Charlie pulled off his other boot. "Had an Uncle Ed, once. But I ain't ever knowed a 'Eddie' before."

"Then it'll be easy to remember me."

Charlie chuckled as he blew out the lamp and eased himself onto the rumpled bed. "Maybe you're right."

She hoped she was wrong. She wanted to kill Rafe and be gone by Monday—before Charlie got to know her very much, if at all.

In the dying firelight, Eddie watched Charlie pull a blanket up over his head. She lay down on the saddle blanket next to the fireplace and doubled the quilt over her.

Before the fire had lost any of its glow, Charlie was asleep, snoring like a sternwheeler's horn in an autumn fog on the Mississippi.

The sound made her wish she were in Missouri.

The next morning, Eddie convinced Charlie to stay and work at the claim while she went after her belongings. Words like "claim jumpers" and "back to working the mine faster" worked real well.

"I should be back by nightfall," she said, more to give herself some leeway than because she believed it would actually take that long. She was sure she could get the camp packed onto the mules in an hour, retrieve the wagon and repack it and be back on the road by noon. That would get her back to camp by late afternoon.

Charlie was cutting saplings to use in the lean-to when she left on Jewel. He waved as she crossed the clearing. Snoring, burnt food, and all, she was already beginning to like him.

The cut-off to Florissant came well before Cripple Creek, but still she worried about meeting anybody else on the road. She watched the horizon in front of her and stayed at a gallop a good part of the way. Once she started up the trail to her camp, her peace of mind returned. When she saw her tent, she felt even safer. She rode into camp the same way she had for weeks—without any doubt in its security.

Eddie quickly moved things out of the tent and onto the mules. If she hadn't set aside the chamois to wrap her mirror when she began to pack, she probably would not have noticed it was missing. She stood in the doorway of the empty tent, perplexed at how the mirror could have disappeared. It was too heavy for a pack rat to carry off....

Suddenly, she began to see the camp with different eyes—those of an intruder. The ground was covered with boot tracks. Were they all hers? Why hadn't she checked before she started packing? She forced herself to laugh at her folly in thinking someone had stolen the mirror. Who would sneak into someone else's camp just to take a mirror?

She tucked the unneeded chamois in Orville's pack, grabbed

the mules' lead ropes, and mounted Jewel. Silly as the idea of a mirror-stealing intruder was, she looked back every hundred feet as she rode away to be sure the patch of dirt she'd just left was still vacant.

The spot where the wagon was hidden was undisturbed. The tangle of brush she'd used to cover the rig had settled into a single, multi-spiked thicket of deadfall. But there were no evidence that someone else had been there.

Eddie rolled up her sleeves, took off her hat, and got to work. She grabbed a tree limb and pulled. The wood snapped in her face and gouged her forehead. She grabbed a different branch and began to tug on that. When it snapped, it tore a gash in her forearm. Before she gave up and took the time to hitch up the mules to do the work, both arms were bleeding and she had a broad scrape on her cheek.

Luckily, the limbs she had been able to pull out proved strategic. The mules freed the wagon from the rest of the debris after hauling away just three loads of dead branches and brush.

Eddie inspected the wagon. The blood stains were still too obvious, but there was nothing she could do. Hopefully Charlie wouldn't recognize it as blood.

All the same, she rearranged the boxes so the red-brown splotches were hidden. Then she transferred the supplies that had been on the mules to the wagon.

The rig looked like a gypsy wagon. Jerrod would have been embarrassed at the lack of symmetry and balance. That was a plus. It certainly didn't look like the wagon she and Jerrod had started out in a month ago. Had it been that long?

She hitched up the mules, tied Jewel to the back of the wagon, and boosted herself onto the driver's seat. The rig had settled into the soil, and she wasn't sure it would move when the mules pulled. She held her breath as she signaled them into motion.

With a dry groan, the wheels turned, and the wagon inched forward.

She had to take the road with the heavily-loaded wagon. It was near noon, which made the odds of meeting someone much higher. She thought about ways to make herself look different. Instead of pulling the hat back over her hair, as she now did by habit, she left it off. The dust she'd raised in freeing the wagon had covered everything with a dingy brown film. She smudged the blood that had oozed from the wound on her forehead with the back of her hand, recoiling from the stickiness she felt in the process. Her own mother wouldn't recognize her.

The mules made better time than she'd hoped for. They were already in sight of the turnoff south when she noticed a cloud of dust on the horizon. Whatever it was, it was moving toward her—fast. The stage? She couldn't make it to the turnoff before whoever it was reached her.

Nothing in the meadow was big enough to hide a wagon, two mules and an extra horse. And the trees and rocks beyond it were too far away to reach in time. She looked at the jumble in the wagon. Much of it would fall off if she tried to cross the soggy meadow. She clenched her teeth to force the fear out of her mouth. She was going to have to let whoever was coming simply ride by.

As the cloud got closer, Eddie could make out the shape of the stagecoach. The sinking feeling in her stomach lessened. She put her head down and talked to the mules, urging them as far to one side of the road as they could get. She slowed the wagon but didn't stop completely. She needed to be able to make the mules run if the situation got bad.

The stage rumbled by in its usual hurry. Only the driver touching his hat brim to acknowledge Eddie as another human told her it wasn't an apparition.

Just after the turnoff, she came to the rutted area she'd worried about since morning. Sweat trickled down her neck as she coaxed the mules through the bumpy mess. When they made it to the flat ground on the other side, she let them rest. She wiped the grime, sweat, and blood from her face onto her shirtsleeve.

The road between Florissant and Cripple Creek was still in view, but her rig was partly hidden from it by an aspen grove. She couldn't see much from where she was, but sound still carried well. She heard hoof beats. But she couldn't see enough to make out the riders.

Eddie readied the reins to move out. Then she reconsidered. She was probably better off where she was. She wouldn't know who was coming until it was too late to move, but most likely, they'd stay on the road going west and not see her at all. If they came south, though…

Two horsemen galloped by on the main road so fast Eddie barely had a chance to assess them. The glimpse she got was enough—Rafe and Scoot. They were already beyond earshot by the time she realized who they were.

She slapped the reins over the backs of the mules. "Hee-yah!" The mules sprang forward. She prayed she wouldn't lose the load on the first curve.

After about a mile at lunatic speed, she slowed the mules so she was sure she didn't miss the turnoff to Squaw Gulch. Her heart didn't stop pounding until she started up the trail.

The rest of the trip was an exercise in patience. The trail up the gulch was wide enough for the rig to pass but not on easy ground. Eddie bumped along, talking the mules over hillocks and large rocks and wondering if the wagon would lose a wheel before she got to camp. Some places were so narrow she couldn't believe it when the wagon actually fit between the boulders. Finally, the rig creaked into the clearing in front of Charlie's cabin.

A brand-new lean-to had sprouted on the mine side of the cabin while she was gone.

She pulled the wagon up near the cabin, set the brake and jumped down. "Charlie," she yelled. "Where are you? The lean-to looks great!"

No answer.

"Charlie?"

From the direction of the mine she heard the faint ring of what sounded like steel against steel. Hesitantly she approached the ominous hole in the mountainside. The ringing got louder. "Charlie?" She moved inside the mine mouth and started down the tunnel. In an instant she'd been swallowed into darkness. The ringing stopped.

"Charlie?"

She heard shuffling farther into the blackness. "That you, Eddie?" More shuffling.

"Yeah."

"You're back early." The crunching noise of boots on crushed stone got louder.

"Yeah."

"I'm coming."

"Take your time. I'll wait here."

The cool, darkness of the mine felt like velvet, which was not what she had expected. She saw a tiny light dancing in the black beyond her and watched as it grew. When Charlie got closer, she could finally make out his form—and the candle he carried in a funny little holder.

Charlie looked around him at the tunnel. "Pretty good claim, eh?"

Eddie looked around as Charlie had. All she could see was the darkness.

"Got a vein with good show. I'm followin' her straight in."

Eddie remembered what Billingsley had told her about the Rule of Apex and wondered if that was wise. The vein belonged to whoever claimed it where it outcropped highest on the surface. Why was he digging *in* if he had to go *up* to claim the ore? She didn't say anything.

She and Charlie walked to the mine mouth. He snuffed his candle, removed it from the wire holder and placed it carefully in a box that held other plain white candles, setting it upright so the melted wax would re-solidify in place. He jammed the pointed side of the holder into a timber and walked into the sunshine.

Eddie was right behind him. The pain of bright daylight caught her by surprise. She put her hands over her face.

Charlie let out a good-natured cackle. "You'll get used to it. Just shield your eyes with your hands for a minute, and you'll be fine."

Eddie shaded both eyes with her hands, opening one eye, then the other slowly. She could see again. "How do you work without any light?"

"That miner's candle's plenty once you get used to working with it."

She wasn't so sure.

"Come see what I built." Charlie was beaming like a kid with a butterfly.

She followed him into the cabin. The window nearest the mine had been turned into a short door. Beyond it was an area as large as her closet at home, tall enough that she could stand only in the few feet nearest the cabin wall. Chinks between the saplings of the roof-wall let in both air and sunlight. The floor had been carefully scraped and leveled. Fresh balsam boughs were already laid over a log frame as a bed. The quilt was folded carefully at the foot.

Charlie had put his heart into the project along with his elbow grease, she knew. It was the oddest bedroom she'd ever seen, but it was hers. "This is perfect, Charlie." A single tear of gratitude trickled down her cheek. She brushed it away, glad Charlie probably hadn't seen it.

Charlie grinned. "Ya like it, eh?"

" It's the best lean-to I've ever seen." It was the only lean-to she'd ever seen.

They went back outside, and it was Eddie's turn to be the kid with the butterfly. "Let me show you what's in the wagon," she said, tugging on Charlie's sleeve. She ran to the freight wagon, grabbed the nearest bundle, and plopped it on the ground. Sharing her bounty with Charlie would be easy after seeing the lean-to.

Charlie's eyes got wider and wider as she unloaded more and more, but he said nothing.

She continued unloading, smarting from his lack of enthusiasm. Within a couple hours, she'd found a place for everything from the wagon. The tools went to the storage area just inside the mine portal. The assay equipment, books, lantern, and clothes went into her sleeping area. "There. That's all of it." She slapped the dust off her hands and checked the empty bed of the freight wagon one last time.

"No. That ain't all of it."

"I thought you'd be pleased, just like I am with the lean-to."

"That's too much stuff for two kids." His tone was terse, and the tenderness she'd felt from him earlier was gone. "You and a brother wouldn't have assay equipment and books—"

"He was older'n me, and he *was* an assayer. Why don't you want to believe me?"

"Just don't seem like an honest story." Charlie was making furtive glances at the wagon.

"He graduated from the Missouri School of Mines—"

"And that's iron oxide in the wagon bed, right?" He could see more than she thought.

"No, that's blood. It was there when we bought the wagon. The livery man told us somebody had hauled an elk carcass in it."

Charlie shook his head. "I wanna believe you, but—"

Eddie looked at him. A mixture of anger and frustration brought her close to tears. The story was near enough to the truth. "If I'm honest enough to show all this stuff to you, why don't you trust me enough to believe I came by it honestly?"

Charlie didn't say anything.

"We could have just gone back into town and spent money you didn't need to on tools we already had—" The anger was gaining on the frustration, but still tears seemed about to brim. She jumped into the wagon and sat down on the driver's seat, grabbed the reins, clicked the mules into motion, and guided the rig across the clearing.

She was unharnessing the mules when Charlie came up.

"Guess you're right, boy. If you're man enough to tell me it's yours when you didn't have to tell me you had it at all, I should be man enough to believe you."

Eddie was too angry to respond.

"I said I was wrong. Ain't that enough?" Charlie's voice was edged in anger. "Jesus," he exploded. "Having you around is like tryin' to please a goddamn woman!" He threw his hands in the air and marched across the clearing, muttering.

His words hit Eddie like a punch in the stomach. Her behavior had almost betrayed her twice in two days. "I'm coming, Charlie," she yelled. "Wait up."

When she reached him, he put his arm around her shoulder, like her father had often done with Jerrod. His step lightened. "Come on," he said. "Time to rustle up some beans and bacon."

She followed behind him half-heartedly. It was a place to stay and food, sort of. Sunday would come. Then she would finish her business with Rafe and end the masquerade.

CHAPTER 11

Rafe stood in the mountain sunlight and stared at the abandoned campsite. His head throbbed with the friendly pain of too much whiskey. At least he knew where this headache had come from—and how long it would take to get rid of it, which was more than he could say of Edwina Sinclair and the headaches he'd had since they'd stopped her damn wagon.

He scratched his neck as he considered the woman. "How the hell did she know we were coming?"

Twenty feet from him, in the middle of what had recently been a camp, Scoot stooped to inspect a fresh pile of mule droppings. "Bet she hasn't been gone four hours."

"Damn!" Rafe kicked the closest thing he could find—a rotten tree stump. He watched it pull loose of the gravelly dirt and slither down the slope below him. "I'm gonna get her!"

"Why, Rafe?" Scoot had an independent look about him that Rafe didn't want to see.

Rafe began to pace as he recited the reasons. "She tricked me. She stole my gun. She stole my horse. Am I supposed to just let all that pass?"

"She stole more'n your horse, Rafe Pettibone."

Scoot never called Rafe by his last name. In fact, until that moment, Rafe hadn't been sure Scoot even knew his last name. "She stole your common sense." Scoot slammed his fist into the palm of his other hand. The horse next to him shied at the display of anger.

Scoot's reaction bothered Rafe, too. Scoot never got his dander up.

"You ain't been worth shit since we stopped their wagon."

Rafe knew he needed to get that hard, sensible look off Scoot's face if he wanted him to stay around. "Calm down, Scoot. Ain't no need to get worked up about it. We'll find her." Rafe tried to grin at his buddy, but his lips stuck to his teeth. He wet them with his tongue and tried again. "Hell, we're gettin' real close. We can track the mules—"

"Not likely." Scoot's anger was now clearly carved into his words. "Already looked." He pointed. "She walked 'em up on the rocks there. Ain't no way we can tell where they come off that ridge."

"Then she knows we're on her tail. She wouldn't be worried if she didn't think we were after her."

"Naw, Rafe. We ain't after her anymore." Scoot grabbed his horse's reins from the pine bough where he'd looped them and mounted. "I ain't waitin' any longer for you to come to your senses. You've turned into a stupid fool because of that woman." Scoot's horse began to move.

"But how'm I gonna rob folks by myself?"

"You ain't gonna rob folks, Rafe." Scoot was next to Rafe now. He stopped the horse and glanced down at him. Shaking his head slowly, a look of unhappy resignation formed on his face. "You're the one that's been robbed. She stole your judgment along with your pants." He urged his horse forward and moved away.

Standing by himself, the pain of last night's liquor hammering in his temples, Rafe resisted the helplessness that threatened to wash over him. "I'll get her," he bellowed into the sunshine. "I'll get her as sure as the sun comes up in the morning!"

"No. No. No. You hold the drill steel like *this*. Now, try it again."

Crouched in the light of her miner's candle, Eddie struggled to grasp the inch-thick shaft of steel so the chisel end was against the mark Charlie had made earlier with the candle on the end wall of the tunnel.

"Now bring the singlejack against the blunt end. Hard. Like this." Charlie hit the flat end of his drill steel with the short-handled sledgehammer squarely. Pieces of rock chipped away. "Then you turn the steel, like this. See?" He rotated the shaft of steel a quarter turn. Then he hit it with the singlejack again. More stone chipped away. A small hole had begun to form in the rock wall.

Eddie repositioned her steel and tried to hit it, hard and straight, with what he'd told her earlier was a four-pound hammer. The singlejack grazed off the side of the steel and hit her knuckles. She shoved them in her mouth to stanch the pain.

Charlie shook his head. "I thought you said you knew somethin' about mining."

Eddie's arm ached from swinging the singlejack. Her knuckles were raw. "I said I knew something about the *ore*," she said through clenched teeth.

She lined up the steel on the mark again and took a side-arm swing with the singlejack. The blow hit cleanly. Chips of rock slaked away from the chisel end. She turned the steel a quarter turn and swung again. Another straight hit. She had a start on her first drill hole.

Until she'd gotten the steel in over an inch, she was afraid to talk, fearing she'd ruin her progress with the distraction. But there were too many questions to abstain from conversation for long. If she was going to be a miner, even for a few days, there was a lot she needed to know. "How deep do we make the holes?"

"Thirty-six inches."

Eddie took the drill steel out and looked at it. It was only about eighteen inches long.

Charlie laughed. "We'll switch to longer steel once we need it."

"How many holes do we have to drill before we can blast a round?"

"In here, we can make do with sixteen."

"Sixteen!" Eddie jumped up from the crouch she'd been in. "I'll be dead before that!"

"I can get a round drilled in about two days—when I'm not wasting time trying to teach a nincompoop."

She went back to work.

Charlie waited until Eddie had managed a few more successful blows. "Now watch me again. There's more ya gotta do to get it right." He pulled his steel out of the hole and picked up a long skinny tool. "This here's a 'spoon.'" He handed the tool to Eddie.

It looked homemade—a teaspoon blunted and fitted with a three-foot long, heavy wire handle. She played with the feel of it and gave it back to him.

"See how we've been workin' this steel? Get her in a few inches, then scoop her out with the spoon. Otherwise you're working the same pieces of rock all day long." He worked the spoon into the hole he'd been drilling in the wall, pulled it out filled with bits of stone, dumped it, and worked it back in to pull out more.

"Coax a little water in the hole now and again to keep the drill steel cool. See?" He held his canteen gingerly and sloshed a bit of water into the horizontal hole he'd just cleaned in the rock face.

Eddie's arm throbbed from the hammer blows that had connected. "It takes so long to get even a little bit of a start. How am I ever going to drill an entire hole?"

"Ain't likely if you quit before you start." Charlie's voice was crusty. "Keep working at it. You'll be surprised what you get done."

By the end of the day, Eddie had finished three holes. Charlie had finished seven.

When they came out of the tunnel, the sun was gone. Eddie was too exhausted to walk straight. Her hands were numb from the hammer and steel. Her arm ached worse than the time she'd broken it falling off a horse. Her leg muscles stung from crouching to drill a hole near the floor of the tunnel, and her back muscles screamed from reaching to drill one at the top of the face. And she felt like she hadn't eaten in a week. Even burnt beans and moldy bacon sounded good, as long as she could collapse onto her bed once she'd eaten it.

"Tomorrow, we'll finish up the drilling and blast," Charlie said as they entered the dark cabin. He lit the lantern.

Eddie looked at him blankly.

He gave an exasperated grunt. "We'll put the giant powder in the holes we've drilled and blow it up when we leave the mine tomorrow night. Then we can muck on Sunday."

Eddie had already sat down and was rubbing her shoulder. When she heard what he'd said, she turned and stared at him in disbelief. "We're gonna work *Sunday*?"

"' Course." Charlie was bustling around the kitchen—cutting bacon, stirring beans, hauling down the cracker tin.

"Do we ever take a day off?" She was careful with her phrasing so she sounded like a boy instead of some pious church lady. Shoveling rock on Sunday didn't suit Eddie's needs in the least, but it wasn't church she needed the time for.

"Fourth o' July," Charlie said thoughtfully. "Course we just had that—"

For twenty-one days straight, Eddie and Charlie worked in the mine from before the sun came up until after it went down. For all Eddie knew, daylight could have been abolished. Every morning, she asked herself why she kept going back into the mine. She felt foolish with her answer.

Being in the mine and working with the rock made her feel close to Jerrod. He'd talked about what it was like to be underground so much when they were still back in Missouri that she felt like she'd been with him on his trips down the dark tunnels of the mines he'd gone into as part of his schooling. Even though this mine was in Colorado, working in its cool darkness made her feel close to him because she was close to what he loved.

She knew she had to deal with Rafe. After twenty-one days, she was beginning to hope that she could do that and still work the mine with Charlie. And that she could honor Jerrod in doing both things.

And after twenty-one days, the wagon was almost full with good ore—or, more accurately, with the ore that Charlie thought was good.

Eddie was convinced he was tossing the best stuff on the tailings pile. A wide streak of discoloration was evident on the ceiling of the mine as they followed the quartz vein deeper into the mountain. When she checked a piece of rock from the ceiling that had been dislodged when they blasted an earlier round, it had looked just like the Stratton ore she'd assayed for Tess.

Billingsley had told her the richest ore often got discarded because it looked so plain. She hadn't believed him—until she'd watched Charlie sorting the rock they hauled out of the mine. The real wealth was in the rock Charlie was tossing as gangue— waste rock not worth the trip to the mill. She had to find a way to make him put the dull gray rock he was discarding in the ore wagon.

With each day's work in the mine, Eddie's concern over the need to drill up—to get at the best ore, which Charlie was ignoring, and to assure his right to mine it—intensified.

They'd just returned to the cabin after mucking out another round. As she lit the lantern near the dry sink, she again pondered how to broach the subject with Charlie.

She started supper, slightly optimistic. After three days of burnt bacon, she'd talked him into relinquishing the cooking chores. Maybe this persuasion would be as easy.

Preparing their evening meal had already become a soothing ritual for Eddie. She carved the mold off the bacon and tossed the strips of meat into a clean pan. After coaxing the coals in the fireplace back to life, she stirred the beans and put them on the fire. But nothing in the routine gave her any ideas on how to talk to Charlie about how he was mining the claim.

Finally, she just blurted it out. "How come we ain't drillin' up, like everybody else?"

Charlie acted like he hadn't heard her, but from the set of his shoulders, she knew he had. He'd heard her all right, and he was peeved she'd asked the question.

She knew, even briefly accepted, that she should drop the subject and wait until he was in a better mood. But each day she didn't speak meant more muscle and powder spent going in the wrong direction.

She rehearsed the words a half-dozen times more in her head before she let them out of her mouth. "The discoloration on the ceiling in that middle stretch is just like the ore I assayed from Stratton's mine—"

Charlie turned to face her, more fire in his eyes than she would have ever expected. "I decide how we work this claim," he said. "I ain't listening to gibberish from a kid barely out of short pants."

"Yes, sir," Eddie said, striving to project meekness even though she didn't feel it.

"Don't ever question what I decide to do with this claim again, ya hear?" His tone was more conciliatory than before, but he was still angry.

"Yes, sir."

"Yes, who?"

"Yes, Charlie," she said with a resigned sigh.

"That's better."

No, it wasn't, she told herself. But there wasn't anything she could do about it.

She carried the pan of bacon to the fire, which was flaming eagerly. Crouching to get the proper angle, she wedged the pan against a burning log and held it over the hottest coals. She concentrated on frying the meat. If he didn't want to mine the good ore, fine. She had no responsibility to make him rich.

Sometimes, he was an impossibly crotchety old man. But she kept thinking about the problem. How could she convince him? Living on beans with a bonanza just above your head was ridiculous. The ore was there—the more she thought about it, the more convinced she was of that fact. She had to find a way to convince him.

"You cook even better 'n me," Charlie said from behind her. "Where'd a kid your age learn to cook like that?"

Eddie knew the question was a peace offering, but she wasn't sure she wanted to make peace. "My brother made me learn," she said. The lie didn't bother her at all. Charlie wasn't willing to hear the truth. Why should she worry about telling it?

"What's this brother's name?"

"Jerrod," she answered. She appreciated that Charlie was trying to make amends for his tyranny of a few minutes ago, but she wasn't interested in conversation, especially not about her "brother." She'd thought about Jerrod the whole time they'd been underground that day, and the pain of losing him was more acute than ever.

"You loved him a lot, didn't you?"

"Yes," she said in less than a whisper. She wanted to change the subject but couldn't think of anything to say.

"I'm sorry he's gone." Charlie moved to the fireplace and put his hand on her shoulder.

"So am I." She brushed the tears away with her sleeve. The ache of missing Jerrod was as much a part of her as her sore right arm. At least in the mine she felt close to him. But she'd resigned herself to the fact that losing him had left a hole in her heart the size of a house.

"Sorry." She sniffled and struggled to smile up at Charlie. "Crying's for sissies and girls. I won't do it again."

He chuckled softly behind her. "Crying's for anyone who's lost something important."

Eddie turned and looked up at him. She felt awful when she noticed tears in his eyes. It was like she'd just walked on the grave of someone he loved. Full of remorse and not wanting him to ache alone, she asked softly, "Who did you lose?"

Charlie waited a moment before he answered, staring into the distance, a tear rolling down each cheek. "She was such a pretty one," he said from somewhere far away. "Golden hair. Eyes like sapphires." His voice cracked with heartache. "I loved her more than my own life, than all the rest of life combined," he said with an anguished tone that made Eddie's heart ache.

"What happened?" Eddie moved the beans and bacon away from the heat and stood. She walked to the table and sat down.

Charlie came back across the room and sat down across from her. He looked at the table rather than at her. "I was young and hot-tempered. Her brother made fun of me, and I vowed revenge. He lost his arm in the prank I pulled to get even." The tears brimmed in his eyes as Charlie choked on the words. "Her family turned on me. Her pa vowed to never let me see her again. She died a year later—" He was sobbing quietly. "I never got to see her again."

Eddie patted Charlie's arm gently.

Finally, he looked up at her and smiled through his tears. "Who knows? If I hadn't been so stupid, I mighta had a kid of my own, like you."

Eddie smiled back. "It's an honor for you to think that."

They sat in shared silence until Charlie muttered dejectedly, "I was a fool. Revenge is always wrong."

Her eyes hardened into dark stones. "But sometimes, you *have* to take revenge—for the sake of justice." She crossed the room to put the food back on to cook. "Sometimes, what the other person did is so wrong it can't go unanswered." She stirred the beans and pulled them into a hotter part of the fire, then held the pan of bacon over the flames again.

"Not really." She heard Charlie's tired voice behind her. "You just tell yourself that to justify whatever it is your fool pride convinces you needs to be done to heal the slight."

"But what if he killed someone?"

"There's the law to help you then. Ain't no reason in this day and age to take care of it yourself."

She fumed as she fried the bacon. He was wrong. Jerrod deserved revenge. And no one was going to get it for him if she didn't.

Charlie rolled up the sleeves of his shirt, preparing to eat. "Any fool that takes the law into his own hands in this society is doing it out of pride and nothin' more."

Eddie concentrated on the cooking, trying to keep the scream in her head from getting out. How could she leave the task to someone else? No one else cared. The heartache was hers.

She dished up the bacon and beans and put the cracker tin on the table. Working side-by-side in the near darkness of the mine had let her know Charlie better than plain dinner conversation would have ever allowed. His wisdom on most subjects was hard won from his own mistakes. Maybe what he said about revenge was right. She didn't want to believe it. What was there to live for if not to avenge Jerrod's death?

They'd eaten most of the meal before Eddie finally spoke. "Would you like me to read to you tonight?"

More than a week before, Charlie had asked her to read the newspaper to him. Even though the paper was three weeks old, Charlie had enjoyed each bit of news, even the society page. The stories about the tea parties and women's meetings had made him giggle like a little boy looking at pictures of ladies' underwear. She'd read to him every night since that first night when he'd asked.

"I like it when you read." He pushed himself up from the table and shuffled over to the bed. "But I got somethin' different than the newspaper for tonight." He reached under a rumpled pillow and pulled out a small, thin book. He carried it back to the table and handed it to Eddie.

Eddie was astounded. An English woman's love poems. "*Sonnets from the Portuguese*? Where did you get this?"

"Found it in a book store in Colorado Springs, maybe ten years ago. Lots o' them Englishmen in the Springs." He took back the book. "I like it," he said defiantly. "Sort of reminds me of Emma."

Eddie put out her hand to take the book again. When Charlie gave it to her, she thumbed through the pages, noticing how worn some of them were. She wondered how to sound like a boy and still answer him. "This looks like a nice book," she said. "I'd be honored to read it to you."

"Boys should know about love," he said gruffly.

Then Charlie plunked back down on his chair. "Getting low on crackers." He said the words as if they'd been discussing the subject of supplies for the last half hour.

His need to change the subject made Eddie want to wrap her arms around the old man in a happy hug, but she just stood there, holding the little book. May as well play along, she decided. "You're right. And if we can afford some flour and lard, I know how to make a passable biscuit." She thought of Irene.

Charlie grinned. "We can manage flour and lard."

He leaned back into the chair. "Maybe we should go into the Creek one day this week. One more round and we'll have enough ore to take a wagon load to the mill. We can save a trip up the gulch with the wagon if we head to Cripple Creek from Mound City." He stroked his chin whiskers. "Wednesday, maybe."

Eddie was afraid to believe what she'd heard. "I'd like that fine," she said, trying to hide her enthusiasm so he wouldn't think about changing his mind.

It didn't seem like the supplies they needed would fill the

wagon. And, if she remembered correctly, the Rosebud Mill was in Mound City—a little town only a few miles west of the turn-off they'd taken up Squaw Gulch from the main road. That Charlie would concede a whole day to deliver a load of ore and then go on to Cripple Creek to get supplies seemed miraculous to Eddie.

"Since there's two of us," Charlie said slowly, "you can bring the wagon back to camp soon as we've loaded the supplies. I'll ride the mare back later—after I've had a shot at the poker table."

"But you don't have money for poker—"

"I will after I take the ore to the mill." He cackled light-heartedly.

"But we need supplies—"

"We'll get 'em. I'll only play with what's left."

"But—"

"Quit sounding like a goddamn wife!"

After a few seconds, his scowl transformed into a confident grin. "Besides, I always win. And I feel a sizable lucky streak comin' my way."

The wife comment kept her from saying anything more, but she lacked his confidence in a lucky streak. Any two-bit cheat could beat a blind man. But at least his decision to go to Cripple Creek meant she could get some advice about the ore he was throwing away. Maybe she could talk to the marshal. And maybe he would help.

Irene was rolling biscuits at the table in the Red Velvet's kitchen just as she did each morning. And as she had on each of the last twenty-two mornings, she was thinking about the fact that she wouldn't be sharing them with Eddie.

For the hundredth time, she asked herself if she should go

to the marshal. For the hundredth time, she came up with the same answer. She had nothing to tell him. She'd seen no killing, witnessed no robbery. Much as Rafe Pettibone deserved hanging more than most of the men who'd already been hung, there wasn't a single thing she could do to get the marshal to bring him in.

She couldn't keep Rafe away from Eddie either. She worried constantly about what might happen to the girl. And there wasn't anything she could do to keep Eddie away from Rafe. Helpless was the worst of all feelings.

She pushed the rolling pin gently over the soft dough, trying not to let her worries turn into tough biscuits.

A knock on the screen door startled her.

Her shriek was followed by a good-humored, masculine laugh from the back porch. "Sorry, Ma'am. I sort of thought you were used to having folks around." Marshal Gruen stood grinning on the other side of the screen door. "Eddie told me you made the best biscuits in camp. Thought maybe I'd ask for the chance to sample one."

Irene opened the door and looked at the lawman blankly. She forced a smile. "Come in." She motioned him inside. He hadn't come looking for biscuits.

"You don't believe me?" The marshal's eyebrows were raised in mock indignation.

She shook her head slowly, praying he hadn't come to tell her he'd found Eddie's body.

"What's a man got to do for you to believe him?" The marshal laughed a nervous laugh. He cleared his throat. "All right. So I came for a biscuit and to see about Eddie. You can throw in a cup o' coffee out o' pure generosity if you're inclined."

Irene grinned at him. No wonder Eddie had liked talking to him. He didn't dance around a subject like most folks. "Just let me get these in the oven, and I'll get you some coffee." She cut twenty biscuits in a series of swift motions, slipped them onto a pan, and put the pan in the oven.

"Sorry I wasn't cordial," she said as she brushed flour from her hands. "I got a lot on my mind these days, and sometimes it gets the best of me." She poured a cup of coffee and handed it to the marshal. "Would you like to take a seat?"

"Much obliged." He pulled a kitchen chair out from the table, turned the chair around and sat on it backwards. "Got any sugar?"

"Sorry." She brought him the sugar bowl and a spoon. "I thought someone rough enough to be the marshal would drink it straight."

Marshal Gruen laughed at the remark and stirred two spoonsful of sugar into his coffee.

She looked at him out of the corner of her eye as she cleaned up the biscuit scraps and flour on the bread board. The nervous feeling in her stomach bothered her, but she couldn't make it go away. Was the Good Lord giving her a sign that she should tell the marshal about Eddie? She'd promised not to tell anyone and had felt like a traitor after telling Tess. Was the marshal's visit a sign—or a trap that would only get Eddie into more trouble?

Irene took her time with cleaning up the kitchen. If the Lord was sending her a message, maybe he would make it just a little bit easier to decipher.

The marshal made a nervous attempt to clear his throat. "Haven't seen Eddie on Bennett Avenue lately. Is the boy ailing?"

The marshal's use of "boy" in the question reminded Irene that Eddie had more than Rafe Pettibone to deal with. "He doesn't work here anymore," she said slowly, trying hard not to let the loss she felt show in her voice.

"Oh." The marshal stopped stirring his coffee and smiled. "He get on at one of the mines?"

"Don't know." Irene wanted to hit him with the rolling pin for looking so happy about Eddie no longer being at the Red Velvet.

"You mean he left without telling you where he was going?"

She didn't want to admit that Eddie had left without even saying good-bye. "Maybe he just needed a little time away from the Creek—"

"But he had nowhere else to go. He's...he's an orphan."

"He can handle himself," Irene heard herself say.

"Who can handle him—" Tess was moving into the kitchen from the hallway, looking less like death than usual for ten o'clock in the morning, but still in her wrapper. She stopped when she saw the marshal's back at the table. "Oops! I'll be right back." She whirled and hurried up the stairs.

The marshal turned to look, but Tess was already gone. "What was that all about?"

"We don't usually have guests in the kitchen," Irene explained.

He jumped up, turning the chair back under the table as he did. "Didn't mean to intrude."

Irene motioned him back to the table. "She's knows you're here now. She'll be mighty put out if she hurries to dress and you're gone when she gets back down." She pulled out a chair and pushed the marshal gently toward it. "Besides, those biscuits'll be done in another five minutes." She hoped the distraction of the biscuits would last until Tess returned. She peeked into the oven for effect. "Yep. Five more minutes should be plenty."

"Who was that?" The marshal seemed flustered, like he suddenly realized where he was and knew he didn't belong there.

"Miss Tess."

"She always come down here half-dressed? Even with the boy around?"

"She wasn't half-dressed. You didn't even see her." The marshal's comment irritated Irene. "Are you in charge of what we're allowed to wear at home now, too?" She put her hands on her hips and looked at him sternly. "She just wasn't beautiful when she came down, marshal. A woman in her trade has to look beautiful *whenever* the public sees her."

"Oh," the marshal said weakly.

Irene went back to the stove and checked the biscuits again, knowing the more often she checked, the longer they would take. Come on, God, she prayed, tell me what to do. She busied herself dusting flour off surfaces in the kitchen that had no flour on them. Meanwhile the marshal alternately stirred and sipped his coffee.

After what seemed like a week, she pulled the golden biscuits from the oven. Carefully taking a small plate from the cupboard, she placed three biscuits on it and laid it in front of the marshal. Then she set out butter and jam and a knife.

The marshal grabbed a biscuit, then gingerly tossed it from hand to hand. "Hot."

It was Irene's turn to chuckle. What did he expect straight out of the oven?

He returned the crusty round he'd been tossing to the plate. He held the edge of the biscuit with the tips of his fingers as he split it open and slathered it with butter and jam. Carefully, he picked up half and blew on it. Then he took a bite. Closing his eyes, he chewed slowly. "Lord above, the kid was right. These are mighty fine biscuits."

"Of course, they are," Tess boomed as she reentered the kitchen. She was in a blue-gray day dress, the most discreet gown in her wardrobe. "What did you expect, marshal? Hardtack?"

Irene breathed a sigh of relief. The sign was clear—God wanted Tess to handle it.

"What brings you to Sin Street, Marshal?" Tess's confidence was enough to fill the whole kitchen. "You seen anything of our runaway errand boy?"

Irene drew a deep breath. Old as she was, she had a lot to learn about handling men.

The marshal buttered a second biscuit. "Ain't seen him in over three weeks. Thought maybe you folks knew his whereabouts."

Tess smiled brightly. "He just plumb up and left one day."

"He's not at one of the mines?"

"Not that I've heard." She shrugged. "You know boys, marshal. They get a harebrained idea and—"

"Eddie was different," the marshal said through another mouthful of biscuit.

"Maybe," Tess said, batting her eyelashes for effect. "But however different he was, he's gone all the same."

"I can see that," the marshal said tersely. He turned to Irene. "Mind if I take that third biscuit with me?"

"That would be fine," Irene said.

He split the biscuit open, smothered it with butter and jam and closed it again, then took a clean handkerchief from his trouser pocket and wrapped the biscuit carefully. He stood, nodded to Tess and then to Irene. "Thanks for the hospitality," he said looking at Irene. Then he turned to Tess. "If you see Eddie, let him know I'm worried about him."

"We'll do that," Tess said as she showed him to the door. She watched the marshal as he went down the steps and into the side yard. Then she went to the side window and watched until he was half a block down Myers Avenue.

Irene waited through the whole process for the rebuke she knew was coming. But at least the Good Lord had given her the sign. It was not her place to tell the marshal.

"Phew. That was close." Tess wasn't angry.

"You aren't upset I let the marshal in the kitchen?"

"Why would I be upset? All he came for was a biscuit."

Irene began to wring the cloth of her apron. "But he was asking about Eddie."

"He didn't learn much, did he?" Tess seemed entirely too calm.

"But you told Eddie she should *go* to the marshal—"

"She hasn't."

"But if you think she should go to the marshal, why didn't we help the marshal go to her?"

"We don't know where she is. But even if we did, it would be wrong. She's got to *choose* to go to the marshal."

"I still don't understand."

Tess offered a big confident smile. "If Eddie goes to the marshal, she has control of the situation. If we send the marshal to her, she doesn't." She stroked her temple. "Maybe there's another way to help her."

"How?"

"I'm not sure yet. I need to think about it."

CHAPTER 12

SITTING ON THE narrow, flat examining table waiting for the doctor to return, Rafe was becoming more and more convinced his trip to Colorado Springs had been a mistake. He told himself he'd come purely out of boredom. The ladies and the liquor in the Creek weren't the same without Scoot checking in once or twice a day.

Still, the headaches were getting in his way. He'd even mentioned the blind spells when the doctor had started asking questions. All he really needed was for the doctor to give him medicine to get rid of the spells. Then he could get himself a new gang, kill Edwina Sinclair, and get back to business.

He could put up with the headaches. Headaches were a part of his life—seemed like he'd always had them. But surely, the doc could give him something that would make the spells where everything went black go away.

The whack with the skillet had to be what made his skull rage in pain and made his thinking go fuzzy. It was probably what caused the minutes of blackness, too. The blind spells were the thing that worried him most. A man had to be able to see to shoot. If a man couldn't shoot, he was worthless.

But in the doctor's office, he'd been too embarrassed to admit what had really happened with the skillet. Instead he'd told the sawbones he'd been kicked by a horse. It was close enough.

The short, round, balding man returned, puffing from exertion. "I'm sorry, Mister Pettibone. Sometimes things take longer than one expects." He'd been gone on an "emergency" errand for fifteen minutes. Rafe could smell whiskey on his breath.

"Now, about these headaches...." The doctor's fat face looked uncomfortable. "You say there was a problem before the horse kicked you?" The doctor looked at Rafe for confirmation.

Rafe nodded. "Headaches, yeah. But not the rest."

"And now you've had some problems thinking? And with seeing things that aren't there?"

Rafe nodded again.

"And you have short periods of blindness?"

Rafe nodded once more, but he was losing patience. Why didn't the man tell him something he didn't already know?

The doctor chewed his lip. "Mister Pettibone, I need to ask an embarrassing question."

Rafe looked up. "Yeah?"

"Do you associate, ah..." The doctor cleared his throat and tried again. "Have you spent time with the, uh, soiled doves?"

Rafe grinned. "'Course, Doc. What red-blooded man don't?" His chest puffed with conquests recalled.

The doctor's face looked pinched. "How long?"

"Since I was in the Army." Any simpleton knew armies and whores went together.

"And when was that?"

Rafe was becoming irritated. "Hell, I don't 'member. Joined up when I was seventeen."

"So maybe fifteen, twenty years ago?"

Rafe shrugged. "Thereabouts."

The doc said nothing for what seemed like an hour. Just stood there, chewing the corner of his mouth.

"Doc, I ain't here on a social call. I got other things to do."

"Of course." The doctor looked straight at Rafe and drew a deep breath. "I can't help you, Mister Pettibone."

"Just something for the blind spells," Rafe said, hating the panic rising in his throat.

"Not for the headaches or the blindness or the insanity and paranoia that comes next," the doctor said, shaking his head sadly. "No treatment helps this far into the French pox."

Rafe scrunched up his face in a confused look.

"Syphilis," the doctor said. "You're in the advanced stages of syphilis, Mister Pettibone."

Rafe looked at the rumpled, whiskey-fortified doctor as if he had four heads. Then he jumped off the creaky table and grabbed his shirt. "You're full o' shit." He left without another word—and without paying the bill.

By bedtime Tuesday, Eddie was as excited as a school child on the brink of summer vacation. Charlie was still planning to go to Cripple Creek the next day, and he still expected her to go along. Even bringing the wagon up the gulch alone afterward didn't dampen her spirits. She'd managed the loaded wagon over the rough terrain before. She could do it again without a problem, even if she would be hauling giant powder.

Going to Cripple Creek meant she could do the three things that had become most important to her. She planned to talk to the marshal and put the responsibility for apprehending Rafe where it belonged. Then she would find Bob Womack, the expert on Cripple Creek ore, so she'd have better ammunition to convince Charlie to mine the deposit up and to take the gray rock to the mill. And she would talk to Irene.

Charlie's words on revenge had echoed in Eddie's ears again and again since the night he'd said them, reinforcing her earlier decision to talk to the marshal. She couldn't point to the exact moment she had changed her thinking about killing Rafe. She'd thought about the possibility of getting the marshal to deal with Rafe over and over after the conversation with Charlie about revenge. Now, she was completely convinced she should relinquish the problem to the marshal. He was the law. She needed to trust him. It pleased her that her decision hadn't changed even once in the last two days.

Once she'd gotten the marshal to deal with Rafe, she could

get on with her life. She wasn't sure what that meant. The mine was more important to her than she wanted to admit. She liked the freedom the West allowed, too. But Charlie wasn't likely to let her stay on once he knew she wasn't a teen-age boy. In fact, she wasn't sure he'd ever talk to her again once he found out. He was a proud old man. He wouldn't like it that she'd put one over on him.

Her mind drifted to what Bob Womack would tell her. She tingled at the thought of having the first man to find gold in Cripple Creek tell her that her ideas about the ore and how to mine it were right. The task of talking to him would not be simple. In casual conversation, she'd learned from Charlie that Womack had a problem with whiskey. Once he'd had too much, he was willing to tell the world what others had told him in confidence. She rehearsed her story one last time as she lay on the fir bough mattress. Bob Womack had to understand the set-up to give her any useful advice. But she needed to avoid putting the claim at risk by giving him more details than he absolutely needed because he might announce them to the whole town.

Just before she fell asleep, she thought of Irene. Eddie missed the warm kitchen and the easy atmosphere of the Red Velvet a lot, but she missed Irene's kindness and understanding even more. If the mill and supplies and her other errands didn't take too long, she'd have time for a long visit with Irene before she headed back. That is, if Rafe and his ruffians weren't watching the Velvet. Eddie set her heart on them being somewhere else.

Before she knew it, Charlie was banging a pan in her ear, his usual technique for getting her out of bed in the morning.

"Come on, young'un! Out o' the sack. We're burnin' daylight."

Eddie opened her eyes and looked through the cracks in the lean-to. It was even earlier than he usually woke her. "It's still dark."

She pushed herself from under the warmth of the covers and rubbed the sleep from her eyes. "Mornin', Charlie." Following him into the cabin, she walked past him and out the door to the outhouse. Eddie enjoyed the walk across the yard. The birds were just starting to chirp encouragement to the sun as it waited to begin its reach into another cloudless sky. The breeze was just strong enough to remind you it was there. It was going to be a good day. She could feel it.

They hurried through breakfast. Before the sun was entirely up, they had the mules hitched to the wagon full of ore and Jewel saddled. Eddie let out a small sigh of relief when she inspected the horse in the growing daylight. The quick re-dye job she had done on the mane and tail the night before in the dark looked better than she expected. Hopefully, she could get by with taking the horse into town one more time. Charlie needed a mount if he wasn't coming back with her, and she'd been unable to come up with a convincing argument for him not taking the horse. Pulling the wagon with one horse and one mule hadn't appealed to her either.

The trip down the gulch into Mound City, where the mill was situated, was easier than she'd expected. They pulled into the little town before mid-morning.

Tucked into the valley a few miles the other side of the main road, Mound City was an odd collection of rough buildings and tents with no main street. The only thing that looked permanent was the mill.

They took their place at the end of the line. Four wagons were in front of them, each waiting to deliver ore. Eddie noted they all held the same kind of ore Charlie had sorted.

Charlie pulled the brake and settled in for the wait. "Looks like some other folks been having a go of it, too."

Eddie smiled and nodded. She couldn't help wondering about the ore that wasn't there. Were the other miners throwing away the high grade like Charlie was? She'd started stockpiling the gray rock from the ceiling after Charlie refused to include it in what they put in the wagon each time they mucked a round. Each day, she added to the mound of the nondescript rock behind the woodpile, hoping Charlie wouldn't find out what she was doing until after she'd gotten a legitimate assay and some convincing advice.

As the wait dragged on, she began to dwell on the other errands she had to run once they got to Cripple Creek, feeling the minutes she might have spent with Irene evaporate as they waited at the mill. "How long do you think we'll be here?"

Charlie chuckled. "Anxious to get back to the good times, eh?"

Eddie frowned. "Naw. I just got some of my own errands to run when we're done—at least if we have time for them." They *had* to have time for them.

"I suppose you could take the horse into town and go to the Mercantile and the grocer right now. We can get 'er loaded up pretty quick if they know what we need ahead o' time."

"Yes, sir!" Eddie stood, readying herself to get down from the wagon. She wanted to see the mill. But getting into Cripple Creek with enough time to get her own business done was critical. There would be other chances to see the mill.

She stopped as she grabbed the seat back to jump down from the wagon. "Oh, no! The list!" When she'd last seen the supply list they'd carefully prepared, it was on the table in the cabin.

Charlie grinned, pulled a slip of paper from his shirt pocket and handed the list to her. "I can't read it, but I can remember to bring it." He cackled with laughter as Eddie blushed at forgetting. "Order just what's on the list," he admonished as she jumped down from the wagon. "No penny candy."

"Yes, sir."

"Yes, who?"

"Yes, Charlie."

"I'll be along to pay up in another hour or two." He reached into his pants pocket and pulled out a battered pocket watch, which he handed to Eddie. "Here. You can keep track of the time better if you have this. I don't want to be waitin' around for you." He gave her a fatherly smile.

Eddie accepted the watch and returned the smile. "Thanks. I'll be careful with it." She put the watch in her pants pocket.

She freed Jewel from the rear of the wagon and mounted. "Where'll I meet you?"

"Wait for me at the Mercantile."

Eddie knew he meant Taylor's Mercantile. He'd boasted several times that they had the best giant powder and blasting caps in the state. Giant powder was all Charlie ever called it. It had taken until they blasted the first round for her to realize he was talking about dynamite.

"And go to Watt's Grocery, not any of those upstarts."

"Yes, Charlie."

Old Man Watt had been kind to him when he needed it, and Charlie would patronize no one else. Charlie had already told her the story twice in the three weeks she'd been with him.

She nudged Jewel into motion and waved to Charlie as she started toward Cripple Creek.

Eddie had almost forgotten the stunning beauty of the surroundings south of town. Now she soaked it in as she rode, taking huge visual gulps of blue sky, trees, and mountain peaks and storing them away for when she and Charlie returned underground. Well before she expected it, she found herself looking down on the Creek from the road into town. Her carefree mood disappeared. From here on, she had to be prepared to encounter Rafe and his hoodlums anywhere. She pulled her hat lower over her face and urged the horse forward.

As she worked her way onto Second Street, she decided on a bolder strategy than she had initially planned. Though she was ready to leave Rafe to the marshal, that didn't mean Rafe was ready to give up looking for her. Although only mid-morning, she decided to check the saloons before she started on the provisioning chores so she was sure of where he was. She left Jewel behind the undertaker's shop on Second Street and worked her way down Myers Avenue on foot, carefully checking the street and then peering over the swinging doors of each dance hall and saloon. They were all doing a booming business, but Rafe was not among the clientele.

After using half an hour on the project, she realized ruefully that she now knew a lot about where Rafe wasn't, but she was still didn't know where he was. She'd just have to take the risk.

At Taylor's Mercantile, she ordered blasting caps, fuse, more drill steel, a wheel for the wheelbarrow, and what seemed to her to be enough dynamite to tunnel to Rhode Island. Then she went on to Watt's Grocery and piled up a sack of flour, two tubs of lard, a case of canned peaches, six slabs of bacon, four tins of crackers, and enough beans to feed a small Mexican village indefinitely. She checked the list and double-checked the total. Hopefully Charlie had gotten a decent deal at the mill—they were going to need a lot of money for all the things she'd had the two merchants set aside. "Charlie will be in shortly to pay for it," she told Old Man Watts.

"Salt Lick Charlie McGill?" Old Man Watt wrinkled his already wrinkled face into a toothless grin. "Ain't seen Charlie in so long I thought he moved on."

"Naw. He's too ornery to go away." Eddie liked it that the toothless old man was Charlie's friend. Charlie deserved friends. "You'll see him in the flesh in another hour or so." Old Man Watt nodded his head in satisfaction.

She checked Charlie's watch—still a bit early for him to be in town, but too little time to do any of her own errands. She retrieved Jewel and started toward the designated rendezvous point. Rather than riding, she decided to walk the horse back up Bennett to Taylor's Mercantile.

She'd only gone a hundred yards when she heard the pounding of horses' hooves behind her, closing fast. She leaped to the side of the street, pulling the horse behind her. The horse ended up between her and whatever was coming down the street. Eddie felt the edge of the boardwalk against her leg. She peeked over the saddle to see who was in such a hurry as the rider went past. Sure enough, it was Rafe. He continued down the street at a gallop, forcing pedestrians and other riders to jump out of the way in front of him.

The horse he was riding was an ugly yellow thing, but it was fast. Having seen it, Eddie knew she'd recognize it instantly if she ever saw it again. An ugly horse for an ugly rider—she liked the symmetry of it.

She patted Jewel's neck as she peeked around her and watched Rafe head toward Myers Avenue on the ugly dun. Good. Now at least she knew where he was.

When she arrived at the Mercantile, Charlie was pulling up from the opposite direction. She walked over to the wagon. He was grinning like a kid.

"Seventy dollars a ton!" He cackled loudly. Then he leaned toward her and lowered his voice. "We're onto something, Eddie. We're gonna be rich." He reached in his pocket and pulled out a fistful of coins. Still grinning, he counted nine silver dollars into Eddie's hand. "Three weeks wages, fair and square."

Somehow, Eddie had thought she'd never see the money. She grinned back at him. "Thanks, Charlie."

Charlie scanned the pile of goods stacked on the porch in front of Taylor's Mercantile. "That ours?"

"Yep. Mister Taylor said he'd have his boy load it. I'll start while you handle the bill." She'd load the supplies all by herself if it meant they finished faster.

Charlie got down from the wagon and went into the store.

By the time the Taylor boy came out to help, all that was left to load were the blasting caps.

"Careful with those," Eddie said. "I saved a spot in the middle front like your grandpa suggested." Even with its special wrapping, Eddie respected the box of blasting caps. If the box detonated, it would blow her and the load to smithereens. She wouldn't forget that on the way back to camp.

Charlie stepped onto the porch, still counting his change.

"Mister Watt will be happy to see you," Eddie said as she tied Jewel to the back of the wagon.

"Reckoned he would," Charlie said, a glint of mischief in his eyes. "He's lookin' to get even at the poker table, most likely."

Her worries about Charlie's plans to gamble at cards dissolved. If Old Man Watt was the kind of man Charlie chose to play poker with, it would be just for fun.

At Watt's Grocery, Eddie again did the loading while Charlie paid up and traded friendly insults with Old Man Watt. By two in the afternoon, the wagon was full. The supply errands were finished.

Eddie untied Jewel and handed the reins to Charlie. "How long you gonna play?" Faced with the immediate prospect, she didn't like the idea of going back to the claim alone.

Charlie seemed to be lost in thought. "Got some business at the records office first."

His errand puzzled Eddie. The records office was part of Walter Tinsdale's law office. His clerk had the responsibility of recording the unpatented claims that were staked in the District. Charlie had recorded his claim over a year ago. What could he be doing at the records office? She wanted to know but was afraid to ask.

"You sure you'll be all right by yourself?"

Charlie let out a hoot. "Spent sixty-one years bein' all right by myself. I reckon I'll be all right one more night." He laughed again.

Eddie rubbed her foot in the dirt, feeling foolish for having even had the thought. "I'll see you when you get back then."

Charlie struggled to get up on Jewel. When he'd finally settled into the saddle, he gave Eddie a haphazard salute. "Start back by five if you want to make it in daylight."

"Yes, sir."

"Yes, who?"

"Yes, Charlie." She watched his back as he and the horse moved slowly down the street.

To get on with her own business, she had to find a place to leave the wagon. She moved it into the alley next to the Mercantile and spread the tarp over the packages, hating the feel of the blood stains that still remained on it as she folded it around the load. She secured the covering with some cord and gave the wagon a final inspection. Leaving the mules harnessed for two or three hours before they headed out bothered her, but she couldn't think of a way to avoid it.

Bob Womack came first. The longer she waited, the more likely he would be drunk—or so she'd heard. Then she'd see the marshal, since he'd be in the office doing paperwork by then, and then Irene—the best for last. She headed for Crapper Jack's Saloon where Bob Womack was usually ensconced at the corner table by noon.

When she walked in the door, she immediately recognized the lanky, disheveled prospector. He was just the way Irene had described him weeks earlier.

The idea of her actually talking to him began to seem preposterous. She didn't belong in a saloon. And he probably wouldn't be able to tell her anything anyway. Before she had the time to talk herself out of it, she walked quickly to the table. "Mister Womack?"

He looked up at her with kind but lonely eyes and nodded.

"I'd like to talk to you, sir." Suddenly, she realized she hadn't thought at all about what she would do if he said no. Charlie, and even Tess, had told stories of how friendly he was. What if they were wrong?

He nodded again, this time toward the chair across from him at the table.

She remained standing. "Can I buy you a drink?" It was the etiquette of the barroom, but she felt strange asking.

He looked at the full bottle of whiskey on the table and then at her. "Got plenty," the sorrowful man said without cracking even a hint of a smile. "What do you need?"

"I'd like to ask your opinion about a mining situation." She looked around the crowded room.

Bob Womack seemed to read her thoughts. He grabbed the whiskey bottle and stood up. "Let's talk outside."

Eddie's heart was thumping as she followed him through the swinging doors and into the alley next to the saloon. He hunched on his heels in the shadows, and Eddie followed suit.

He looked at her earnestly. "East or south of town?"

Maybe this was going to be easier than she thought. "South." "Victor?"

"Not that far. Near Mound City." She hoped that was the right balance between detail and vagueness.

"How far are you down?"

"That's part of the problem. We're going *in* not down—or up." Admitting their mining strategy felt like acknowledging there was a bastard in the family tree.

Womack raised his eyebrows. "Why?"

Eddie shrugged. "It ain't my claim. I'm just working it for wages."

He raised his eyebrows again. "Then why do you care?"

Eddie hadn't rehearsed that question. She shrugged again.

Bob Womack shrugged back. "Mine it up and file it again where it surfaces." His face brightened with interest. "Goin' in on a quartz stringer?"

"Uh huh. That a bad idea?"

"Not if you're gettin' ore to the mill." He took a swig from the bottle.

"But there's darker stuff that I think might be worth more." For better or for worse, it was out.

Bob Womack looked at her, thinking and chewing on his thumbnail. "Got a sample?"

Eddie pulled a dull gray rock from her pants pocket and

handed it to him.

He looked at it carefully, turning it over several times. Then he carried it into the street where there was more light and looked at it again. He handed it back to Eddie. "Mine it. You'll be surprised."

"Will you talk to my boss about it?"

Bob Womack chuckled. "Maybe. Get that piece assayed first." He corked the bottle and started back toward Crapper Jack's.

"I'd planned to do that, sir. Know an honest assayer?"

He shook his head. "Maybe Guyot, up near Mound City. Just don't trust it to Billingsley."

"Yes, sir." Eddie worked to hide her elation at what he had told her about the ore as they walked back into the saloon. "I won't go to Billingsley," she said solemnly.

"You won't, eh?" Clarence Billingsley was standing just inside the door of Crapper Jack's.

"Hello, Mister Billingsley," Eddie said, straining to keep the panic out of her voice.

Bob Womack shuffled past them and back to the table where Eddie had found him.

She followed Bob Womack and leaned over to shake his hand after he sat down. "Thanks for the help, Mister Womack. Maybe someday, I can return the favor."

He nodded. "Go after that ugly stuff." He took another swig of his whiskey.

Billingsley remained where Eddie had first seen him, in front of the only door she knew would get her out of the saloon. She started toward the door, hoping something or someone would distract him so she could get by without talking to him. No luck.

"Well, sonny boy, I haven't seen you in a while," Billingsley said when Eddie reached the door, false friendship oozing from his words. "You must be up to something pretty impressive to be talking to Crazy Bob." The weasel was pinched into a collar too tight for his lumpy neck. "Got a claim somewhere?"

"No, sir." She tried to push past him.

"Not so fast." He poked his index finger in her face. "I saw you with that old prospector earlier today, loading a wagon." His face came close to hers. "That was a lot of supplies. You and him are onto something, ain't you?"

Eddie shook her head in a frenzied, "No."

"Oh, yes, you are." He leveled a calculated stare at her. "And you're gonna tell me what." Half the saloon had stopped to listen to the conversation. Eddie's heart sank at the possibility of having to disclose Charlie's claim to Clarence Billingsley.

"I was just helpin' an old man," Eddie said with the widest grin she could manufacture. "Ain't nothing wrong with that, is there?"

"Not if you say so, Edwina."

Eddie stared at him, wondering if she could bluff her way through by acting like she hadn't heard him.

Billingsley's eyes gleamed with malice. "Rafe Pettibone's been doin' some talkin'," he said. "And I'm pretty good at addin' two and two..." A thick layer of meanness covered his words. "Edwina."

Calm. She had to stay calm. How could she make him think he was wrong? She drew her breath in slowly, looking at him quietly the whole time. "Mister Billingsley, that ain't a damn bit funny. Don't you call me by a girl's name ever again!"

"Why not, *Edwina*?"

Try again. She forced instant calm into her voice and looked at him icily. "My pa used to say, 'If you stand in the barnyard, you're gonna get shit on you.'" She maintained her cold glare, intent on making Clarence Billingsley doubt whatever he'd heard from Rafe.

"The whole town knows Rafe Pettibone is a stinkin' excuse for a human, Mister Billingsley. He doesn't know *shit* about who I am, and your arithmetic ain't real good. I ain't no girl." She pushed her way past him and out the swinging door.

As she walked toward Marshal Gruen's office she struggled

to steady her nerves. Had she planted enough doubt? Would Billingsley do anything even if she hadn't? Probably not. There wasn't anything in it for him if Rafe found her. If Billingsley was going to put effort into something, there had to be money in it for him. Besides, once she talked to the marshal, the problem with Rafe would be gone anyway.

Her mind shifted to her next task. She had to make the marshal believe her. If she was shaking like an aspen leaf when she told him about Jerrod, he'd think she was making it up as she went along.

By the time she rounded the corner onto Bennett, her heart was beating almost normally again, and most of the butterflies in her stomach were gone. She stopped just across from the jail and marshal's office to brush herself off before she crossed the street. She wanted to look as good as she could when she talked to the man she planned to trust for the justice Jerrod's murder warranted.

As she stepped off the boardwalk, the door to the marshal's office opened. Marshal Gruen was smiling as he walked out beside another man who had his head down. Then Eddie noticed the ugly dun horse at the hitching post. Rafe.

She pulled back into the shadows, unable to even blink in her horror. The marshal and Rafe shook hands, and Rafe went to his horse. She stayed motionless in the shadows, stunned into immobility. The images flashed in her head over and over. Rafe and the marshal shaking hands. The marshal smiling. Rafe *walking away* from the jail. All her well-laid plans burst into shards inside her head.

CHAPTER 13

EDDIE'S EMOTIONAL PARALYSIS abated before Rafe was out of sight. In a daze, she followed him at a distance until he went into the Double X. Once sure of his whereabouts, she returned to the wagon and started back to camp. After the hideous revelation, a visit with Irene was the last thing she wanted.

She drove the mules mindlessly, letting them take their own lead all the way to the turn-off. Somehow, she managed to work the loaded wagon up the gulch without tipping it over. She didn't even comprehend that she was driving a wagon or where she was going for most of the trip.

The sun was slipping behind the mountains as she pulled into the clearing in front of the cabin. It was then she remembered the blasting caps and Mr. Taylor's warning. The realization that she could have easily blown herself up on the trail didn't bother her one bit. There didn't seem much to live for anyway.

She was more exhausted than if she'd spent twenty-four hours straight working the mine. It seemed pointless to unload in the near dark. After unharnessing the mules and retying the tarp to keep the supplies secure, she headed for the cabin.

She walked into the dimness and stared forlornly at the fireplace. Mechanically, she teased the banked coals back to a flame. After adding wood to the fire, she looked at the bean pot but didn't move it. At least tonight, she wouldn't have to eat beans. She lit the lamp, took down the cracker tin, put it on the table and just stood there.

A few minutes later she opened the cracker tin, then she closed it and put it back on the shelf.

Absent-mindedly, she picked up the book of poetry and tried

to read. It seemed strange not to say the words out loud. She laid Charlie's watch on the table near the lamp, open, so she could see the face. Minutes seemed like hours as she waited for him to return and struggled with the new development in what to do about Rafe. How could Marshal Gruen be involved with that monster?

Desperate to find something to distract herself, she carried the lamp into the lean-to and rummaged through the mining books Jerrod had brought along. Maybe if she could concentrate on learning more about the ore deposit, her thoughts would stop swirling in stormy circles. She opened book after book, looking at the first few pages and closing them without any interest in knowing more of what they had to say.

After going through fifteen of the twenty volumes Jerrod had insisted on bringing along, she picked up one that felt strangely light. When she tried to open it, the pages seemed glued together. She held the book closer to the lamp and found a clasp holding the book shut. When she unfastened the clasp, hundred dollar bills fell into her lap. She stared at the money as if it had dropped from the sky.

When she thought to count the crisp bills, she found there were ten of them—a thousand dollars. She couldn't stop staring at the money. Finally, she put it back in the book safe and carefully secured the clasp. She restacked the books with the book safe as the fourth book from the bottom, where it had been when she found it. She sat on her bed, staring at the stack, as thoughts of Jerrod and Rafe and Marshal Gruen wove in and out of each other. Could money somehow buy Jerrod justice? Was there someone she could *pay* to kill Rafe?

Finally, she blew out the lamp and collapsed on the bed with a whimper. Nothing ever got simpler.

When she awoke, sunlight was streaming through the cracks in the lean-to. Simultaneously, she heard the morning sounds of the birds and the cabin door slamming against the wall. She jumped up, grabbing her hat and smoothing her clothes, readying herself to greet Charlie.

"Thought you were going to be back last night," she said, looking down to fasten a button on her shirt as she walked into the main room of the cabin. Her line of vision was toward the floor. The first thing she saw was boots. They were not Charlie's.

She looked up at a man in his thirties, just short of six foot, not fat, not thin. His face was tanned but his bald head with its fringe of curly blonde hair was not. He was holding his hat.

"Most people knock." Eddie was peeved and scared at the same time.

His blue eyes gave the impression God had run out of pigment before he finished. But what they lacked in color, they made up for in intensity. His eyes bored into her. "Not if it's your own place."

She looked at him dumbly.

The stranger pulled himself up to his full height, squaring his shoulders and holding his head as if it was on a steel rod. "I won this place in a poker game last night."

"Who *are* you?" Eddie made the question into a clear demand.

The man cleared his throat and stood even straighter. "I'm Ira Kendrick, and I own this mine."

Eddie could barely speak. "You what?

"Dammit, I told you. The old man who owns the place anted it up in a poker game. I have his signature here to prove it." The stranger produced a folded scrap of paper from his shirt pocket.

Eddie took the paper and read it vacantly. "I hereby give all of my current claim to the Tin Rooster Mine to the bearer of this note." "Charlie McGill" was scribbled at the bottom of the page.

In a flash, her imagination went beyond the stranger's explanation. "Sorry, *Mister* Ira Kendrick." She spat the words at him. "But you ain't jumpin' this claim. It belongs to Charlie McGill. I ain't about to hand it over to somebody who just waltzes in."

She glared at the stranger. Where was Charlie?

"I ain't jumpin' it. I own it. Won it fair and square last night." The stranger's eyes sparked with anger.

Eddie felt her own fury building. She grabbed the butcher knife she used to trim the bacon. "Get the hell outta here," she yelled, waving it in front of his face. "Out!"

The stranger backed out of the cabin. Once beyond the point of the knife, he shook his fist. "I'll be back—with the marshal. Then it'll be you that gets the hell out!" He shoved the paper in his pocket as he stomped to his horse.

Eddie heard the hoof beats as he left. Too easy, she told herself. Either he was bluffing, stupid, or a coward. Regardless of which, she had to find Charlie before he came back.

She climbed on Orville and started down the gulch to find him.

Eddie's mind was a jumble as she rode. How had that stiff excuse for a human gotten up the nerve to claim he owned the Tin Rooster? Charlie couldn't have lost the claim. He wouldn't have gambled the Tin Rooster. But he hadn't come home like he promised. Where was he?

She regretted she'd never studied the scrawl Charlie called his signature. As she worked the mule down the gulch, she pondered who might have an honest version of Charlie's name in writing.

Charlie didn't believe in banks. And he didn't write letters. It had amazed her Charlie could even write his name with his sight so far gone. He didn't do it often. Only when he needed credit.

Old Man Watt, she thought with relief. He made *everybody* sign for their groceries when they bought them on account. Charlie told her he'd bought that way for years. With someone who could vouch for Charlie's real signature, they could handle that pompous Ira Kendrick easily—after she found Charlie.

Half a mile up the main road, she found Jewel, still saddled, but astray. Blood stains smeared the saddle.

"Charlie!" She dismounted quickly and began to search the side of the road. "Charlie! Charlie where are you?" She barely recognized her own voice as she yelled his name hoarsely. The uphill side of the road was barren, with only a few clumps of grass in the gravel that had weathered from the huge boulders. She eased her way onto the steep downslope, where the brush was thicker, and descended in panic. "Charlie?" She hurried down the slope. "*Charlie? Answer me!*"

She heard a low moan from below and scrambled toward it. As she came around a scrawny pine tree, she saw him, slumped against a rock and panting. "Charlie!" She rushed to him and began to check his injuries. "What in God's name happened?"

He looked up at her. One eye was swollen completely shut and a huge bruise colored his temple. Scratches crossed the lower part of his face making a grotesque plaid of his skin. He managed a weak smile as he worked at breathing. "Knew you'd find me," he said. His voice was a hoarse whisper. "Knew I could count on you."

Smiling, she gave him a gentle hug. "'Course I'd find you." She felt a stickiness on her hand as she pulled it away from his back. "You've been shot." She stared at the blood on her hand and then at the angry red blotch on the ground behind him.

"Ain't no damned better with a gun than he was with his fists," Charlie rasped.

She looked at the hole in his back. From what she could see, whoever had done it wasn't as bad a shot as Charlie was pretending. A great deal of blood had already soaked into the ground where Charlie had been lying, and the wound was still bleeding.

"You're hurt bad, Charlie. I'm going to get you to a doctor."

His face contorted in pain. "No."

"Can you ride?"

He gasped. His breathing was becoming more rapid and shallow. With a concentrated effort, he shook his head once.

"I'll bring the doctor here." Eddie started to scramble back up the slope. Then she hurried back to Charlie. "Want some water first?"

He nodded.

She ran to Jewel and retrieved the canteen, then scurried down the hill again.

Propping Charlie against her knee, she offered him the water. "Who did this to you?"

Charlie grimaced again. "That jackass…" He stopped talking and tried to drink.

She waited as he swallowed, then waited longer as he coughed up blood.

He wheezed a few more breaths. "The mean one—with the gang." He seemed bewildered. "He was lookin' for you."

Her blood curdled. "Rafe Pettibone."

He offered her another weak smile. "Didn't tell him nothin'."

She held him straighter, trying to help him take another drink.

Charlie motioned for her to move the canteen away from his mouth. "About the claim…" He used all his energy to force a broad grin. "That bastard only got what he deserve—" His head fell sideways.

Charlie McGill was dead.

Eddie cradled the lifeless body in her arms and cried, rocking him back and forth like a mother grieving a child.

When Rafe Pettibone stomped into Clarence Billingsley's office, Billingsley was studying his business ledger. Rafe glared at the flabby, sallow assayer. "You said the old man would lead me to Edwina Sinclair." The big plan Billingsley had sucked him into the night before was a bust.

Billingsley looked up from the ledger. "And?"

"And he didn't." Rafe continued to glare.

Billingsley shrugged. "What happened?"

"He laughed at me." Rafe seethed, remembering it.

Billingsley's fat face contorted into a know-it-all smile Rafe instantly hated. "Did you expect a special invitation to visit?"

Rafe looked at him, unsure of whether the attempt at humor was worth a response. "I stopped him on the road, like you said. I punched him around a bit, like you said."

"And?"

"He told me it was none of my goddamn business." Now why had he admitted that?

Billingsley made a noise halfway between a snort and a laugh.

Rafe never had liked the man, but now he was particularly peeved with Billingsley's attitude. Less than twelve hours before, the fat assayer had sought him out while he was busy at the Double X. Billingsley had assured him Edwina Sinclair was dressed as a boy and working with the old miner he was to stop on the road. Billingsley had even come and told him when it was time to leave to follow the old man.

He'd made it sound like a cakewalk. "You said all I had to do was rough him up, and he'd tell me where she was...." Rafe was disgusted with himself for even talking to the fat toad. It wasn't worth his time. "You don't know shit about Edwina Sinclair."

Still Rafe didn't want to give up. Maybe Billingsley *did* know where to find her. And from the way he'd talked last night, working with Clarence Billingsley might give him a way to start another gang.

Billingsley drummed his fingers on his desk.

The ache in Rafe's head reminded him how important it was to find Edwina Sinclair. If Billingsley was going to help him, it was time to get on with it. "Well?"

"Where's the old man now?"

"Dead. I shot him."

Billingsley's mouth dropped open, and he stared at Rafe. His skin got a pasty look to it.

That was a little bit closer to the respect Rafe felt he deserved. But Billingsley didn't change his expression. He sat rigid in the chair, breathing slowly—in and out, in and out—and staring through the window.

Rafe began to wonder if the fat man was having a stroke.

Finally he faced Rafe and eyed him coolly. "I can't believe you were that stupid."

Rafe set his jaw. "He ignored me—walked away laughing when I asked him where she was. Nobody ignores *me*." He took a deep breath.

The assayer sat up straighter in his chair, his face still sickly. He didn't say anything for what seemed to Rafe to be far too long.

Then Billingsley cleared his throat. "This changes things." He drummed his fingers on the desk. "Anybody see you kill him?"

"'Course not." Rafe glared at the assayer again. The geezer was so old nobody was going miss him. "Quit worrying. No one'll even realize he's gone," he said in slow, precise words.

Billingsley worked his pursed lips in a circle. "We'll still do all right. We can find her without him."

He sounded like some official—which made Rafe dislike him even more. He considered choking him, but only briefly. Billingsley was his return ticket to the good times. He could tolerate a little stuffiness to get back into business. And from the sound of it, Billingsley had connections that meant *real* business.

"If we act fast, nobody'll be the wiser." Billingsley stroked his pudgy chin. "Even better, we could make it look like she killed the old man." He thought for a moment, a nasty grin on his face, then sighed. "What a pity we can't take the time. It would be so fitting to have the Law get her for us."

The throbbing headache made Rafe impatient with Billingsley's jabber. "I want Edwina Sinclair. *Now*." His request came out as more of a roar than Rafe had intended.

Billingsley jumped, then went back to sitting motionless at his desk. "Not so fast. We have a few business details to cover first."

"Business details?" Rafe narrowed his eyes. "What the hell's goin' on?"

"I did some checking at the records office this morning." Billingsley leaned back in his chair and clasped his hands behind his head. "The old man re-filed his claim yesterday and changed the ownership—to Eddie Taggert."

"Eddie Taggert?" Rafe disliked people who acted like they knew more than he did. At the moment, he was disliking Clarence Billingsley for a whole lot of reasons. Maybe he *wasn't* worth spending time with. The ache subsided in Rafe's head. He blinked a few times, trying to think.

"That's the name Edwina Sinclair is using as a boy."

Rafe's mind cleared briefly. "Eddie Taggert," he said nodding. "Hey? Ain't that the kid that stiffed the crooked assayer?"

"Yeah. Yeah," Billingsley said irritably.

"That's Edwina Sinclair?" Rafe thought about it for a moment, then grinned. "I'll be damned." He rubbed his chin, recalling Edwina in the shift and then Edwina disguised as an errand boy. "Son of a bitch." Then he remembered Billingsley's earlier statement. "So what are these 'business details'?"

Billingsley nodded. "Once you kill her, I get the claim."

Rafe thought about the demand. He wasn't interested in mining. In fact, he thought people who spent their time underground were dumber than sheep. But the way the fat man's eyes gleamed made Rafe unwilling to agree without some discussion. "Why's that so important?"

"I like mining."

Rafe could tell Billingsley was hiding something. "And you like money. You ain't foolin' me. We'll make it a fifty/fifty split."

Billingsley shook his head. "You gonna work it?"

Rafe looked at his feet. "Nope." He looked up at Billingsley. "You gonna kill her?"

Billingsley's forehead glistened with sweat. "Ten per cent."

"Twenty-five," Rafe said, wondering why he was worrying about it at all.

"Deal," Billingsley said, too quickly. He reached for his writing paper.

"Now what the hell are you doing?" Rafe was anxious to find the woman. The rest could wait.

Billingsley wrote carefully on the paper, then picked it up and blew on the ink to dry it. "We're putting it in writing, Mister Pettibone," he said stiffly. "I find the practice helpful in avoiding unnecessary arguments later." He handed the paper to Rafe.

Rafe squinted at the flowery writing.

"It says—" Billingsley started.

"I can read." Rafe was getting more and more irritated by Billingsley's uppityness. "It says 'Clarence Billingsley and Rafe Pettibone agree to share the Tin Rooster Mine and claim in a seventy-five/twenty-five split, respectively.'"

They both signed the document, then Billingsley folded it and put it in his pocket. "I will keep this on my person at all times," he said with that same snooty air. "That way, it can't fall into the wrong hands."

Rafe was glad *he* didn't have to keep it on *his* person "at all times." That would sure as hell cramp his style with the ladies. He looked at the dumpy assayer. Probably never occurred to Billingsley that he might want to take his clothes off sometimes, he decided with a snicker. "Where's the woman?" Rafe stood tall with his feet apart, intent on showing Billingsley there would be no more "business details."

Billingsley pulled a map from his roll top desk. "I took the location from the claim records this morning," he said as he unrolled the map. "The Tin Rooster—" He stopped and looked up at Rafe. "And Edwina Sinclair—should be up Squaw Gulch, right about here." He pointed to a spot he had circled on the map.

"Damn," Rafe said, studying the map. "I was over halfway there last night."

"This time, you'll get all the way there," Billingsley said. "And you'll kill Edwina Sinclair."

Rafe admired how much nastiness Billingsley could put into a smile.

It was still before noon when Eddie began to see reality through her grief. When she finally tried to think about what she needed to do, the complexity almost paralyzed her. She had to bury Charlie—properly, with a funeral. But how could she get his body to the undertaker without attracting the marshal's notice? For that matter, how could she convince the undertaker not to let the marshal know he'd been killed? There was no way to guess what Marshal Gruen might do. But as a friend of Rafe Pettibone's...

Those were the easy questions. After those came the one for which she feared she had no answer: How could she get to Rafe before he hurt someone else?

Her solution to the first problem was to go back to the cabin, get a tarp and rope, and exchange the horse for the other mule. Once back to where she'd left Charlie, she wrapped his body in the canvas and carefully tied the bundle with some of the rope she'd brought. She refused to let herself cry again.

She managed to get the bundle onto the mule by throwing another piece of rope over a tree branch above the first mule, then tying one end around Charlie's body and the other end to the second mule. When she backed the second mule, the bundle with Charlie's body was lifted above the first mule to where she could position the wrapped corpse, face down, on the mule's back. She tied the load meticulously, then checked it numbly. The shape of the pack did not suggest its tragic contents.

Early that afternoon Eddie rode quietly into town with the pack mule behind her. She took the mules to the back of James A. McCloud's shop, then came around on foot to the front door of the building. She was trying to figure out if Charlie had kin who needed to be notified, as she opened the door.

The gaunt undertaker, who looked mostly dead himself, glanced up from his newspaper when she came in. "Yes?"

"I need your services, sir."

"Where is the deceased?"

The tone of his voice made her think she was talking to a cadaver. For a fleeting moment, she considered taking the body to the meadow where Jerrod lay and burying Charlie alongside her husband.

The undertaker coughed to remind her he had asked a question.

"Oh," she said hating the witless feeling that was overcoming her. "I'm sorry. It's...ah...just a little...hard."

"I understand," he said in deep, solemn tones. "Kin?"

"No...I...ah...worked for him."

The undertaker raised his eyebrows slightly. "Well?"

Eddie waited in confusion.

"Where *is* he? How long will the trip take to get the body?"

"He's out back."

The undertaker's eyebrows raised almost to his receding hairline.

"He was bushwhacked coming back from town last night. I found him just before he died. This morning."

"The marshal know about this?"

"Yes," Eddie lied. "We know who did it." Her eyes hardened, and she set her jaw. "We'll get him."

The undertaker hurried to the back of the shop and out the rear door. Eddie was grateful he was more interested in doing his job than worrying about a killing.

Once they had the body unwrapped and lying on the table, Eddie's grief welled beyond her control. She sniffed back tears.

The undertaker didn't notice. He was busy with the tasks of his trade.

He went through Charlie's pockets, removing his belongings and placing them on a tray. He handed the tray to Eddie.

She looked at the handful that was all that was left of his life—the rabbit's foot charm Charlie always stroked before they blasted, the penny minted in his birth year, a threadbare handkerchief, and ten dollars. Then she took it all in her hands.

She held Charlie's belongings silently. "I don't know his next of kin," she finally remembered to stammer.

"Don't worry about it, kid. He probably doesn't have any." The comment seemed so easy for the undertaker. He could have been talking about debts or potatoes—the emotion level would have been the same. "He'll have to go in the pauper's section, ten dollars ain't quite enough—"

"He deserves a funeral, sir. That's the least I can do." Eddie fought not to let the tears begin to flow again.

"Come on, kid. He was old. If he doesn't have money for a funeral, no one's here to mourn him anyway."

Her eyes glistened, and she clenched her quivering jaw. "How much would a funeral cost?"

"Twenty dollars," the undertaker said in a kinder voice.

"If I use his ten, I can give you nineteen right now." She sniffed again.

The sallow man looked at her, his mouth puckered as if he'd eaten something sour. "All right. I'll do it for nineteen."

She handed him the silver dollars Charlie had given her the day before and the ten dollars from Charlie's pocket.

He laid the money on his desk.

"It's important he have a service." She put the little tray on the desk and traced her finger slowly around its edge. Then she stopped and stood quietly, thinking. She wanted to hold Charlie's lifeless body just once more, but made herself stand with her hands at her sides instead. "And some flowers."

Funerals were blurring together in Eddie's head. Her father's long procession in the bleak St. Louis winter, Candace's, which had seemed more like a party, and the one she dreamed of giving Jerrod—all of them blended in her mind with the task of burying Charlie.

The undertaker's face assumed one of those abominable, sick-angel smiles. "You want a minister, I presume?"

Eddie nodded.

"Shall we have the service in the morning? Maybe ten o'clock?"

Eddie could tell from the look on his face that he expected her to be the only mourner. "I need to tell his friends...."

"I can only get it in the *Crusher* day after tomorrow," he offered.

They wouldn't see it soon enough to attend the funeral. She smiled wanly. "Please do that. But I'd like time to let his friends know before he's—"

"I understand. Would two o'clock tomorrow afternoon be better?"

She nodded tiredly, already making a list of the folks in town she'd need to talk to before she went back to camp. How long would it take for her to tell the people who knew Charlie that he had died? Who even belonged on the list?

"Now, what kind of coffin would you like for Mister McGill?"

Eddie worked numbly through the same decisions she and Tess had made only weeks before for Candace. She wanted these choices to be consistent with the way Charlie had lived. This time, she selected the simplest options—a plain pine box, no musicians, no funeral procession. She focused on paying respects to Charlie rather than succumbing to her own grief. It didn't help that Jerrod's face was etched in her mind as she responded to the undertaker's questions.

Once she had the grim details under control she went to see Old Man Watt. He was restacking sacks of flour in the back room when she found him. "Afternoon, Mister Watt."

He pushed the last sack onto the top of the pile and turned to see who had spoken. Once he realized it was Eddie, he went quickly back to his work. "Figured you'd be around." He began to muscle a fresh barrel of pickles to the front of the store.

"Then you know?"

"Don't know why the hell he anted it up. We all told him not to." He pulled his lips tight in frustration and shook his head.

"Charlie wanted out of the game, but that Kendrick fella kept goading him into another hand. That jack-ass *knew* Charlie couldn't see." Old Man Watt stopped rolling the heavy barrel and looked up at Eddie. "Charlie was holding three aces and the two of clubs when he lost the Tin Rooster. He said he thought he had four aces." Old Man Watt shook his head thoughtfully. "It was almost as if he actually knew he didn't have four aces though. He walked away from the table after that hand giggling like a little kid." Old Man Watt shook his head slowly. "A ten dollar bet. He anted up everything he owned on a ten dollar bet."

Eddie listened, not understanding what she was hearing and wishing she didn't have to tell Old Man Watt that Charlie was dead.

"He thought it was some funny joke. I could still hear him laughing after he'd walked out of the saloon."

Eddie didn't want to think about it. None of it made sense. Charlie'd had ten dollars in his pocket when he died. Why would he bet the mine instead of betting the money? She wanted to hide somewhere and let the ache overpower her. Instead, she dredged up what she could find of her resolve. "There's worse news."

The old storekeeper stopped shaking his head and looked at her.

"Charlie's dead, sir." Saying the last word reminded her of the "yes, who?" game she and Charlie had played, and the tears began to stream down her face.

"Dead?" Old Man Watt looked blankly for a place to sit down. "How?"

"Shot in the back. I found him this morning, just before he died."

Old Man Watt staggered out the back door of the grocery, leaned against the building for support, and stared at nothing. "That just ain't right," he mumbled. He didn't seem to realize Eddie was still beside him. Then his eyes darkened in fury. "The marshal know who done it?"

"I know," Eddie said with slow, cold firmness. "And I aim to take care of it."

Old Man Watt watched her before he spoke. "If I was ten years younger, I'd help." Then his eyes glazed over. "Charlie McGill was a good man. He didn't deserve to die that way."

Eddie wanted to agree, to rage on about the demon who'd done it, but Mister Watt wouldn't understand. "His funeral is tomorrow afternoon," she said quietly. "Who else needs to know?"

Old Man Watt returned to the moment. "I'll take care of that. Me and Charlie go back a long way—knew him when we was both hustling grubstakes in California." He wiped a tear from the corner of his eye. "He was always there when I needed him." He smiled at Eddie, biting on his quivering lower lip. "I'll make sure his friends know."

"I'd be obliged."

He touched Eddie on the shoulder as she moved to leave. "Let the marshal handle it. You're only a kid. You could get hurt—bad."

"I have to do it, sir." Tears streamed down her face as she mounted the mule.

CHAPTER 14

THE SIMPLE ACT of entering the tunnel of the Tin Rooster Mine made Rafe sweat. Being under the earth wasn't just a waste of time. It was like begging to be buried before you were dead. He held the kerosene lantern high, trying to cast the most possible light into the darkness. Each step he took required more courage than the last. It seemed as if he'd walked a mile in the blackness, but the tunnel still went beyond where he stood with the lantern.

To hell with what Billingsley had told him about going to the end of it. He'd come in far enough. He'd rig the blast where he was standing.

Holding the lantern close to the ceiling, Rafe looked for cracks where he might wedge the dynamite he'd carried in with him. Six sticks, Billingsley had told him. Six sticks was enough to be sure Edwina Sinclair didn't get out. He'd brought along eight sticks just to be certain. Now all he needed was a place to put them.

The ceiling was craggy but not cracked. In the middle of a dark splotch on the rock, a shallow hole had been drilled, long enough for one stick. He pushed a stick of dynamite into the hole and packed mud from the floor around it to keep it from falling out. The dynamite was hidden, but the fuse hung down in front of his face. He coiled the fuse and pasted it to the ceiling with more mud. Now he just had to do seven more.

Lowering the lantern, he searched the walls of the tunnel. Along the wall on his left he found a series of cracks that looked like they might be big enough to hold more than one stick. He worked at the cracks with the prospector's pick Billingsley had given him until they were broad enough to wedge three more sticks of dynamite into them. About ten feet farther down the tunnel, he found similar cracks on the other wall and put the other four sticks there.

Billingsley had cut the fuse lengths for Rafe before he left town, but Rafe had insisted on taking extra fuse. Rafe chuckled as he looked at the fuses Billingsley had cut, discarded in a heap with other mine debris. The fat assayer wasn't going to blow him away with the woman that easily. The fuses were now three times as long as Billingsley had cut. That would give Rafe plenty of time to get out before the dynamite went off.

He held the lantern high and inspected his handiwork. Unless Edwina Sinclair stopped and looked *real* hard, she'd never notice the stuff he'd just set up. Hell, he *knew* where it was, and the light was so bad he could barely see it.

He planned to uncoil the extra long fuses after she went farther into the tunnel. That wouldn't have been possible if he'd followed Billingsley's instructions to the letter. He puffed with pride at his good thinking and skill. Maybe he'd use dynamite more often.

Now, it was only a matter of waiting until she came into the mine. Then—good-bye Edwina Sinclair.

Once the work was completed, the blackness began to close in around him. The spooky feelings he always had when he couldn't see daylight started to bother him. Rafe picked up the lantern and hurried out of the tunnel into the sunshine.

Pulling out his pocket watch, he timed himself as he climbed to the spot on the side of the gulch that he'd chosen as his lookout, which was where he'd also set up his camp. Hidden behind some large rocks and a stand of aspen, he could see the clearing in front of the cabin as well as the mouth of the tunnel. Three minutes. He could return to the tunnel, going downhill, in even less time once Edwina Sinclair went into the mine.

This time, it was going to be a cakewalk.

For the entire ride back to camp, the guilt of being responsible for Charlie's death gnawed at Eddie. The burden had become almost unbearable by the time she reached the clearing in front of the cabin. Her mind replayed everything she could have done to keep him safe, over and over. If she hadn't stopped to help the day she met him...If she'd told him to stay away from Rafe Pettibone...If she'd found a way to get Rafe behind bars before he could hurt the lovable old man... Why was everything always a jumble of incomplete "ifs"?

Charlie was dead. She had to live with that.

After she put the mules in the corral, Eddie started toward the cabin. After several steps, she stopped. She didn't have the heart to go in the cabin alone. At least not yet.

She turned toward the portal of the mine. Maybe the darkness and the cool, stable rock would calm her. She grabbed a candle and absent-mindedly lit it as she moved through the first ten feet of the tunnel. The flicker of the candle flame reflected dimly off the walls as she strode into the darkness. She didn't feel like she was in the mine. She didn't even feel like she was inside her body.

When she walked by the discoloration on the ceiling, a numb thought about the drill hole she'd begun on the sly entered her mind, but she didn't bother to even look up at it. Was it only yesterday that Bob Womack had told her to mine the gray rock and work the vein from where it surfaced? None of that made any difference now. She came to the end of the tunnel.

All of their work tools were neatly set against the face, waiting for Charlie and her to start drilling holes tomorrow morning. Her tomorrows were gone. Again.

She turned over an empty dynamite box and sat on it, staring at the rock wall as the candle flickered in her hand. Was there a way she could at least keep Charlie's spirit alive? If there was, it probably had something to do with the Tin Rooster.

As she sat, discarding idea after idea for honoring Charlie, she thought she heard scuffling in the tunnel. Settle down, she told herself. She just wasn't used to being in the mine by herself.

But her skin prickled, and she sensed an eerie need for caution. She heard a distant hiss, but thought she was imagining things. She listened harder, trying to identify the familiar noise. She got up and began to walk back toward the mouth of the mine. The hissing seemed out of place and prolonged. Then she realized what it was. Lit safety fuse!

She hesitated, wondering whether she could find the fuse and get past it and out of the tunnel before the spark reached the dynamite. But whoever lit the fuse was probably outside waiting for her. She ran back toward the end of the tunnel, looking frantically for some sort of cover.

As she dove under the disabled wheelbarrow that Charlie had propped against the wall, the tunnel erupted in a deafening roar. Her candle blew out. Out of the blackness, rocks came hurtling down the tunnel as if they'd been thrown by some angry giant.

Before the first fury had finished, a second blast detonated. More rocks crashed against the wheelbarrow, adding the racket of the clanging metal to the din. Pieces of rock stung her legs, and she pulled herself into an even tighter ball underneath the overturned wheelbarrow.

The noise lessened, and the rocks stopped banging against the metal. She lifted its heavy weight off her and peered into the darkness.

Wham! The tunnel exploded with another blast. A cabbage-sized rock hit her leg as she scrambled to get back under the wheelbarrow. Several smaller rocks hit her arms. Flying shards stung her face before she finally regained her safety. The roar, the rain of rock, and the stinging, smoke-filled air combined in a terrifying fury that convinced her she was already in hell.

With unexpected speed, silence returned to the tunnel. Eddie strained to hear. Only the occasional roll of a rock that required a flatter resting place broke the silence.

She peeked out from under the wheelbarrow, afraid to leave its armored confines. In the distance, she saw a square of light—the portal. At least the only way out of the mine hadn't been completely blocked by the blasts.

She grasped the wheelbarrow, preparing to lift it off of her. As she moved, her left leg screamed in jabbing pain. The wheelbarrow fell back on top of her, and she passed out.

Rafe rubbed his hands in glee as he watched smoke billow from the mine. "You're dead at last, you miserable bitch!" He'd heard the three explosions, his smile broadening with each successive rumble. Now his gaze was fixed on the mouth of the mine. Did he need to go in to be sure she was dead? Billingsley had said it wouldn't be necessary—if she didn't die in the blast, she'd die from wounds or lack of water in a day or two. Still, maybe he needed to be sure. He watched as the smoke and dust began to lessen. The tunnel had been spooky enough the first time. Billingsley knew about mines. If he said Rafe didn't need to go back in, that was good enough

Rafe grabbed the bedroll he'd expected to use and the rifle he'd had ready and headed for his horse. He was back in business.

Marshal Gruen didn't like dealing with drunks, especially drunks who bothered him while he was trying to get through his paperwork. The sun's rays suggested supper time, but the bleary-eyed man sitting across from him didn't seem hungry enough to leave. "Explain it to me again," he told the lush. "I can't figure how someone who was there when you first got there could be a claim jumper."

The drunk tried to sit up straight in the chair. "I won the claim in a poker game, but that damn kid run me off it."

"What kid?" The whole story wasn't making much sense.

"The kid that was there!" The drunken man was angry again.

"How do you *know* he doesn't own the claim?" The marshal said it to be ornery. The idea of a kid owning a claim was preposterous. "What does this kid look like?"

The drunk gave a weak shrug. "Ordinary, I guess. Sort of skinny. Not too short. Brown hair. Maybe sixteen or so..."

"There must be ten kids like that walking on Bennett Avenue this very minute."

The man across from him sat sullenly.

"Tell you what Mister—"

"Kendrick, Ira Kendrick," the drunk slurred.

"Well, Mister Kendrick, I ain't about to go chasing people off mining claims without hard evidence. So we'll do it right and proper." The marshal leveled his "fair judge" look at Ira Kendrick. "You come back here Monday with a signed affidavit from the clerk over at the records office saying the claim you won exists and is in the name of the man you won it from, and I'll go with you to evict this 'kid' you're worked up about." He got up. "That'll give you three damn days to sober up. You come back drunk, the only thing I'll help you with is getting out my door."

Ira Kendrick got to his feet. "Some law you are. The kid might steal all the high grade between now and then!"

The marshal looked at him with pity. "You've never been in a mine, have you, Mister Kendrick?"

"N-n-n-no," Kendrick stammered.

"Figured as much." Marshal Gruen walked the crybaby to the door. The whiny, spineless ones—who wanted you to take care of all their little squabbles for them—were the worst part of being the marshal.

When Eddie came to, the weight on top of her made her afraid to move. She lay motionless in the blackness, trying to recall enough of what had happened to figure out where she was and what she had to do. The smell of burnt powder stung her nostrils and made her head throb. Finally, she remembered the explosions and realized it was the wheelbarrow that had her pinned. She pushed herself out from under it, using her right arm and leg for leverage.

She thought she'd seen light from the mine mouth after the last blast, but, now, she was in total darkness. Had there been more explosions while she was unconscious?

Out of sheer exhaustion, she finally gave up trying to think and just listened. The tunnel was quiet, which gave her no idea of what her chances were of getting out. She listened harder. In the silence, she thought she heard a coyote howl. Then she decided she was imagining things. It couldn't already be night.

She felt along the floor of the tunnel until she touched the rock of the wall and pulled herself up. Pain screamed in her left leg, but she was able to stand. She could walk on it—the leg wasn't broken—but each step brought excruciating pen. She took a deep breath and began to slowly work her way along the tunnel wall.

She was all turned around and couldn't remember how close to the end face she'd been before the first explosion. The lack of a sense of direction made her unsure whether she going further into the mine or working her way out.

Eventually her muddled mind told her she could get out no matter which way she was heading. If she came to a dead end, all she needed to do was turn around and she'd be going the right direction. Before she took each step, she felt around carefully in the rock strewn tunnel to be sure she had good footing for the next one. As she gained confidence in what her body

was still willing to do and in her belief that she was getting closer to the portal, she moved faster.

She could feel the wind from outside the portal when she
tripped. She tumbled over a small boulder and crashed into the
debris on the tunnel floor, scraping her face and arm. After a
few seconds, she pulled herself upright and took a careful step
in the direction she'd been going, ignoring the setback. Her
steps were small and slow, and she took extra time to make sure
each step was safe before she made it.

Step by faltering step, she worked her way along the wall,
frustrated that she couldn't see the end of the tunnel. Finally, a
sound reached her ears—the whoosh of the wind in the aspens.
She smelled the freshness of the outside air as she touched the
timber of the portal. She was out—and it was night.

When she stumbled into the open, her first sensation was the
smell of the evergreens. But her joy at the scent was replaced
by caution almost instantly. Everything was still, which didn't
mean much. She squinted in the darkness of the new moon,
wondering if the quiet might be broken by a gunshot at any
second and not knowing from where it was likely to come.

She knew without thinking that Rafe had set the blast. She
wouldn't just wait for whatever he decided to try the next time.
Limping from bush to rock, rock to tree, she reached the make-
shift corral. Too weak to saddle up, she eased Orville out of the
corral and got up on him bareback,

The only fragment of a plan she had as she started down the
gulch was to find Irene. How she could get Rafe into the hands
of an honest lawman was still a fuzzy half-thought. But her resolve was rock-hard and crystal-clear. Two crooked lawmen
were not enough to stop her. No one else was going to die because she'd failed to deal with Rafe Pettibone.

When she got to the edge of Cripple Creek, she left the mule
in the corral at the livery and limped quietly down the side
streets until she was near Irene's shack. Then she ducked into

the alley. Her whole body hurt. She was exhausted.

Eddie knocked softly on Irene's whitewashed door and waited. When she didn't hear any response, she knocked again, more loudly.

This time, someone inside began moving around.

She knocked again.

A sleepy voice asked, "Who is it?" The door opened a crack at the same time.

Eddie kept her voice low. "It's me."

"Who's 'me'?" The door opened a bit farther, and Irene's kind brown eyes peered into the darkness of the alley.

"Eddie," she whispered more loudly.

The door opened wide, and Irene's arms enveloped Eddie in a hug. "Eddie! Lord above!"

"I need help," Eddie said as Irene held her tight. "Can I come inside?"

Irene let Eddie out of the hug, hurried her into the shack, and closed the door. She slipped shut a lock Eddie hadn't heard open and closed the curtains.

After lighting the lamp, Irene took a closer look at Eddie and gasped. "What happened?" She brought the lamp up to Eddie's face. "You look like you just fought Gentleman Jim Corbett. There ain't a patch o' skin on your face that ain't scraped or bruised or both!"

Eddie managed a thin smile as she slumped into one of Irene's two chairs. "Bad, huh?" The pain was starting to differentiate itself into the separate sensations of stinging and aching. She *felt* as if she'd just gone ten rounds with Gentleman Jim.

Irene hurried to get a fire going in the stove and put a teakettle of water on to heat. She glanced over her shoulder at Eddie as she pulled bandages and a jar of salve from a shelf.

The next thing Eddie knew, Irene was dabbing a warm, wet cloth on her face. She realized she must have dozed off in the chair.

"Looks like you've been bouncing rocks off your face," Irene said.

"That's about what happened." Eddie winced as Irene worked on a particularly tender spot.

Irene washed each scrape on Eddie's face with the soapy cloth, drying each one gently before moving to the next. "What's the rest of you look like?"

Eddie took inventory of where she felt pain. "Nothing's broken." At least that's what she hoped. "I think there's probably a big bruise on my left leg, and my arms are scraped up pretty bad." She was talking in a monotone and barely noticed her own voice. "There was a lot of rock flying in the explosions."

"The what?" Irene stopped working on Eddie's wounds and looked at her squarely. "Girl, you got a lot o' story to tell—"

Eddie waved the comment away. "I just need to get fixed up enough to go after him. I'll tell you what happened later."

Irene returned to her ministrations. "You ain't going after nobody in the shape you're in."

The sternness in Irene's voice made Eddie sit up straight. "If I don't, I'll be in worse shape than this." She studied Irene's face for a few seconds. "If I don't, I'll be dead. Or someone else will be dead because I didn't."

But the weight of all the events of the day before and the pain in various parts of her body were pushing on her with a power she couldn't resist. She struggled to stay awake as Irene applied salve to the cuts on her face.

"Lie down on the bed," Irene said. "I can do the rest of you easier there."

"But I'm all dirty."

"I know how to wash a sheet. Now lie down."

Eddie gingerly stretched out on her back.

She woke when the thin light of early morning was just starting to peek through the curtains Irene had drawn the night before. Eddie pushed herself out of the bed, embarrassed she had taken Irene's sleeping place for the whole night. As she stood, she felt her knees buckle. Steadying herself with a firm grip on the washstand, she searched the room for Irene. Finally Eddie found her, nestled in several quilts and sleeping peacefully on the floor in the far corner of the room.

Another wave of guilt rolled over Eddie for denying Irene her own bed. But the guilt was quickly replaced by fear—of having exposed Irene to the same danger she had unintentionally put Charlie in.

Irene rolled over and opened one eye. Then she opened both eyes and grinned at Eddie. "Thought maybe I dreamed you came back." She looked at Eddie's hands, clinging determinedly to the edge of the wash stand for support. "You're upright, but you ain't ready to be." She got up from her pile of quilts. "Get back in bed."

"I could've slept on the floor."

"Wasn't lookin' for volunteers."

"You can't take care of me, Irene. It's not safe."

"That's for me to decide." Irene moved to the bed and put her arm gently around Eddie. "And I can't decide much until I know what's going on." She helped Eddie sit on the edge of the bed. "Lie down."

Eddie shook her head.

"Then just lie back if you start to get lightheaded." Irene patted Eddie gently on the shoulder. "I'll make us some coffee. We can talk while I get dressed."

Eddie wasn't sure talking was a good idea. Rafe Pettibone had killed two good people because of her. Talking took time. And time gave Rafe the chance to find her again and to hurt someone else.

"It's just not safe."

Irene stopped putting ground coffee in the pot and marched to the side of the bed. In an uncharacteristic gesture, she waved her index finger in Eddie's face. "Don't tell me 'bout 'safe.' I've been through the Underground Railroad. I've seen my whole family slaughtered in front of my eyes by evil men who said they were the Law. For forty years, I've carried the burden of getting out alive when they didn't. Don't talk to me about safe." Her eyes blazed.

Eddie stared at Irene.

"You think you can take care of this alone just 'cuz it's happening to you. There's folks here ready to help, and you *need* them to help you." Irene put her hands on her hips and burned a hole between Eddie's eyes with her glare. "Ain't it about time you got this problem solved?"

Eddie was still too exhausted to fight the tears that welled in her eyes.

Irene leaned toward her and wrapped her in a warm, firm hug. "You don't have to do whatever it is alone, child. You gotta understand that."

"All right," Eddie said weakly. "But you have to promise to be careful. Very careful."

"I can do that." Irene finished making the coffee, pulled a chair next to the bed, and sat down. "I'll get the coffee once it's boiling. You just start talking."

Eddie pulled her feet up on the bed and leaned back into the pillow. It felt so good to just lie down on a bed. "It's Rafe Pettibone."

"Figured as much."

She told Irene everything she remembered about what she'd tried to do to deal with Rafe. She told her how Charlie had also warned her about revenge and how he had taught her mining. She told her about Charlie's death and his funeral the coming afternoon. But when she had finished and had stopped talking, she felt restless and began to fidget.

Irene watched her intently as she poured two cups of coffee. "There's something else, ain't there?"

Eddie nodded sadly.

"May as well get it out."

Eddie swallowed hard. "It's the marshal." She hated the idea that he could be involved with Rafe.

"Marshal Gruen?"

"Yes."

"What about him?"

"He's thrown in with Rafe Pettibone."

Irene's big brown eyes grew wide. "Lord Almighty." Then her face screwed up in a perplexed frown. "That just doesn't seem likely when you think about it."

"Charlie—and what you said about killing—convinced me I needed to go to the marshal and have him deal with Rafe. I was planning to do that on Wednesday, when Charlie and I came to town." Eddie gulped, remembering all that had happened since that trip less than two days ago. "As I was coming across the street to see him, the marshal came out of his office with Rafe, and they shook hands."

Irene stood stone still, not a muscle in her body moving. "That sure changes things."

"Yeah," Eddie said, the tiredness of a hundred years weighing on her. "It means I have to kill Rafe Pettibone myself." She sighed. There didn't seem to be any other way out. It was no longer a matter of revenge. It was a matter of survival—hers and anyone's who happened to befriend her.

"There are other lawmen."

Eddie felt disloyal at the irritation Irene's comment generated inside her. "Like the one in Florissant?" The ratio of honest lawmen to crooked lawmen seemed pretty dismal.

"No, like Colorado Springs." Irene sat looking at her calmly as she spoke. "The county sheriff is bigger than Rafe Pettibone. I'd bet my life on it."

Eddie wanted to tell her she might be doing just that, but decided against it. "And how do I get Rafe Pettibone and the county sheriff to meet? Invite them to an ice cream social? 'Oh, by the way, Sheriff, this is Rafe Pettibone. He's a murderer. Do arrest him once you finish your cake.'"

Irene tried unsuccessfully not to laugh. But her levity was momentary. "Maybe we could capture Rafe and then take him to the marshal."

Eddie opened her mouth to refute the idea, then closed it without saying anything. If she could get Rafe bound and gagged, maybe she *could* get him down the pass to Colorado Springs and safely to the El Paso County Sheriff. Surely the county sheriff was beyond Rafe Pettibone and his gang.

"Maybe that would work," Eddie said slowly, thinking of how it might be done as she uttered the words. "Do you think Tess would be willing to help?"

Irene let out the breath she'd been holding. "She already told you she would."

Eddie remembered the note. "When can we talk to her?"

Irene grinned. "I'll talk to Miss Tess first thing, once she's up. Then maybe you can talk to her this afternoon." Her face flattened into seriousness again. "But you've got a funeral to attend." She reached for a garment on a hook behind the door—a long, green, lightweight cape with a hood. "Wear this when you go—with the hood *up*. And be careful. No telling what that man will try next."

Irene had managed to get dressed and ready for work while they were talking. She picked up the things she'd laid out to take with her to the Red Velvet and opened the door. "I'll try to have Miss Tess back here by three o'clock." She smiled again, then gave Eddie a mother's stern look. "You be careful, you hear?"

CHAPTER 15

SEEING CHARLIE'S COFFIN made Eddie feel hollow, as if the very juice of life had been sucked out of her. Staring at the pine box, she used every drop of resolve she could muster to keep her tears from starting again.

The ache was overwhelming. She tried to keep hold of reality, but the minister's words disappeared on the wind, uncomprehended, unheard. No more chances to read to the lovable old coot, no more lessons in mining. She strained to accept that Charlie was dead, but her heart screamed in protest.

She didn't feel the dirt when she tossed a handful into the grave at the minister's cue. Who could she learn from now? The hymn seemed meaningless even though she'd chosen the song especially for its simple message of hope. She remembered his wrinkled, whiskered face. No, she would not accept his death. For now, she let the ache prevail. Perhaps acceptance would come later.

Mumbling something to the undertaker and minister when the service was complete, she headed back into town from the cemetery. She was glad she had chosen to walk. Enveloped in the numbness that had overtaken her when Charlie died, she thought it odd she could function so normally. Her legs still moved. Her voice still responded when a question was asked of her. She could still make out rain clouds on the horizon. How did all those things happen when she was so dead inside?

As she walked down the cemetery hill, the green cape Irene had insisted she wear twisted around her to where it was difficult to walk. She stopped to pull the fabric away from her legs.

"Myrna, how kind of you to come," a female voice said from behind her. Someone grabbed her elbow and forced her to continue down the hill. "Just keep walking, dear. We'll keep up with you." The voice was both loud and familiar.

Eddie glanced next to her. Tess gave her a small smile but kept the grip on her elbow.

Another woman had appeared on her other side, walking almost in front of her. Jolene. The two of them seemed intent on moving Eddie somewhere—quickly.

Tess leaned toward her, grabbed her around the waist, and said under her breath, "Keep moving. Clarence Billingsley's been trying to see what's under that hood the whole service." She accelerated the pace until they were almost running. "Come on. We're going to convince him you're somebody else."

Tess's voice became as loud as if she were speaking at the service. "We're so sorry to have Charlie gone. It's such an awful thing. You met him in Leadville, right? How nice of you to come all the way to Cripple Creek on such short notice."

"Oh, it was the least I could do," Eddie said in a falsetto. She felt as if she was supposed to play-act and run a foot race simultaneously. And every time she caught enough breath to say something, Tess started on another babbling string of false information in response. But they were moving fast, thanks to Tess's support. Even with all the chatter, they reached Myers Avenue almost as quickly as if they had been in a carriage.

"You'll stay the night, won't you, Myrna dear?" Tess clutched Eddie's waist even tighter as they walked up the front steps of the Red Velvet. "It'll be wonderful to talk about Leadville."

"If it won't be a bother," Eddie warbled. "I'm exhausted from all the travel."

Tess shut the front door the instant their skirts had cleared it, then started Eddie up the stairway. "Wait in my sitting room."

As Eddie trudged up the stairs, she glanced over her shoulder and out the window of the front door. Clarence Billingsley was standing in the street. She hurried up to Tess's room and peeked from behind the curtain in time to see Billingsley turn and hurry up Myers Avenue.

"I doubt he's convinced," Tess boomed as she entered. Jolene and Irene followed Tess into the room.

"I don't understand what he's got to do with this," Eddie said.

Tess flipped her auburn curls. "It undoubtedly has something to do with money. Other people's money."

"Maybe he thought I was someone else." Eddie wanted to hope. Her life was complicated enough at the moment.

"The devil likes company," Irene said. "I wouldn't be too fast to decide he and Rafe aren't in it together."

Then Eddie noticed Jolene. "What have you got to do with this?"

The youngest dove stood quietly just inside the door, her eyes as big as saucers. "I owe you," she said softly.

Eddie's thoughts drifted back to the afternoon in the yard of the Red Velvet. "Not really." If Rafe had been in jail where he belonged even then....

Tess cleared her throat to bring the group to attention. "We need a plan, Eddie boy—"

They all broke into laughter.

She began again. "We need a plan to get Rafe Pettibone."

"I have one," Eddie said, "but I'm going to need some help."

Irene beamed.

Eddie looked at Tess self-consciously. "If you don't mind sullying the Red Velvet with the likes of Rafe Pettibone, feminine wiles are the best weapon we have."

Tess grinned. "I think I'm going to like this."

Afternoon light streamed through the windows of the Double X as Rafe stood nose to nose with Clarence Billingsley. "No damn way I'm standing watch at a whore house waiting for a dead woman to walk out the front door." The dull pain of his usual headache was intensifying.

"Shhhh." The fat weasel looked around the barroom.

A few other patrons were on the opposite side of the room, intent on their own conversations and alcohol.

He leaned toward Rafe and said in a stage whisper, "If she is at the Red Velvet, you damn well better get back there and make sure she doesn't get away."

Billingsley kept his eyes leveled on Rafe, which made Rafe stand up taller so Billingsley had to look up.

"Someone was hiding in a long, hooded cape at the funeral. I tell ya it was Eddie Taggert. I could just sense it."

"You got no sense at all, you idiot!" Rafe slammed his bottle on the table. "She's dead, dammit! I used two more sticks than you told me. Her and everything else in that tunnel are blown to kingdom come!" His head was beginning to pound.

"Shhh, will ya?" Billingsley looked over his shoulder, then back at Rafe and glowered. "Just quit arguing and get over there!"

Rafe looked around the room. No one but the bartender was paying any attention to them. And the bartender was too far away to hear their conversation. Rafe recalled his last departure from the Red Velvet as he turned back to Billingsley. "Ain't no sense in *watching* a brothel."

"You got to," Billingsley yelled.

The bartender put a shotgun on the bar. "Keep it friendly, boys." His voice was loud enough to hear him in the next saloon.

Rafe had an odd gratitude for the barkeep's remark. When Billingsley yelled, his head hurt even worse.

Billingsley smoothed his rumpled vest. "If you watch the Velvet, I can go out to the claim and check the rubble from the blast." He looked at Rafe coolly. "Or would you rather go back into the mine and make sure the job's done?"

Rafe glared at Billingsley, furious that it made sense to do what the son of a bitch said. He sure as hell didn't want to go back into that hole. "I'll watch the Velvet." He looked at the full bottle of whiskey on the table, then at the dance hall girl waiting for him at the bar.

"Take your whiskey with you," Billingsley said.

Small consolation, Rafe told himself.

"I should be back before midnight. You can get back to the Double X then."

Rafe grunted. He preferred to be at the Double X now.

"I'll come get you at the Velvet once I'm sure—" Billingsley coughed. "Once I'm sure of *things*."

Rafe grunted again. He grabbed the bottle of whiskey and headed for the door.

He squinted with the pain of the bright sunlight. He didn't like the set-up. Being where Tess Temany could march him around with a shotgun in his back again had no appeal whatsoever. Edwina Sinclair was dead, and Billingsley's plan was a waste of time. He glared at the fat man. "If she's dead, like I told you, you owe me a whole night with a good whore."

"Fair enough," Billingsley said. "But get your sweet ass down there first. Let's just hope she didn't get away while we were wasting time 'discussing' it." He turned toward his office, then turned back. "And watch *both* doors. Understand?"

Rafe was still muttering when he sat down on the porch of the Sweet Alice Dance Hall, directly across from the Red Velvet. No doubt about it—Clarence Billingsley was a genuine pain in the ass. Watch the back door, too. How was he supposed to park himself in two places at once? What an idiot!

The dollies were inside, and he was outside. At the moment, dreaming about what they might be doing was the best he could do. That stupid Billingsley. Next he'd have him watching the cemetery to be sure the old man didn't rise from the dead.

Once Tess, Eddie, and Irene had worked out the details of the plan, Tess showed Eddie into Candace's room to get ready. Being upstairs at the Red Velvet seemed like a completely different place to Eddie—she felt almost like a foreigner. She couldn't relax—she didn't understand the customs of this previously forbidden domain. But even more, the thought of getting close enough to Rafe to pull the plan off unnerved her.

The Velvet was gearing up for its usual evening business. Dinner, which was always served at eight, was still more than two hours away. Eddie would not partake in those festivities. She, Tess, and Irene had planned a separate party, which she would host alone—later.

Eddie let Candace's filmy peignoir slip off her shoulder, painted a sultry pout on her face, and looked in the mirror. It wasn't Edwina Sinclair staring back. And it certainly wasn't Eddie Taggert. The fact that she didn't even know her own identity bothered her even more. She wasn't sure she could remember how to be a woman. She'd never known how to be a harlot. Worst of all, she was beginning to doubt she could play the seductress with Rafe successfully a second time.

She stood closer to the mirror and studied the bruises on her face. Jolene had hidden them well with makeup, but Eddie still knew they were there. She threw the filmy fabric of the dressing gown over her face in frustration. Realizing the potential, she drew the cloth gracefully across her cheek. Maybe a veil—

She searched Candace's trunk for something filmy that she could drape over her head. In the back corner at the bottom of the stack of pretty things, Eddie found a large scarf of soft green chiffon. She draped it around her head and across her face. The green matched her eyes almost perfectly.

Tess barely knocked before she bustled in. "Ready?"

Eddie looked at her in confusion. "Now?" Things weren't supposed to happen for another three hours.

"Change of plans. Rafe Pettibone's been sitting across the

street for more than an hour. Drinking." She rubbed a spot of makeup on Eddie's forehead to smooth it. "He's sober enough to seduce at the moment. If we wait, he'll be too drunk to walk across the street."

Eddie's eyes widened. "Right now?" The squeak of a voice didn't seem like hers.

Tess looked Eddie over like she was merchandise. "Jolene did a fine job with the makeup." She walked completely around Eddie. "And the chiffon gives you an exotic look. Your skin looks perfect behind the veil." She studied Eddie again, this time shaking her head in disapproval. "But we've got to do something about that hair." Her eyes lit up. "I have it!" She hurried out the door.

In a few moments she was back, carrying an impressive mass of blonde curls piled elaborately on a wig form.

"But that's your French wig—" Irene had told Eddie all about it. The wig had been ordered from Paris to accommodate a particularly wealthy client's desire for a blonde Tess.

"Anything for the cause." Tess carefully positioned the wig on Eddie's head and secured it with a half a box of hair pins.

Eddie looked at herself, dumbfounded, as Tess turned her slowly around in front of the mirror. "I don't look like me," she said in dazed amazement.

"That's the whole point, isn't it?"

Eddie smiled self-consciously.

Tess smiled back, but slowly. "You can still let me do this part—"

"I know." Eddie looked at her feet, hidden in soft satin slippers instead of work boots. "But that wouldn't be fair." She looked intensely at Tess. "In fact, I don't like it that Jolene will be the one to get him in here. Maybe he'll try to drag her to the Old Homestead shed again—"

Tess put up her hand to still Eddie. "What man with half a mind would take a two-minute sneak in the shed when he's offered a whole night at the best parlor house in town?" Tess's laughter filled the room, then her face reverted to a serious expression. "Besides, Irene will be watching-with the shotgun."

"You sure Jolene'll be safe?"

Tess threw her hands in the air. "For heaven's sake, Eddie! None of us is ever sure we're safe!" She re-draped the chiffon around Eddie's face and over the wig. "Ready?"

Eddie nodded, trying to stop the trembling in her knees.

Rafe looked at the lights as they came on one by one at the Red Velvet. It wasn't fully dark yet, but Tess and her girls were preparing for the evening. With ladies as lovely as the Velvet claimed, the men had a right to be able to see them well. He thought again of enjoying a night in one of those beds. He took a deep breath and let it out slowly. When Billingsley got the mine running, the ladies at the Red Velvet would be happy to kowtow to Rafe Pettibone.

His jaw hardened with the memory of his last encounter with Tess Temany. What an idiot he'd been to let her parade him around like a toy soldier. He should have taken care of her and the Sinclair woman right then and there. Now, here he was sitting across the street like some damn thirteen-year-old waiting for a peek. There was no damn reason to be ogling the shadows in the windows from across the street. He ought to walk right into the place and take what he wanted. Still, the thirte-year-old in him yearned for the peek—or anything more he could get from where he sat doing what Billingsley had assigned him.

The front door opened, and the young, willowy one he'd tried to take in the yard came out and down the stairs. She looked straight at him. And smiled!

Rafe blinked. How much whiskey had he had anyway? He looked at the bottle. It was half gone.

The girl stood in the street facing Rafe and squinting into the late afternoon sun.

He rubbed his eyes. She was real. He knew she was real. He'd already had his hands on her soft, round breasts.

She smiled again and came toward him.

Rafe could hear his heart beating in his throat when she crossed the street and walked up the steps to the porch of the Sweet Alice.

"Evenin', Mister Pettibone," she said demurely.

Rafe nodded, afraid his tongue would fall out of his mouth if he tried to speak.

She stood next to him, close enough that he could feel the cloth of her skirt on his arm.

He felt like he was fastened to the porch. The smell of her perfume made him giddy. This was too good to be true. What the hell was going on?

She slowly circled the toe of her shoe on the boards of the porch next to him. "Mister Pettibone?"

He looked up at her, frantically stuffing his doubts in the farthest corner of his mind.

"Miss Tess would like to make it up to you for the last time you were at the Velvet."

Her voice was almost a coo, and Rafe took a few seconds before the words themselves registered. "Huh?"

"Miss Tess has a special lady for you if you'd like to come inside."

Again he had a difficult time comprehending the words.

She looked at him intently, waiting.

He felt his willpower melting into the boards beneath him. "Now?"

She nodded.

Rafe stood, corked the bottle and grasped it by the neck. Surely Billingsley wouldn't mind if he watched the doors from the inside.

Damn fine that the stupid madame had come to her wits. He wouldn't need whiskey tonight, but he carried it with him anyway. He walked behind the girl as if she'd put him in some hypnotic trance, not seeing anything but her waist and the graceful movement of her hips. Her last words registered in his consciousness, as they started up the stairs of the Red Velvet. "Who's this 'special lady'?"

She turned, offering him a winsome smile. "She's beautiful," she said dreamily. "From Europe..." Her voice dwindled into a sigh.

"She good-lookin'?" Rafe growled the question, trying to find some clue that Tess Temany's "gift" was a nasty joke.

"Myrna? Oh, yes! She's so lovely...."

Something had to be wrong with this. "Is she...is she sane?" He didn't want no lunatic.

The girl looked at him impatiently. "Of course."

They reached the front door of the Red Velvet, and she showed him inside. Five or six of the whores smiled at him from their seats in the parlor. He ran his tongue over his lower lip.

Tess Temany appeared from out of nowhere. She was smiling, too. "Evenin', Mister Pettibone." Her breath seemed like silk. "Would you like to go to your room? Myrna is waiting for you." She took his whiskey and set it on a small table next to the stairs.

"Myrna?"

"Your special lady," the girl who had come for him at the Sweet Alice whispered.

Rafe wet his lips, feeling somehow too large for his clothes and too clumsy to take a step.

Tess looked at him, waiting for an answer.

"Yes," he blurted. "Yes, that'd be fine." He was Rafe Pettibone, outlaw gang leader. Why was he letting these women fluster him? He hated it that they controlled what he wanted. But he wanted it all the same.

"This way," Tess said, still smiling. She started up the stairway.

"Only—" She stopped and smiled seductively at him. "We don't allow guns upstairs." She stared calmly at the gun holstered at Rafe's hip. "Would you leave it here in the hall, please?"

The request came with so much honey, Rafe would have licked the sweetness from the words, given the chance. He unbuckled the holster and presented his gun and holster to the girl. He could handle any woman, with both his hands tied if necessary. Besides, he still had the derringer in his pocket and the knife in his boot.

Tess turned back to the stairway. "This way," she said sweetly.

Rafe kept pushing the doubts from his mind. The ladies had invited him in. Billingsley didn't need to know. He could check out the place and have a good time, too. As he started up the stairs, he looked down into the parlor. Smiling painted faces greeted him. None of them was the bitch who'd hit him on the head. All of these faces were lovely. If his luck held, maybe he'd find a way to have them all before the night was over.

When they reached the top of the stairs, Tess led him down the hall. At the third door, she knocked lightly. "Myrna, your guest is here."

The door opened on a tall, blonde woman swathed in a filmy white bedroom thing and a green veil. She waved him in gracefully, but without a word. He heard the door close behind him. He was alone with her.

She didn't move.

His first instinct was to grab her and ravish her instantly, leaving no time for anyone to stop him. But he decided that might get him thrown out. Maybe it would be even better if he took his time like the rich bastards probably did.

She reached toward him gently, her fingers and face both hidden in the veil, and drew her hand slowly across his cheek. She seemed to pull back a bit, but then caressed his forehead lightly with one teasing finger.

Rafe's eyes gleamed with pleasured amazement at the softness of her touch. He'd never let one of them rough whores scratch at him again.

She walked around him in a painfully slow, sinuous dance that kept him a spectator. His eyes focused on the moving curves. His hands, so ready to reach a moment before, hung like lead at his sides. A hot foreign woman—and she was all his for the night. Some little niggling thing in the back of his mind felt wrong. But certain parts of his body told him things were so very right. He reached for her.

She seemed to draw back again, then let him touch her. What a game she played.

She kept up a slight sinuous movement as he held her by the waist. She was slender, but the pulsing rhythm she worked with her body made her seem round. Then she stopped—and backed away.

"What? What do I need to do?" Rafe's eyes widened in his panic to please his silent mistress.

She reached for the top button on his shirt. He undid half of the buttons on his shirt in a frenzy, then tore off the shirt without undoing the rest. Not pausing, he yanked off his boots and socks, then dropped his jeans and stepped out of them. He stood before the mysterious woman, naked and in his glory. "I'm all yours, darlin'."

The woman motioned to the bed and led him toward it, the veil still over her face and the filmy robe still covering her soft body from neck to ankle. She pulled a wide satin ribbon from the sleeve of the robe and patted the bed.

Rafe dutifully sat on the edge of the bed. She kissed him light-ly through the veil. He grabbed at her but found only a handful of the filmy gown in his grasp when he looked at his fist.

She gave a low melodious laugh. The mystery of her face made him hot.

Suddenly, he wasn't sure he wanted to see behind the veil. He'd heard about whores like this. The men who'd had them swore there was nothing better. He shivered, then willingly let her tie his hand to the bedpost with the satin ribbon.

She began to move her hips in and out, back and forth again. She moved to the other side of the bed with another ribbon. Red. He liked it that they were red ribbons. Maybe he should ask her to tie one on the best part of him. Ain't no way she was going to subdue *that*. It already stuck up like a flag pole.

She tied his legs, again with red ribbon, one to each bedpost.

He strained to pull her to him, but the ribbons held. All the better when he finally got her.

She stooped to pick up his clothes. She took the derringer from his pants pocket, the knife from his boot and laid them neatly on the dresser on the other side of the room. Surrender.

He was ready to explode with the want of her. The ache went all the way to his ears. "Now, woman, now! I can't wait. Take me now!"

The mysterious Myrna walked to the wall next to the bed and kicked it three times, then turned to Rafe as she pulled the veil from her head. "I'll take you tomorrow, Rafe Pettibone. To Colorado Springs. God willing, I'll see you hang for the murders of Charlie McGill and my husband, Jerrod Sinclair." She took off the blonde wig.

Rafe's eyes felt like they would burst from their sockets. "You? God dammit! You're dead!"

The door opened, and three other women hurried in. Tess Temany was in the lead. She looked at Edwina, then at Rafe.

Suddenly embarrassed about being without his clothes, he squirmed on the bed, trying to get the coverlet over his privates. The ribbons cut into his wrists and ankles as he twisted.

Tess walked closer and stared directly at his crotch. "Good Lord, Eddie! Why didn't you tell me he has the pox?"

Edwina Sinclair looked at the madam stupidly.

Hell, Rafe thought. She probably never even *heard* of syphilis. But that didn't change his predicament. How the hell was he going to get out of this without anyone knowing that a bunch of women had taken his clothes and tied him up?

That colored woman who'd marched him around before had come in, too. She had the shotgun leveled on him.

Shit! He was gonna get shot, naked and tied up—by a nigger woman. Son of a bitch.

"Okay, girls, let's get this fool's clothes back on," Tess Temany said. She took the shotgun and put it in his crotch. "Only untie one limb at a time. All three of you go to it." They untied his left leg, put his pants leg over his foot and then retied the leg—with the ribbon *and* a rope.

He wanted to struggle with all his might, but the barrel of the shotgun two inches from his privates made him lie still.

"Faster, ladies," Tess said crisply. "We have some entertaining to do." They hurried through the other three restraints, then pulled the shirt over his shoulders and his britches over his hips.

He couldn't believe it. Now in addition to the ribbons, thick, hairy ropes held his arms and legs to the bedposts. He'd have to take the whole damn bed with him to get away.

"One more thing," Tess said. She gave the shotgun back to the colored woman who leveled it at Rafe again. Then the madam went to the dresser, pulled out a small bottle, and measured its contents into a glass. She filled the glass with water and stirred it. As she moved toward the bed, she said, "Help me, Eddie. I'm sure Mister Pettibone would like to sleep well."

The colored woman kept the shotgun aimed at his crotch. Edwina lifted his head while Tess Temany put the glass to his lips. "If you know what's good for you, you'll drink it right down," Tess said as she poured the liquid down his throat.

Rafe drank. Hell, maybe it was poison. That would be the easiest way out of this mess.

They were readying to leave when Tess turned back to the bed. "Where's that scarf?

Edwina picked the filmy green thing off the dresser and

handed it to Tess who folded it deliberately. She pulled the per-fumed handkerchief from her cleavage and stuffed it in Rafe's mouth, then pulled the scarf tight across his jaw. "Sorry, honey. But I don't like any unprofessional singing at my parties."

They blew out the lamp, drew the curtains, and closed the door when they left, leaving Rafe stretched on his back on the bed in a black void. Son of a bitch. And his whiskey was downstairs.

Eddie's heart was still hammering in her ears when Tess led her to the small spare room at the end of the hall twenty minutes later.

"Most of the noise from downstairs doesn't get this far," Tess said. "Maybe you can get a good night's rest."

"I need to wash up first." Her skin crawled with the feel of Rafe Pettibone.

Tess nodded toward a large pitcher and bowl on the dresser. "I think Irene's already brought up some warm water." She opened the drawer and grabbed a bar of soap in each hand. "What's your pleasure? French milled or lye?"

Eddie took the lye soap. That would clean anything.

Tess pulled a simple cotton nightgown out of the same drawer. "Thought this might be more comfortable."

Eddie offered an exhausted smile. "It's been so long since I slept in anything but my work clothes, I'm not sure I can do it." She looked down at the peignoir that she still had on. "I know I'd never be able to sleep in this."

Tess gave her an amused look. "You'd probably be able to sleep in the all together on the back of a buffalo tonight. So much has happened in the last few days you have to be pretty near dead with exhaustion." Tess just stood there and smiled.

Sort of like a mother, Eddie decided.

"You did a good job."

Eddie nodded her thanks.

Tess took a step toward the door. "It's too bad about Marshal Gruen." She sighed. "Colorado Springs is a long way—"

"I *saw* them shaking hands, Tess. I can't trust him for justice if he's friendly with the murderer." She closed her eyes and took a long slow breath. She wanted it to be different as much as Tess did.

"You're right," Tess said. "But it sure would make things easier."

Eddie giggled with fatigue. "Easy hasn't been in my vocabulary for a while now."

"Guess not," Tess said with a soft smile. "I'll make sure Irene wakes you first thing when she gets here in the morning." She turned toward the door again.

"Tess?" Eddie was so tired she wasn't sure the events that had just transpired were real. "Is he really tied to a bed down the hall?"

Tess gave Eddie a motherly hug. "Yes. Now get some rest so you can get him to Colorado Springs."

"I should really go for the wagon tonight. Then I could start for the Springs in the morning."

Tess clucked like a doting mother. "You're just a measly ol' human being like the rest of us, Eddie Taggert. You need some sleep. Until you get it, that wagon isn't going to do you a bit of good."

"Yes ma'am," Eddie said.

"I saved a bit of the laudanum for you, just in case. Do you want it?"

Eddie shook her head. "Is that what we made him drink? Laudanum?"

Tess grinned. "Yep. He'll sleep like a baby."

"Will he die?"

Tess laughed. "He's a big man. The dose he got was a lot less than Candace took." She smiled again as she closed the door.

Eddie scrubbed herself all over twice, then nuzzled into the soft towel Irene had left with the water. Washing up was a luxury all by itself. She put on the nightgown and climbed between the crisp white sheets. Heaven probably didn't feel as good.

Rafe was captured. Eddie knew she should be able to sleep well. But sleep didn't come as easily as she had expected. She still had to get him all the way to Colorado Springs. That wouldn't be easy, but she could do it. Then what?

It was the "then what" that kept her from falling asleep. She wanted to mine Charlie's claim, to show the world he knew what he was doing when he staked it. She wanted to stay near where Jerrod was buried. There was nothing for her in St. Louis. Could she have more than "nothing" here? Or was "here" an impossible dream and "there" an empty necessity?

Maybe one of her father's friends would let her work in his office. The idea made her stomach queasy. How could she spend her life stuck in some room looking at business correspondence for someone she didn't even know?

She remembered the act she'd managed to put on earlier that night. Could she work for Tess? The thought of letting men other than Jerrod touch her made her shudder. Tess's life was not her life. She let out a deep sigh. Her life was in the Tin Rooster Mine. Charlie had lost it. She had to get it back—for him, for them both.

Sleep finally caught up with her as she was counting hundred dollar bills in her head. Maybe there was a way.

CHAPTER 16

EDDIE HEARD A rooster crow and realized she was not at the cabin. As she woke, she twisted to get upright and felt the smoothness of the sheets. Where was she? She looked frantically around the dimly lit room. The Red Velvet.

She sat up in the bed and let the events of the previous night play in her head. They seemed preposterous. But the peignoir was draped on a chair across the room. Had she really worn it? She remembered the red ribbons and tying Rafe to the bed. She needed to see him, tied to the bed and unable to harm anyone. She got up quietly, put on the robe, and crept down the hall.

Jolene was asleep in a chair next to the door of the third room from the stairs—with the shotgun in her lap. Eddie tiptoed by her and peeked through the keyhole.

Someone was wiggling on the bed. She could see ropes tied to the bedposts. How much of her memory was real? She slowly turned the knob on the door and pushed it open once the latch lifted. She looked back at Jolene, who continued to sleep undisturbed, then looked through the tiny crack in the door that she'd allowed herself. Rafe was on the bed, awake and struggling against the restraints.

When she entered the room, she felt like a moth flying into a flame. He was tied well. She didn't need to be afraid. Why had she come to look? She didn't know. Maybe she needed to see him up close to prove to herself she was not afraid.

As she came around the bed, Rafe stopped squirming. His eyes opened wide in fury, and he stared his hatred at her. His jaw moved, and Eddie heard short muffled grunts that would have been words without the gag. Cuss words, no doubt.

Then his face contorted into a mindless grimace. In seconds, his eyes became lost in what seemed to be some sort of intense pain. Eddie watched as his face solidified in a vacant stare. She moved her hand in front of his face. He was blind. Could laudanum do that?

She shook her head to clear her thinking. "Not this time, Rafe Pettibone. You're not going to get me to fall for this trick." She stared at him hard, hating without qualification. "You're going to Colorado Springs," she hissed through clenched teeth. "You're not going to trick me into untying you." She turned quickly and hurried back to her room.

Right and wrong, good and bad blended in her head as she lay on the bed trying to figure things out. Without trying to, she fell back to sleep.

The sun was streaming through the window when she heard a knock on the door.

"Come in," she said timidly.

Irene pushed open the door and bustled in with a tray heaped with food. "Thought you might appreciate a little nourishment." She placed the tray on the bed next to Eddie. Milk, coffee, biscuits, and leftovers from the party the night before.

The scent of the biscuits made Eddie's mouth water. She hadn't had enough to eat in the last three days to keep a chickadee alive. Her stomach announced the oversight with a deep growl.

Irene laughed. "Maybe I didn't bring enough." She moved toward the door. "You know where the kitchen is if you're still hungry after you finish this."

The tray held even more than Eddie had expected—chilled shrimp, devilled eggs, applesauce, a chunk of Virginia ham, and a big slice of chocolate torte.

She ate it all. Then she got out of bed to get dressed. The bruises and scrapes didn't hurt nearly as much as they had the day before. She got into her ragged work clothes without much pain.

When she came downstairs to the kitchen, she poured herself more coffee.

Irene was busy making pies.

"Wish I could help," Eddie said wistfully. She'd rather peel a whole tree full of apples than say goodbye to the Tin Rooster. Ira Kendrick might own Charlie's mine, but her heart was buried there in the rubble.

"Can if you want," Irene said. "You're welcome in this kitchen anytime."

"Got a job to do," Eddie said with resignation. At least fetching the wagon and mules would mean she'd be out in the sunshine. She poured a cup of coffee and sat down at the table. "If I ask you a question, will you give me an honest answer?"

Irene put on a peeved look. "I ain't ever give you nothin' but honest answers." Then the peeved look turned to a pout. "You're the one who's short on honest answers."

Eddie ignored the jab. "Do you think a woman could mine for gold?"

Irene raised her eyebrows, and nodded sagely. "Depends on the woman, I suspect." She gave Eddie an inquisitive sidelong glance. "You thinking about goin' into mining?"

Eddie answered with an impatient cluck. "I'm already 'into' mining. I just don't know how to stay there."

Irene didn't say anything.

Eddie gulped the coffee, got up from the table and put the cup on the dry sink. "I'm thinkin' of trying to buy the Tin Rooster from Ira Kendrick."

Irene raised her eyebrows as far as they went. "What you gonna use for money?"

"Jerrod left some, maybe it would be enough."

Irene shrugged. "If it is, then I guess there'll be a woman mining gold in Cripple Creek."

Eddie grinned and moved toward the back door. "But first, I need to deliver a skunk."

"Maybe you ought to have someone go with you." The concern in Irene's eyes made Eddie realize how lucky she'd been to choose the Red Velvet when she'd needed a job.

"Naw. I'll be fine. Rafe's upstairs, safe in bed."

They laughed together.

"But maybe that Billingsley fella—"

"I'm more worried about getting the wagon down the gulch than about Clarence Billingsley." Eddie hoped Irene wouldn't challenge her bluff. She smiled reassuringly. "I'll be fine."

There was no sense in putting Tess and Irene in any more danger than she already had. No one else was going to die because she hadn't dealt with Rafe Pettibone. And God willing, Clarence Billingsley was too much of a coward to do anything, and she would be fine.

Eddie rode the mule slowly down Bennett Avenue, scanning the faces of everyone she passed on her way out of town. She had a piece of business she needed to finish before she got the wagon, and Bennett Avenue was her best chance to get on with it. Maybe she could find Ira Kendrick without asking Old Man Watt where he was.

As she made eye contact with the passers-by, she smiled and nodded. Not having to worry that the next face might be Rafe's was a benefit she hadn't anticipated.

The town was growing so fast that she recognized only a few of the pedestrians and riders she passed, but the storekeepers who were outside were ones she'd gotten to know when she was running errands for Tess. Eddie looked up the street, smiling with the pleasure of being part of a community. About a block away, she spotted Marshal Gruen striding purposefully in her direction—with an angry look on his face. Her smile faded.

Hunching into her jacket and pulling her hat over her forehead, she urged the mule across the street, then slipped off, and led him into an alley. Please, God, just a little luck, she begged.

Now was not the time for a friendly chat with Marshal Gruen. In fact, after seeing him with Rafe, she knew there never would be again.

Before she moved out of the alley and onto Carr Street, she glanced back at Bennett Avenue. The marshal walked on and hadn't noticed her. Pity the poor soul he's going to talk to, she thought.

The attempt to avoid the marshal brought her more than a "little" luck. Ira Kendrick was standing outside of Mrs. Fogarty's boarding house, across the street from the alley she'd just come out of.

Eddie held onto the mule's reins, crossed the street in determined strides, and walked up to Ira Kendrick before she could lose her confidence. He had turned away after she'd first glanced at him, but the combination of the build and the fringe of blonde hair around the pale bald pate was unmistakable. "Mister Kendrick?"

He turned and, once he recognized her, scowled. "What do you want?"

"I'd like to buy the Tin Rooster from you, sir." She forced a smile. Being civil to him was a necessity if she was going to get the mine back. It was hard to do. He was as spineless, heartless, and totally unpleasant as she'd recalled from their first meeting.

"Go away," he growled. "I own it, and I'm gonna keep it."

"But I'm willing to pay."

"With what?" He sneered. "I suppose you was doin' dog work just for fun." He gave a repulsive laugh. "You ain't got money." He waved a hand at her clothing, letting the sneer take over his whole face. "You look like a beggar."

Eddie was wearing what she'd had on in the tunnel. Self-consciously, she looked down at her tattered clothes. Then she looked back up at him, her jaw set and her eyes blazing with anger. "It ain't what I wear, mister. It's the money I got." She wasn't sure she'd be able to hold back the anger building inside her. "It would only take ten dollars to cover his bet. That would make you even. I got that much."

Ira Kendrick scowled harder. "Don't make a damn bit o' difference what the bet was. *I own that mine.*" He stuck his finger in Eddie's face. "You got that straight?" He wagged the finger back and forth in front of her eyes. "And come Monday morning, I'll be back with the marshal to run you off."

Eddie refused to let her eyes focus on the finger he was jabbing at her. She closed her eyes to help herself stay calm. "How about *a hundred* dollars? She opened her eyes for effect. "That's ten times the money you put up."

"You're wasting your breath."

"It's not a very good mine," Eddie said, trying to make her voice sound small.

"Then why do you want it?"

"He was like a pa to me—"

Kendrick snorted.

She groped for something that might make a difference to him. "Wouldn't you want to keep something you worked on with your own pa?"

"Hell, no." His eyes hardened into watery blue ice.

Eddie tried not to feel the urgency boiling inside her. Maybe shame would work. "Ain't nothin' important to you but money?"

"Nope," Ira Kendrick said comfortably. "Not a damn thing."

"Then I'll give you a thousand for the Tin Rooster." Her last hope.

Silence. He studied her face. "A thousand dollars?"

"Yes." She stared at him without blinking.

He looked at her clothes again. "If *you* got a thousand dollars, *I* must be President Grover Cleveland."

Eddie balled her fists, fighting not to let her anger explode into words.

"Go away," Kendrick said again. He put his face so close to hers that she could feel his breath. "Go away—from me and from my mine."

Eddie turned, fighting the tears of fury that burned in her eyes. "Have it your way," she muttered through clenched teeth. "You miserable son of a bitch."

Each step she took increased her anger. She jerked the mule along behind her on the lead rope until he finally balked. Orville stopped in the middle of Second Street and brayed in protest.

The mule's rebellion brought her to her senses. What in the world had gotten into her? She had to get Rafe to the county sheriff. Here she was, *walking* the mule to get the wagon. At this rate, she'd be back to the Red Velvet just in time for Christmas. She patted Orville's neck to calm him, then climbed up on his back and urged him into a trot.

The banging on the back door of the Red Velvet brought Irene from the dining room where she was putting away the silver from the night before. "I'm coming. I'm coming," she said as she hurried into the kitchen. "Don't put your fist through the door."

Marshal Gruen stood on the porch, his hand poised to hammer on the door again. When he saw her, he let his arm drop. "Irene Haney, you got a heap of explaining' to do."

She looked at the marshal, wide-eyed at his behavior.

"You may as well let me in, or I'll haul you off to jail for bein' an accomplice."

Irene opened the door, still staring at the marshal and wondering if he'd been chewing on locoweed or something. She motioned to the kitchen table with its four chairs. "Have a seat," she said with a thin veneer of calm. "And start at the beginning—accomplice for what?"

"You know damn well what." He was clearly furious.

Irene couldn't think of any reason that he should be—except for their reluctant boarder upstairs. There was no way the marshal could have found out about that.

He grabbed a chair and sat down, then stood up again. "Why'd he do it?"

She put a cup of coffee down in front of him, then stood with both her hands on the edge of the table. "I can't answer your questions until I know what you're talking about." She looked at him earnestly. "Would you please start at the beginning so I can figure out what this is all about?"

The marshal seemed to relax a bit. He sat back down at the table and put his head in his hands.

After slowly pulling out a chair, she sat down across from him. "Why did who do what?"

The marshal raised his head and cleared his throat. "Why did Eddie Taggert kill Charlie McGill?"

"*What?*" She looked at him with her mouth open, sure now that he'd lost his mind.

"Clarence Billingsley left my office a few minutes ago. He signed a sworn statement saying he saw Eddie kill Charlie McGill—on the road to Victor." The marshal's face was gray. He shook his head sadly. "It's hard to believe Eddie could do a thing like that."

Irene watched him quietly, not sure whether a glass of cold water in his face or a thump on the head with the rolling pin would bring him to his senses faster. She decided on simplicity. "Marshal, you've gone stark raving mad."

He glared at her belligerently. "You think I like this? You think I *want* to believe this?"

"I think you're an idiot to believe it."

"Billingsley said he saw the murder."

"Wouldn't be the first time he saw something that wasn't there." She shook her head. "Eddie wouldn't kill anybody. I couldn't even get her...er...ah, I mean *him*...to kill flies in the kitchen." Irene prayed the slip had gone unnoticed.

"But Billingsley says—" The marshal put his head in his

hands again.

"Why would Eddie kill an old man she was friends with?" Irene folded her hands in front of her on the table, trying to make herself stay calm.

Then she realized she'd slipped again. Unless she was an "accomplice," she wouldn't know Charlie McGill was an old man... and that Eddie was a "she".

The marshal seemed to miss both slips, and she was grateful.

"Billingsley claims McGill changed the claim to Eddie's name. Maybe Eddie was out to swindle the old man all along." He shook his head in frustration. "Why else would Charlie McGill have signed it over?"

"Do you know for sure, he did?"

The marshal squirmed. "I'll find that out when the records office opens on Monday."

"Does Eddie seem like a swindler to you?"

"Damn it, Irene. I want to believe he didn't do it as much as you do. But there's a witness for God's sake!" He ran his hand through his hair. "I can't just pretend Billingsley never came to me. I gotta think like a lawman."

"You're thinking like a donkey." Irene let the insult fester for a moment. "Who was it made Clarence Billingsley look bad a few weeks ago? Maybe Billingsley's just sore about that." She narrowed her eyes for effect. "Who was lying that time?" She glared at the marshal as if the look itself could make him change his mind. "Besides, when he left this morning, Eddie was talkin' about trying to *buy* the mine from Ira Kendrick."

This time, he caught the slip. "So you *have* seen him. And he agrees that sissy pants Kendrick owns the claim? This just don't make any sense."

Irene tried to steer him back to safer issues. "Why would that fat toad Clarence Billingsley know about the mining records anyway?"

Marshal Gruen's mouth drew up in a grimace that she guessed

he wore as a thinking pose.

"I'll bet the truth's a whole different story than what Billingsley's told you."

The marshal looked up, concerned, confused but with a glimmer of hope in his eyes. "You might be right. That puny claim is getting a lot of attention." Finally, he asked the question she knew was coming. "Have you seen Eddie since Wednesday?"

This was not the time to lie. Irene nodded.

"He here now?"

"No."

"Will he be back?"

Suddenly, an incredible racket broke out upstairs. Candace's room was directly above the kitchen, and Rafe was throwing his weight against the bed so hard it banged against the wall. The clanking repeated, again and again, almost in a rhythm.

Marshal Gruen looked up at the ceiling. A piece of plaster dropped into his coffee cup. "What the hell?"

Irene jumped up from the table. "They're moving furniture." She tried to make herself look even more anxious than she was. "I'm supposed to be helping them." She began to wring her hands. The noise stopped.

The marshal got up. "When will Eddie be back?"

"This afternoon, around three."

Another series of thumps. The marshal looked up as he moved toward the door. He shook his head and returned to the subject. "I'll be back at three-thirty." His gaze locked with Irene's. "You have him here. Understand?"

"Yes, sir." Irene knew she meant it. What she didn't know was how she was going to make it happen.

Before the marshal was off the back porch, Irene had hurried up the stairs. When she got to the room where they were keeping Rafe, Tess was already at the dresser, mixing up another dose of laudanum.

Tess grimaced. "Noisy bastard, huh?"

Irene groaned. "With really bad timing."

Eddie looked at the items in the wagon, going over the list in her head one last time. The tarp, the ropes, her clothing, Jerrod's books—and the book safe—were all loaded in the wagon bed. The rest belonged to Ira Kendrick now. She thought of Charlie's singlejack and the spoon he'd designed himself. Ira Kendrick wasn't worthy of them. But they were his, and she had to leave them.

She moved to the front of the wagon. Her prospector's pick leaned against the seat. She picked it up by the handle. The weight of it in her hand made her feel strong. If she had to, she could bring the pick down hard—into anything or anyone. She slid the pick under the front of the seat.

While she was bent over storing the pick, she pulled a bundle from under the seat. The efficient smell of gun oil greeted her nose when she opened the bundle. The two guns she'd practiced with so earnestly earlier in the summer lay nestled in Jerrod's heavy coat. Both guns were clean and loaded. Hefting one, then the other, she thought about the little bit of target practice she'd allowed herself an hour earlier. On seven of her twelve tries, she'd hit the dead-center of the spot on the tree stump she'd used as a target. The rest had been close. Poppa would still be proud.

If she needed to use a gun, she could. But she didn't want to. Charlie and Irene were right—killing was wrong.

She dismissed the thought of putting one of the revolvers in her belt when the idea crossed her mind. Until she was hauling Rafe, she didn't have any reason to be armed. She rewrapped the guns and put them back under the seat. Once she'd delivered Rafe to the county sheriff, she'd hand him the guns, too.

She looked toward the portal of the Tin Rooster, then at how far the sun had progressed through the sky. She was already running late. She wanted to go into the tunnel—to feel the coolness of the rock, to inhale the smell of mining one last time. But if she went in, she was afraid she might not be able to make herself leave. The grief of losing Jerrod and Charlie and the mine might weigh her down in the darkness to where she'd just sit there until she turned to dust.

Still she dallied. It would be nice to know if the blast Rafe had set had caused much damage. Maybe it was bad enough that Ira Kendrick wouldn't want the mine. She laughed to herself and shook her head. That jackass wanted the mine to spite her, not to work it. He probably wouldn't even recognize a ruined tunnel as a problem. And if he did, he'd blame the damage on her.

She climbed onto the wagon seat, released the brake, and clicked the mules forward. Skillfully easing the team onto the narrow trail with Jewel tied behind the wagon, she started for Cripple Creek, never letting herself look back.

Wildflowers danced in the breeze even in the steep terrain of the gulch. The brightness of the day and the beauty around her made her smile in spite of the situation. She tried not to think about never seeing the place again. She put her whole focus on keeping the mules moving.

Once she got to the main road, she pushed the animals to go faster and faster, as if her life depended on their speed. But she had no life, and the speed didn't matter.

She had to stop thinking that way. Maybe she just had to get this task done before the next became clear. Once she got Rafe to Colorado Springs, maybe then her future would take some hint of a shape.

When she reached the Red Velvet, she left the loaded wagon at the back of the lot. She unharnessed the mules, rubbed them down half-heartedly, and tethered them. She was exhausted but knew her fatigue was more from her state of mind than the work she'd done. She checked Charlie's pocket watch while she climbed the steps to the back porch. Quarter 'til three. She'd made good time. Real good. So what?

When she reached for the screen door, it opened before she even touched it. Tess and Irene were both standing just inside the door. Eddie looked from the painted face to the dark face and back. "What's wrong?"

"We have a problem," Tess said.

"A *big* problem," Irene said solemnly. Her usual grin of greeting was missing.

Tess took Eddie by the arm and moved her into the kitchen. "Billingsley's told the marshal he saw you kill Charlie."

Eddie leaned against the door jamb, trying to think. That worthless imitation of a human. Was making him give a customer an honest price that much of an affront? "Guess that means I have to leave right now." How was she going to get Rafe in the wagon in broad daylight without attracting attention?

"I don't think so," Tess said. "Irene convinced the marshal that Billingsley might be lying. If you run away without talking to the marshal, you'll make that fat sissy look like a hero."

"And I'll look guilty as sin." Eddie plopped dejectedly on a kitchen chair.

"The marshal's already talked to Irene," Tess said. "He even threatened to arrest her as an accomplice." She started to pace the kitchen. "Why are men so willing to believe such complete blather?"

Eddie couldn't help but smile. Tess was usually the champion of all males still capable of walking upright.

"The marshal will be back at three-thirty," Irene said. "And he told me I better have you here." Irene's face was a mix of regret and fear. "I ain't never been to jail." She squared her shoulders and held her head straight. "But I'll go if you need me to."

Eddie's chest felt like she was inhaling lead.

"We've decided it's up to you," Tess said in her business voice. "If you want to run, we'll put up as much ruckus as we can to distract him."

"Does he know Rafe's upstairs?"

Tess and Irene both smirked.

"Naw," Irene said. "But he thinks we're pretty noisy when we move furniture."

Tess gave a quick laugh, then turned serious again. "I think you need to talk to the marshal."

"But he's pals with Rafe—"

Irene was shaking her head slowly. "The marshal felt real bad about what Billingsley told him. The pain was all over his face." She gave Eddie a knowing smile. "He wasn't hurtin' for Charlie McGill. He was hurtin' for you."

"So you think I should talk to him, too?"

Irene didn't answer.

"We both think you should make up your own mind," Tess said. "But maybe it's worth trying to find out if you saw what you thought you saw."

"I *saw* them shake hands."

"And Clarence Billingsley says he saw you kill Charlie McGill," Tess said.

"But he's lying!"

"The truth gets lost in a lot of different ways," Irene said softly. "Anybody ever give you something that was in a box, inside another box, inside still another box? What you're looking for takes a while to find when it's that kind of situation."

"But if they're friends, he'll let Rafe get away." Eddie's eyes widened at the thought of it. "Then none of us will be safe. He'll kill us all—and Jolene, too."

"That's true," Tess said. "That's the risk. But think about it, Eddie. Was the man you had coffee with so many times someone who could be friends with Rafe Pettibone?"

Eddie's head swirled with confusion. The decision couldn't be postponed. "I don't know what to do!"

"Then do the thing that *feels* right," Tess said.

Eddie stopped struggling. Could there be a respectable reason for the marshal to shake Rafe's hand? She couldn't imagine one. Still she wanted to trust him—had wanted to trust him all along. But if he was dishonest, like the marshal in Florissant, the risk was too high. She couldn't chance letting Rafe run loose again.

Finally she found what she thought was a workable compromise. "We won't tell him we have Rafe," she said. "And if he takes me to jail, then someone else has to get Rafe to the sheriff in Colorado Springs."

Tess and Irene nodded.

Eddie brushed a hand over her ragged clothes. "I guess I need to be honest with him about who I really am." She looked at the pocket watch. "Ten minutes to become a lady—unless he shows up early."

CHAPTER 17

WHEN IRENE USHERED Marshal Gruen into the kitchen fifteen minutes later, Tess and Eddie were already sitting at the table. Eddie had put Jerrod's now-ragged jacket on over her clean skirt and blouse. Her face was scrubbed. She'd placed her battered hat lightly over her hair, which Tess had managed to comb into a reasonably feminine style.

Eddie raised her head slightly when the marshal sat down across from her. "Howdy, Marshal Gruen."

The marshal cleared his throat. "I haven't seen you in a while, Eddie." His voice had a tone to it that reminded Eddie of the night her father had told her that her mother was dead.

"Been busy." She still didn't look up.

The marshal cleared his throat again. "Son, let's not make this any harder than it already is."

"Yes, sir." She thought of Charlie and their game.

"I have a witness who says you killed Charlie McGill."

"I didn't, sir." She waited a moment before continuing. "I found Charlie the morning after he was shot. He told me who did it before he died."

"Who?"

"Rafe Pettibone."

Marshal Gruen exhaled loudly. "That's sure as hell more believable. I've had a feeling that bastard belonged in jail since he showed up in town." Then he tightened himself back into his official business expression. "Why would an arrogant, hard-drinking son of a bitch like Rafe Pettibone bother with an old man, especially one who didn't have any money?"

Eddie looked up at the marshal, letting him see her face. "Rafe was looking for me. Charlie knew where I was."

As the marshal watched, she stood and took off the hat. Irene helped her with the jacket. "It's a long story, marshal," Eddie said. "Where would you like me to begin?"

The marshal stared as if he were seeing Christ in the second coming. His face got red all the way past his hairline. "Begin with who you are." He turned to Irene. "Could I have some water?"

Eddie sat down again.

While Irene fetched the glass of water, the marshal fidgeted with a nickel he had fished from his pants pocket.

Irene set the glass of water down in front of him along with a shot glass of whiskey.

The marshal looked at the liquor and raised his eyebrow, but said nothing. Then he looked at Eddie and repeated his request. "Tell me who you are."

Eddie's mouth was dry as sand when she said the words she had practiced so carefully the week before. "I'm Edwina Taggert Sinclair, widow of Jerrod Sinclair, who was murdered by Rafe Pettibone on June fifth between here and Florissant."

The marshal went rigid when he heard the word "murder." He slowly picked up the shot glass and downed the whiskey in one gulp.

"Tell me everything," he said, with a quaver in his voice that belied the calm he was trying to project. "Start at the beginning and tell me the whole story, every detail."

Eddie told him about the hold-up, Jerrod's death, her abduction, and her escape.

The marshal sat quietly as she talked. Too quietly, she worried. Was he going to throw her in jail once she finished?

She described the rest—her experience with the corrupt marshal in Florissant, Rafe's attack on Jolene, Charlie's death, and the blast at the mine. She told him about all of it. But she did not tell him they'd captured Rafe and had him tied to a bed upstairs.

Irene and Tess stayed at the table with her the whole time. When she finished her story, it was almost five o'clock. She looked at the marshal and said slowly, "I didn't kill anyone, Marshal Gruen. The worst I did was lie to you and," she nodded to her friends at the table, "to Tess and Irene." She continued softly. "They've forgiven me for that. Will you?" It felt good to ask.

The marshal nodded, almost imperceptibly, but kept sitting there. He didn't seem ready to speak, much less leave.

"Is there anything else you need to know?" Eddie wondered what she could have missed.

"Why didn't you come to me?" The marshal choked on the words.

The silence that came after the marshal's question banged on her ears like a spoon on a pot bottom. His question had changed their roles. Suddenly, she was the betrayer instead of the betrayed. She groped for an answer, even an inadequate one, but nothing came.

Finally she had to say something. "I wanted to. But I couldn't. It didn't seem like there was anyone I could trust—at least not at first." She smiled at Tess and Irene. "Then, when I did try to come to talk to you about it, you were with Rafe."

The marshal jumped up. "What? Why the hell would I be anywhere near that scum—'cept to put handcuffs on him?"

"You were shaking hands with him."

The unbearable silence returned. Then the marshal muttered "Son of a bitch" under his breath. He looked at Tess and Irene, then fixed his eyes on Eddie. "He came to see me a few days ago, babbling about some woman he wanted me to arrest. Something about getting hit on the head with a skillet by some woman who had seduced him."

Tess and Irene both looked at Eddie with raised eyebrows and smirks.

Eddie could feel her face getting red. "I didn't seduce him," she muttered. "At least not…"

The marshal hadn't heard her. He seemed lost in some recollection, shaking his head in what seemed to be amazement. Finally he spoke. "I was trying to get him to leave. I walked him to the door thinking he would get the hint. When he went outside, he stuck out his hand. I shook it just so he would keep going."

Tess shook her head in disbelief.

The marshal chuckled. "I washed my hands as soon as I went back inside." He resumed his look of control. "I'll get up a posse and start hunting for Pettibone as soon as it's light tomorrow." Then he scowled. "And I'll get to the bottom of Billingsley's lies when the records office opens on Monday."

He looked at Eddie. "You made a passable lookin' boy," he said matter-of-factly. "But you make a mighty handsome woman." He seemed embarrassed.

Eddie fidgeted in response to the compliment.

"I'm sorry I lied to you," Eddie said, feeling as bad as if she'd told the untruths to her imaginary brother. She sighed. "And I'm still sort of lying to you."

In unison, Tess and Irene sat up straight in their chairs.

"You don't have to hunt for Rafe Pettibone. We took him last night. He's upstairs, tied to a bed."

Marshal Gruen studied each of them, with a peeved look on his face. "Is there anything *else* you have to tell me?"

"Yes," Tess said. "He's drugged at the moment. You probably wouldn't need a posse if you took him right now." She hid her smirk behind her sleeve. "What a waste of laudanum."

"Goddamn," the marshal muttered as he got up and moved toward the back door. "Why bother with a marshal? We got us a bunch of women, flouncing around subduing dangerous criminals by batting their eyelashes." He moved to the door. "Goddamn."

Tess laughed as the screen door closed behind him. "He'll get over it. Time will supply a kinder version of his part in the turn of events."

The marshal came back in fifteen minutes with three burly men. Together, they untied Rafe from the bed, retied his hands and legs, and carried him out the front door, intent on getting him to the jail while he was still subdued with laudanum.

For some reason, they took the red satin ribbons with them.

The mid-morning sun beamed through the small, barred window up high in the back wall of Rafe's cell. Even that little bit of brightness bothered him. His head pounded with more fury than usual. One night in this stinkin' jail was more than enough. How the hell was he going to get out of this fix if he couldn't even think?

A skinny man sat in the chair at the far end of the room, just outside the bars. He held a Winchester on his lap, but kept nodding off, then catching himself with a snort. He'd sit bolt-upright for a minute or two, then he'd start to nod again. The keys were on a nail right behind him. Maybe there was a chance once he fell asleep. Rafe began to think of what he could use to reach across the ten feet between them and get the keys without waking the deputy.

As the deputy was finally drifting into his dreams, Rafe heard a slight scraping noise behind him. He turned to the window, shielding his eyes. Someone outside was lowering a string with a folded slip of paper on it into his cell. Rafe grabbed the paper and opened it.

In his flowery hand, Billingsley had written:

> *Distract the guard. I'll take him from behind. Tear up this note, then tug on the string twice so I know you've read it.*

Rafe wadded up the note and threw it in the corner, then tugged twice on the string.

Eddie knew that even though it was almost ten in the morning, everyone else at the Red Velvet was probably still asleep. It was Sunday. That meant Irene wouldn't get there until four in the afternoon. Eddie had the whole day to accomplish her one remaining task—take the guns to Marshal Gruen.

That left too much time for her to think and too little time to hope. She hadn't been able to come up with a way she could stay in Cripple Creek. Her only option was to go back to St. Louis. But every time she thought of St. Louis, she started to cry. She didn't want to go back. She wanted to work the Tin Rooster. Tears trickled down her cheeks again, and she brushed them away.

Maybe a nice friendly chat with the marshal—about something other than Rafe Pettibone—would help. But would he even talk to her anymore, now that he knew she wasn't an orphaned boy?

She hurried downstairs from the little room on the second floor where she'd slept. Although dressed in women's clothes, she'd jammed the old hat down on her head because she couldn't get used to the feel of not wearing it. As she came to the bottom of the stairs, she glanced in the mirror. She still didn't recognize herself. She shook her head in frustration.

Quietly, she let herself out the kitchen door and walked to the back of the lot where the loaded wagon stood. She climbed up onto the seat and reached underneath it for the bundle wrapped with Jerrod's coat. Unfolding the coat one last time, she gazed at the blue metal and wood of the two handguns.

She didn't want them—didn't need them—in her life. It was time to take them to the marshal. He might even be able to leave the office for a cinnamon roll and coffee "like old times" if she was lucky.

She rewrapped the bundle and wedged it behind the wheel where she could reach it from the ground. Then she jumped down from the other side of the wagon and came around to retrieve the guns. Once she had the parcel firmly under her arm, she started walking to the marshal's office.

She walked in the middle of the street, where she could soak in the most sun, and looked around her with a new sense of freedom. She wondered if prisoners felt this much exhilaration once they could walk where they chose again. Then she thought of all the heartache of the last weeks and sighed. She'd earned her joy.

As she walked the last block of Bennett Avenue before the marshal's office and the jail, she started to whistle. Maybe she'd still be able to find a way to stay in Cripple Creek. Maybe she'd think of it before the stage left tomorrow morning for Florissant where she'd board the train to Colorado Springs and then St. Louis.

"Deputy! Hey! You! Dumb shit deputy! I'm hungry." Rafe took a tin coffee cup and rattled it across the bars. "Don't I got a right to get fed around here? I need some food, dammit!" His head screamed in agony at the noise.

The deputy jumped up from his chair and rushed to Rafe's cell. He held the rifle loosely in one hand and pulled a watch out of his pants pocket with the other. Squinting at the watch, he stood in front of Rafe's cell. "It's only ten o'clock." he said with authority. "Missus Fogarty don't bring your lunch 'til noon. Now stop all the rack—"

Billingsley, who'd snuck in during Rafe's performance, hit the deputy solidly with the butt end of a revolver. The lawman crumpled to the floor. Grabbing the deputy's hands, Billingsley tied them behind the unconscious man's back. He glanced around feverishly. "Where are the keys?"

Rafe nodded toward the opposite wall.

Billingsley yanked the ring of keys from the nail and hurried to the cell door. He handed Rafe the revolver. "Here. Hold this while I open the lock." He put the key in the lock and turned it.

The cell door creaked open.

Rafe rushed out. "Much obliged, Clarence." Maybe old Billingsley wasn't such a waste of time after all.

Billingsley put his hand on Rafe's shoulder and stopped him.

When Rafe turned to look at him, he felt the ice of the fat man's glare.

"This time, get it right," Billingsley said firmly. He gestured toward the gun Rafe still held. "Maybe you can do better with a gun."

Rafe grinned. "I got me a gun and daylight. This kind of killing's easy. I can do it blindfolded."

"Your horse is in the alley. Pick your time to get her, but for God's sake, don't shoot her in town." Billingsley's face gleamed with more than sweat. "And do it soon. *I've got to have that mine.*"

Rafe suspected the greedy look on Billingsley's face was because of something he found in the tunnel. Well, he wasn't going to do any more of the fat boy's dirty work for a measly twenty-five per cent. He squeezed his eyes to make the pain behind them abate momentarily. "What'd you find in that mine that's got you so fired up?"

Billingsley put his finger to his mouth. "Shhhhh."

Together they listened as the front door to the marshal's office opened in the next room.

CHAPTER 18

EDDIE OPENED THE door to the marshal's office and looked around. The office was empty. She thought about asking the deputy—who'd be guarding Rafe in the jail room—where the marshal was, but decided she already knew. She closed the door to the office, certain that the marshal was already at the Tea Cup Cafe. The possibility of a cinnamon roll—and a good talk—made her want to hurry.

She came down the steps from the marshal's office, turned left, and started across the alley next to the jail. Out of the corner of her eye, she noticed something move farther into the alley. She turned to get a better look. The ugly dun stood saddled and waiting.

Eddie moved into the alley to get a better look at what she thought she was seeing.

Rafe watched as Billingsley stuck his head into the marshal's office and looked around, then motioned for Rafe to follow him.

Probably no one there in the first place, Rafe thought. It was just a way to change the subject. He wasn't about to let Billingsley avoid the issue. "What did you find in the mine?"

"Not now!" Billingsley's voice was sharp, sort of like Rafe's old man.

"Yes, now." Rafe stood in the middle of the marshal's office, one hand holding the revolver and one hand holding Billingsley up on his toes by the front of his shirt. "I ain't gonna settle for twenty-five percent."

Billingsley's bald head gleamed with sweat. "All right! All right! We'll make it fifty-fifty."

Hot damn, Rafe told himself. He must have found something pretty rich to agree so easy.

The sunlight was intense as Rafe and Billingsley went out the door. Rafe squeezed his eyes shut to keep out the brightness. When he opened them, it was as if someone had thrown a black cloth over his head. Son of a bitch! This was not the time for one of his damn spells.

Before Eddie could think of what to do about the dun, she heard boots tromping across the porch of the marshal's office.

"You can get it done in four days, can't you?" Eddie recognized Billingsley's voice, then a footfall on the stairs of the porch.

Rafe's snarl of a laugh came in answer to the assayer's question.

She leaned against the side of the building, shaking with combined fury and fear.

"I can't wait any longer than that, you hear?" Billingsley sort of wheezed, then cleared his throat. "You've got 'til Wednesday to kill her, Pettibone. Get it right this time."

She still couldn't see why Billingsley would want her dead.

With a start, Eddie realized she was within inches of being discovered. She lunged the ten feet between her and the horse, dodged around it, and ran farther into the alley. Frantically tugging at the bundle to free one of the guns, she scurried behind a pile of firewood. Her fingers felt the curve of the revolver's grip as she crouched behind the wood. She pulled out the gun she'd taken from Rafe the night she escaped.

The pile wasn't very good cover, but it was better than standing in the open—at least, for the moment. Eddie looked resolutely at the gun, then peeked out from behind the woodpile to see what was going on at the entrance to the alley.

"Four days," Billingsley said again. "Any amateur could do the job with that much time.

For once, Rafe was glad Billingsley was a windy bastard. If he kept talking, Rafe could use the direction of the wheezy voice to know where he was going and keep up with him. "Don't worry," Rafe said, feeling more confident than he had in a month. "It won't take near that long." Once he could see again, that she-devil was a goner.

"Get it right this time."

Rafe ignored the insult but moved with Billingsley's voice again, doing his best to act natural as he moved through the blackness his eyes refused to dispel.

"Hurry up!" Billingsley's voice was down the porch stairs. "If the marshal comes back while you're diddling around, we've both had it."

Still as high-falutin' as ever, Rafe fumed as he went down the stairs toward the voice. At least the jackass hadn't noticed he couldn't see.

When Rafe heard a horse snort, he turned smoothly toward the sound. He shoved the gun Billingsley had given him casually into his belt as he walked down what he hoped was the alley next to the jail. Damn. He'd dealt with the blindness before. It would go away—it always did. But how could he buy the few minutes he needed so Billingsley didn't catch on? Son of a bitch.

Eddie came out from behind the woodpile, the revolver cocked and aimed at Rafe as he stopped next to the horse. "Stop right there, Rafe Pettibone."

Rafe's head came up, but he seemed unable to focus his eyes. She wondered if the laudanum from the day before was still affecting him.

Billingsley shrieked. "It's her, dammit! It's her! Get her now!" Rafe pulled a revolver from the waist of his pants and took three slow steps into the alley toward Eddie.

Eddie jumped back behind the wood pile.

"Get her!" Billingsley screamed the command, then stood still in the middle of the alley pointing toward her hiding place.

He had to be really hateful to want her dead over a little business deal. It didn't make sense. Nothing made sense anymore. She tried to watch Billingsley, to find out if he had a gun, without taking her eyes completely off Rafe. Billingsley moved down the side of the alley toward her, waving his arms and yelling. But from what she could see, he didn't have a gun—at least not in his hand.

Eddie heard Rafe cock his gun and watched him as he aimed down the alley. He seemed lost.

She didn't want to shoot. But she couldn't let him get away. Now that she'd let them know where she was, she was as good as dead if she didn't get him to give up. "You're not getting away, Rafe. Throw down the gun!"

Billingsley rushed toward her. He was ten feet from her when Rafe's gun roared. The assayer fell on his face next to the wood pile. Blood puddled beneath him.

"Billingsley?" Rafe's voice sounded like a child's. "I got her, didn't I, Billingsley?"

Eddie took her eyes off Billingsley. "No," she yelled, her voice laced with firmness. "You got him, not me, Rafe. Now throw down the gun." Please throw down the gun, she begged in her head. Maybe he really couldn't see. No decent person would shoot a blind man.

Instead of giving up, Rafe fired off three shots in quick succession. The third one splintered a piece of firewood just to the left of her head.

Eddie clenched her quivering jaw and re-cocked the gun. Rafe Pettibone was not going to terrorize her or anyone else anymore. She aimed at Rafe's chest and squeezed the trigger.

The sound of the gunshot seemed to come from two directions. Eddie watched as if she were underwater—Rafe pitched slowly forward and fell to the ground. He didn't move. A dark patch grew in the dirt under his belly. She let the gun fall from her hand.

Marshal Gruen rushed into the alley as she collapsed next to the woodpile.

The next thing she knew, the marshal was shaking her shoulders gently. "Eddie? Are you all right?"

When she opened her eyes, he smiled.

"Are you hurt?"

She shook her head.

"You sure?"

She nodded, then looked toward Billingsley's body.

"Dead. Both of them." He helped her sit up, then glanced at the two bodies. "Some gunfight."

"I didn't want to kill anyone."

"Sometimes, there's not much choice."

She felt as if she'd lived too long.

"Odd. He must've' shot his buddy." The marshal didn't seem to want an explanation.

"I really didn't want to shoot him." She felt awful. After Irene's advice and Charlie's teaching, it had come to this anyway. Maybe she had wanted to shoot him. He was dead, regardless. And she'd killed him. She'd failed *everybody*.

"He's got two bullet holes in him." Marshal Gruen pulled her to her feet and put his arm around her shoulder for support. He walked her toward Bennett Avenue and his office. "Either one of them would have been enough. We both killed him."

She stopped walking and looked up at him, worried that her

mind had stopped working in the pandemonium. She asked for an explanation with her eyes.

"You shot him in the heart," the marshal said. "So did I."

"You shot him in the back?"

"Sometimes, there's not much choice."

"But..." Eddie stopped her words, but her mouth stayed open. The concepts of right and wrong seemed suddenly useless.

CHAPTER 19

EDDIE WAS AS nervous as the day she got married. It was Monday morning, and the records office would open for business in five minutes. She smiled at Marshal Gruen, who had come with her claiming he needed to know the truth as much as she did—to deal with Ira Kendrick. Eddie crossed her fingers, rubbed Charlie's lucky rabbit's foot, and muttered, "Please, God, let it be true," as she paced in front of the records office.

A wiry young man with freckles opened the door and nodded for them to come in. He hurried back to his desk and sat down. Once in his proper place, he looked up at them and smiled. "May I help you?"

"We need to check a mining claim," Marshal Gruen said.

"Name?"

"Marshal Hugh Gruen."

The clerk smiled meekly. "I know that, sir. I need the name of the claim."

"The Tin Rooster," Eddie volunteered.

The clerk smiled with satisfaction. "Don't even have to look that one up. Just changed hands last week. I remember 'cuz I wished I'd been the kid working for that old man."

Eddie couldn't endure another second of suspense. "Well, whose *is* it?"

"Charlie McGill gave it to a boy that worked for him—kid by the name of Eddie Taggert."

She shrieked and began to dance around the room.

Eddie didn't care that the clerk was staring at her as if she'd gone into a seizure.

Marshal Gruen grinned at the clerk and shrugged. "I need to

see the official notation, please. There's a dispute."

The clerk relaxed back into his job. "Let me get the claim records. It will only take a minute." He got up and hurried toward a door that led to another room.

After a few minutes of dancing around, Eddie managed to calm herself enough to act like a reasonable adult. She beamed at the marshal. "Thank you for telling me." Marshal Gruen had explained why Billingsley had wanted her dead before he escorted her back to the Red Velvet after the shooting.

Now he seemed almost disappointed that the claim was Eddie's. "You sure you want to get into mining?"

"More than anything."

"It's back-breaking, dirty work."

"I know." She smiled softly, remembering all the plans she and Charlie had made for when they "hit it big."

"And it might be worthless."

"I know there's good ore, sir." She'd studied that rock—drilled it, mucked it, read about it in books. And Bob Womack had agreed with her.

"It's not much of a place for a woman."

"It's the place I want to be." She looked at his face, trying to find the words to make him understand how important it was to her to work the Tin Rooster. She couldn't think of any.

He looked at her thoughtfully. "If that's what you want, I guess you earned the right to try."

She smiled. "Thank you." The words were too little to reflect how much she wanted him to accept her desire to work the mine. But they were all she could come up with.

The clerk came puffing back, carrying a heavy ledger book that he dropped with a thump on his desk. He opened it and thumbed the pages quickly. "Here it is." He pushed the book toward the marshal.

Eddie peeked around the marshal to read the entry herself. "Tin Rooster Mine, Squaw Gulch, from Charlie McGill to Eddie Taggert." A description of the location of the claim followed.

"Thank you," the marshal said after taking enough time to have read it twice. He turned to Eddie. "Anything else you need to know?"

"Nothing I can find out here," Eddie said.

The marshal raised his eyebrows.

"I need to see how much damage Rafe did to the tunnel."

"Let me go with you." The marshal seemed tense.

Eddie looked at him, trying to find a way to have him not worry. "I'm going to have to go in there alone eventually." As she said the words, she realized she wasn't ready for that yet. She hesitated. "If you'd like to come with me, I'd be pleased," she said quietly. She looked down at the ladies clothing she had on. "But I'd better not go in this."

The marshal nodded.

"Meet you at your office in fifteen minutes?"

He nodded again.

She set out for the Red Velvet, running in spite of the skirt.

Marshal Gruen was walking out of the records office when Ira Kendrick arrived. The marshal nodded in recognition, but Kendrick walked past him as if he were invisible and on through the door like it was to his own house. The marshal went back inside. The kid behind the desk might need some help. Besides, this was probably going to be fun.

"I need an affidavit of ownership for the Tin Rooster mine." Kendrick stood his full height and glared down at the clerk with a haughty look on his face.

The marshal liked him less sober than drunk.

"Well, I'll be damned," the clerk muttered. He pulled the record book that still sat on the corner of his desk toward him and opened it to the page he had just shown to the marshal.

"Why do you need an affidavit?"

"None of your business," Kendrick said stiffly.

"He needs to show it to me." Marshal Gruen moved to the desk and smiled at the clerk. Then he turned to Ira Kendrick. "Mornin', Mister Kendrick." He smiled a genuinely fake smile.

Kendrick's shoulders stiffened. "I can handle this."

The marshal smiled again. "Maybe." He noticed the clerk wiping his face with his handkerchief.

Kendrick turned to the clerk. "Just make me up the affidavit."

The marshal chuckled. "You might want to look at what the record says first."

Kendrick grabbed the book out of the clerk's hands and skimmed the page. His face clouded with fury as he read the entry. "He tricked me!"

The marshal couldn't help himself. A broad grin covered his face. "Looks like."

"But that ain't legal! He put up that mine and I accepted his bet in good faith." Ira Kendrick's words sputtered with spit.

"As I recall, he gave the bearer of the note 'all of his current claim.' Seems to me that blind man you were playing for a sucker saw a whole lot better than you did."

Kendrick's hands opened and shut in fury, and he worked his mouth around in a circle, chewing the inside. "Who is this Eddie Taggert?"

"Not anyone you need to know."

"He stole my mine!" Kendrick's face was contorted in red ridges of rage. His nose was taking on a hint of purple.

The marshal hoped the silly grin on the clerk's face didn't get him clobbered.

Instead of going after the clerk, Kendrick grabbed the front of the marshal's shirt. "You get him out of my mine!"

Marshal Gruen put his hand over Kendrick's fist and forced him to relax it and let go of the shirt. He pushed Kendrick to arm's length and glared at him. "No, Mister Kendrick," He said firmly, "I will *not* get 'him' out of 'your' mine. The mine belongs to Eddie Taggert, good and legal. And she's going to work it."

Kendrick stopped before the words he'd planned to utter came out of his mouth. His face froze in a fury that surprised even Marshal Gruen. "She? *She!* A *woman* stole my mine?"

The marshal's patience was wearing thin. The man was too pathetic to be funny. His strongest desire was to throw Kendrick into the street. Instead, he made one last attempt to reason with him. "You have no claim to that mine, Mister Kendrick. You never did. Let it go and get on with your business."

Kendrick continued to work his mouth. "No. It's mine. I won it fair and square."

The marshal shook his head. "Either get control of yourself or get out of Cripple Creek." He dared Kendrick to utter another word with the scowl he leveled at him.

Kendrick's lip curled, uncurled, curled again. Then he stomped out the door and down the street.

Marshal Gruen turned back to the clerk and winked. "Ain't it fine when things turn out the way they should?"

Fifteen minutes after Eddie had left the marshal at the records office, she was dressed for mining and standing in front of the jail holding the lead rope of one of the mules.

The marshal came up just as she was preparing to go inside to see where he was. Eddie watched his shoulders relax as he looked at her in the work clothes that were familiar to him.

"It's about an hour's ride," she said, trying to make some kind of conversation.

He nodded. "Nice day for it." He scanned the blue sky and smiled.

Eddie was too excited about the mine to think of anything else once they were on the road. But the awkwardness of their earlier conversation made her reluctant to even try to talk to the marshal about mining.

The marshal wasn't very talkative either. He seemed more lost in his thoughts than upset. In fact, he was more withdrawn than she had ever seen him. Could a woman owning a mine make a man react that way, she wondered. They rode the entire way to the turn-off without talking.

As they worked their way up Squaw Gulch, Eddie's own mood took on shadows. What if the explosions Rafe set had ruined the tunnel? Worse yet, what if someone else had jumped the claim while she was in town?

When they rode into the clearing in front of the cabin, she breathed a relieved sigh. "It looks like no one's here."

The marshal gestured toward tracks in the yard. "Those are different."

She got off the mule and looked at the imprints in the dirt. "Billingsley?"

"Probably. But let's take this slow. You wait here."

Eddie wanted to run directly to the mine, but she honored the marshal's request and stayed where she was. He checked the cabin and the spring house. He even looked in the outhouse to be sure no one was waiting to ambush them. Then he returned to where she waited.

"Now?" She asked the question like a kid.

"Guess so."

Eddie ran to the mine, found two candles, and had them lit by the time the marshal had walked across the clearing. "You'll love it!" She handed him a candle and started into the darkness. She felt like she'd come home. Even if she barely made enough to live, this was where she belonged.

She climbed through the jumble of rocks to the spot in the tunnel where she'd noticed the discoloration on the ceiling. She looked around at the debris while she waited for the marshal to catch up. From what she could see, the damage looked like it could be repaired. As she turned to view the other side of the tunnel, she noticed the small boulder where she had tripped trying to get out of the mine. No wonder she had scraped herself so badly. It was covered with quartz crystals.

Marshal Gruen came up behind her as she was raising her candle to see what was above her. He raised his candle as well.

A huge cavern gaped above them, too deep to see beyond. Its sides were lined with a labyrinth of gold filaments and nuggets, nestled in a glittering mass of quartz crystals. Even in the meager candlelight, the lining of the cavern sparkled like sunlight.

Eddie let out a long slow whistle though her teeth, the way Jerrod always did when he saw something incredible.

The marshal asked in a whisper, "Gold?"

"Reckon so," she said out loud.

She could hear Charlie laughing.

THE END

ACKNOWLEDGEMENTS

They say writing is a solitary profession, but if you do it that way, it's usually not very good. I had a lot of help on *Widow Boy*. To the extent the story turned out well, thanks are due to many different angels. (If you think it's not-so-good, blame me alone.)

First to the writers who made me keep going:

Thank you a thousand times to Jimmie Butler and the members of his Colorado Springs critique group in the mid 1990's. That experience was better than an MFA for learning to write fiction that's got a strong story line but still has a heart. The comments were invaluable in revising a very young manuscript, and the commitment of the group to each member's success was compelling and unwavering. Thank you all.

Also thanks to Gayle Gross and The 10-Day Book Club for making me get the manuscript out of the bottom drawer a couple years ago. The excitement of the readers in that experiment was the source of new motivation.

Thanks, too, to my Pacific NW writers' group. We may be free-form in what we discuss in a given session, but my commitment to writing stays fresh because of you guys.

Thanks also to the early readers. Family and friends who read the story and told me what needed to be tweaked were a huge blessing as were those who said things like "When is the movie coming out?"

Special thanks to my son Dave and his wife for creating the woman on the cover. Given their work schedules, that was a miracle. Thanks to Rich Poelker and his son for the loan of a family antique for that photo.

Thanks as well to those who helped make the story historically accurate and technically correct. To my son Mike (a professional geologist), who double-checked all the geology with me on site. Thanks to the Western Museum of Mining and Industry, Colorado Springs, where I learned what mining in the area was like during the Cripple Creek gold rush, both as a docent and in researching specific topics as a volunteer. Thank you to the many experts who wrote or taught courses on the history of the area, the history of mining, and the details of what life was like in Cripple Creek, Colorado in 1893. And thank you to the personal contacts who answered questions about firearms, horses and mules, and other topics on which I was not particularly well-versed. With your help, this is an accurate story. Also thanks to those who actually made the history that's been included in the book. Your willingness to take those risks made for a great setting.

Thanks too to my loved ones who've supported me in writing this and other stories. In particular, thanks to Pete Lloyd for his encouragement.

Thank you to all who were in any way involved. You all made a difference.

OTHER BOOKS
BY MARY LLOYD

Supercharged Retirement: Ditch the Rocking Chair,
Trash the Remote, and Do What You Love

39 Bites of Wisdom: Little Lessons in Getting Life Right
(e-book)

Kaleidoscope I (a book of poetry illustrated by Patt Buell.
Currently in limited supply, but hopefully available as an
e-book once technology allows)

ABOUT MARY LLOYD

Mary Lloyd is a writer. Before she finally accepted that fact, she was a geologist, a college statistics instructor, an organizational development consultant, a marketing research supervisor, a line manager then an executive in the natural gas industry, and a retirement "expert." (Stay away from being an expert—it's a terminally serious life.) She lives in the Pacific NW where the hiking is outstanding and the grandbabies are close. You can contact her by e-mail at support@mining-silver.com or via the Contact Us link on the www.mining-silver.com website.

Dear Reader,

If you liked this story, please tell someone. The success of any given book is no longer a matter for "big business." Regardless of the size of your publisher, it's word of mouth and online reader reviews that make the difference in any book's success now. That's good news for you as a reader—you get to shape what comes through the book pipeline next as never before. So please consider writing a review on Amazon, Goodreads, or any other review site you find useful. (If you haven't done an online review before, give it a try. It's pretty easy—not at all like those high school book reports we all dreaded.)

Also, if you'd like to be alerted to my new books as they come out, please go to http://marylloydwriter.com and click on the mailing list link.

Thanks. Read on!

Mary Lloyd